Praise for *The Truth of Right Now*

★ "A powerhouse of storytelling that feels timely and timeless."
—*Kirkus Reviews*, starred review

"Corthron marks herself as a writer unafraid of taking up
difficult topics relevant to teens' lives."
—*Publishers Weekly*

"Debut novelist Corthron eschews the easy path, especially when Lily, who's
white, displays careless, dangerous naiveté when Dari, who's black, faces
an ultimately tragic interaction with police officers. . . . Its focus on racial
injustice becomes the most powerful of the novel's subplots."
—*Booklist*

"Corthron's writing strikes the right balance of pitchy and pithy—
no words are left unchained or events unraveling as Dari and Lily
experience the highest of highs and the lowest of lows."
—*School Library Journal*

"This isn't always an easy read, but it's absolutely an important one."
—*School Library Journal*, Teen Librarian Toolbox

"Confronts particular issues relevant to today's youth."
—*School Library Connection*

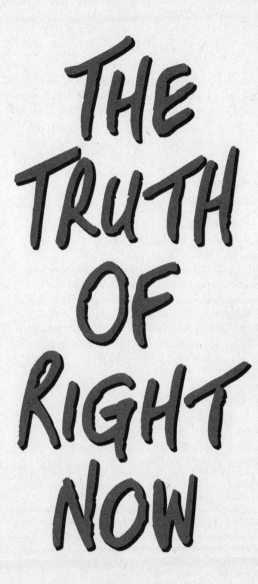

THE TRUTH OF RIGHT NOW

KARA LEE CORTHRON

Simon Pulse

New York London Toronto Sydney New Delhi

SIMON PULSE

An imprint of Simon & Schuster Children's Publishing Division

1230 Avenue of the Americas, New York, New York 10020

First Simon Pulse paperback edition January 2018

Text copyright © 2017 by Kara Lee Corthron

Cover photograph copyright © 2018 by Shutterstock/Nielskliim

Also available in a Simon Pulse hardcover edition.

All rights reserved, including the right of reproduction in whole or in part in any form.

SIMON PULSE and colophon are registered trademarks of Simon & Schuster, Inc.

For information about special discounts for bulk purchases, please contact Simon & Schuster Special Sales at 1-866-506-1949 or business@simonandschuster.com.

The Simon & Schuster Speakers Bureau can bring authors to your live event. For more information or to book an event contact the Simon & Schuster Speakers Bureau at 1-866-248-3049 or visit our website at www.simonspeakers.com.

Cover designed by Steve Scott

Interior designed by Tom Daly

The text of this book was set in Adobe Garamond Pro.

Manufactured in the United States of America

10 9 8 7 6 5 4 3 2 1

The Library of Congress has cataloged the hardcover edition as follows:

Library of Congress Cataloging-in-Publication Data

Names: Corthron, Kara Lee, author.

Title: The truth of right now / Kara Lee Corthron.

Description: First Simon Pulse hardcover edition. | New York : Simon Pulse, 2017. | Summary: "A heart-wrenching debut novel about relationships in its many forms—families, friendships, romance—and how Lily and Dari, coming from different backgrounds and different worlds, strive to find a connection through their differences as they fight against their own individual pasts"— Provided by publisher.

Identifiers: LCCN 2016018605 |

ISBN 9781481459471 (hc) | ISBN 9781481459495 (eBook)

Subjects: | CYAC: Friendship—Fiction. | Love—Fiction. | Family life—Fiction. |

BISAC: JUVENILE FICTION / Social Issues / Prejudice & Racism. |

JUVENILE FICTION / Social Issues / Dating & Sex. |

JUVENILE FICTION / Family / General (see also headings under Social Issues).

Classification: LCC PZ7.1.C673 Tr 2017 | DDC [Fic]—dc23

LC record available at https://lccn.loc.gov/2016018605

ISBN 9781481459488 (pbk)

For Tom, Kia, Mom,
and everyone fighting the good fight with an open heart

PART 1

INVISIBLE GIRLS

How hard would I have to bite my tongue if I want to bite it in half? Is it a sawing motion? Chewing? Or would I have to chomp down hard, ignoring the pain, pushing through until both bridges of my teeth touch? I consider trying it. I won't. But I consider it.

"There's Mexican hot cocoa," she calls out over the noisy grinding of coffee beans. "The good kind. Trader Joe's."

I stare at my arms.

"No, thanks."

"Iced coffee?"

"No. But thank you." I am doing all I can to sound civil. I'm not feeling civil today. I don't like it when my mother pretends to be chipper before eight a.m. She might be even less of a morning person than I am.

She stares at the grinder. Concentrating.

"Maybe you should wait," she says.

I take a breath.

Wait. Skip the first day of school. Few things scream, *Abnormal!*

louder than a girl who can't even stomach the first day of school. *Everyone* is anxious. *Everyone* wishes that one extra week of August could've miraculously materialized. I have to remember that. It's not just me.

I dreamed about it last night. First dream I can remember having in a month at least. In the dream, I walk into my homeroom. Pfefferberg's homeroom, which is from last year, so that makes no sense. I head for my old seat next to the green filing cabinets. It's so quiet, but I hear my footsteps, like my shoes are cement blocks. I sit. Everyone turns to me and no one makes a sound. I can't see their eyes. I almost can in my periphery, but when I try to look directly at someone's face, the eyes vanish. I pray for the bell to ring, for Pfefferberg to enter, for something to distract them from me. Anything. Then I hear something, which is a mild relief from the silence. It sounds like rain, but only a trickle. Maybe the ceiling is leaking? No one's getting wet. A faucet somewhere? A toilet running? No. I look down at my feet and see the puddle growing in volume. I lift my head again. If I stare it'll be obvious. So I sit in it and keep my gaze facing forward as if the piss isn't mine.

"You look like you're a thousand miles away," she says, pulling me back to the present.

If I could be a thousand miles away, I would be. "Let's get a dog."

"Random much?" Mom pours her coffee into a large, lopsided, maroonish mug. She took a pottery class once. "Dogs don't enjoy city apartments."

Now she hovers. She will not sit next to me; too sisterly. She will not sit across from me; too confrontational. She just floats around, pretending that she prefers standing.

"What about a small handbag dog?"

"Is this a real request, Lily?"

I sigh. Probably not. But I'd love a little, adorable diversion right now. Sheila E. disagrees. Purring and sleepy from her breakfast of organic whitefish, she bats at my calf in protest.

"Play hooky," she says. "Let's go to Wave Hill. Somewhere fun that feels like we're in the middle of nature. Want to?"

No. I want you to force me to go to school like a normal mother.

"I have to get it over with," I say, and it's true. "If I wait, it'll just be worse."

She nods, blowing on her coffee.

I leave the table and realize I had no reason to be there at all. I wasn't eating or drinking anything. Autopilot. Before the first day of school we always used to sit at the table and nosh and gossip. My body brought me there, but the rest of me had lost interest.

My backpack is lighter than it should be. No textbooks. No laptop. No notebooks neatly color-coded for each subject. Just my iPod, a pen, and a banana. Good enough.

I head for the door.

"You need money for your MetroCard?"

I look at my mom, with her open, hopeful face, and it's hard not to hate myself. I'm sure she had such high hopes for her daughter.

"That's okay, Mom. I think I'm gonna walk."

More nodding.

"Do you want me to walk you?"

"No." I shut the door behind me and move quickly to the elevator. Inside I watch the numbers counting down to one, feeling as though my soul is being slowly sucked out of me through my butt.

In the lobby, Marcus looks down at whatever the hell he has behind his doorman's desk. For a while, he tried to smile at me. Now he does his best to politely ignore me, which is fine. I step outside onto the sidewalk and look up at the sky. It is a ridiculously beautiful day. The sky is clear as spring water. But then again, spring water isn't blue, so is the sky ever actually clear? No idea, but I now want to taste blue spring water.

I walk down the block and smile, imagining its deliciousness. It wouldn't be a fake blue like in a Rocket pop. It would taste like regular spring water with just a refreshing splash of blueberry juice.

The breeze feels like I'm being kissed all over my exposed skin. I inhale deeply, wanting to savor the beauty of this moment before stepping into the next.

It's going to be a terrible year.

The smell could be worse. Much worse, considering. I lean against the stall door in the third-floor bathroom and close my eyes. The day hasn't been quite as horrific as I had imagined. I walked into my new homeroom and, yes, for that first awful, awful second, I thought I might fall down dead. Everyone snapped their heads over to look at me, but most of them looked away just as fast. A few of the bleeding hearts gave me sorrowful, pitying looks that made me want to hit them. But mostly no one wants to look at me at all. I'm the invisible girl. It's fine. I'm not exactly used to it, though. People used to like me well enough and I used to be . . . well, likable. But then again, what does it mean to be "likable," really? To say all the right things at all the right times? To be funny? To be smart, but never *too* smart? I don't know. And after last year, I'll probably never know.

I am the invisible girl.

A few short months ago, a fate like this would've sent me into a three-day crying jag. Not now.

At least I'll be left alone.

The stall's walls are clean, painted over. There hasn't been enough time yet for them to get refilled with messages about who sucks and who loves who. Nothing to distract me from memories of last period.

Last period was tough.

Mr. Crenshaw was rambling on about some science-y crap. I'd zoned out for a minute, trying to remember a sweet little melody I came up with a few days ago but was too lazy to write down.

While I was searching my brain for music notes, everyone in the room started shuffling around, talking to each other, and moving seats. I'd missed something critical and had no idea what I was supposed to do.

"Uh? What did he say?" I stupidly asked the nearest body, which belonged to Jamie Paulsen. She glared at me with complete disgust.

"We're picking lab partners. Clearly." She got away from me as quickly as she could. I almost grinned. Jamie's still as bitchy to me as ever. I dig her consistency.

I looked around the room, trying to find any possible allies. Neither Jackie nor Tracy wound up in my chem class. Haven't seen them in forever anyway. People quickly paired off and I felt my pulse racing because no one even bothered looking in my direction. But then I noticed Tara McKenzie staring out the window.

"Hey, Tara," I said, practically breathless.

She jumped, startled by my presence. "What?"

"Do you need a lab partner?" I asked, hoping not to sound as desperate as I felt.

She turned back to the window for a moment. I tried to follow her gaze, but saw nothing worth looking at out there. A chain-link fence. A black squirrel fighting a white pigeon. She sighed and shrugged. It was the best I could hope for.

We sat in our new seats. Mr. Crenshaw droned on about our responsibilities to our partner and how class would be split between lectures and experiments and though I seriously did not give a single shit, I paid close attention to avoid another near-humiliation.

When the bell rang and I gathered my things, I felt Tara's hard eyes on me. I didn't know what she was thinking or what she wanted, but I felt like I should say something.

"Thanks. I mean, uh, you know . . ." *Eloquent.*

For the first time in my memory—and I've known her since middle school—Tara smiled. A big, bright, evil smile.

"How does it feel?" she asked. And she left me standing there with my legs trembling and my stomach roiling and a giant knot in my throat. I retreated to the bathroom.

Tara McKenzie.

At five feet zero, she's always been sort of small, not fat, not thin, but somehow shapeless. Pale, sickly-looking skin prone to breakouts and mousy brown hair that's neither short nor long, but always mysteriously in her face. Everything about her defies description, and not in a good way.

Tara the Target.

So many people hate Tara McKenzie. So many of us have teased her over the years. Tara McKenzie who had the pregnancy scare in eighth grade, which led to the rumor that the father of her alleged unborn child was her brother. If that weren't bad enough, the rumor started because no one could believe anyone else on earth would touch her.

A few years ago, she was the object of so much ugly attention. Now it's like she's a ghost no one even bothers thinking about anymore. I am pretty sure that I have never said anything cruel to Tara in my life. But have I laughed at her expense? Yep. Have I ever stood up for her? Nope. I don't think I've ever said a single word to her until today. She's no dummy. I am one of the invisible now and she wants me to know that she knows. Despite my wishfully thinking that I prefer it this way, it kind of feels like death. But then again, how would I know what death feels like?

I flush the toilet and leave the stall. I check myself in the mirror. Surprise, surprise: I look like shit. Pale. Pasty. My white teeth look buttery in comparison to my skin. I really look at myself. A one-hundred-fifteen-pound sad girl with frown lines, bony arms, and an unruly head of long, curly dark hair. I sigh and briefly consider adding lipstick and/or mascara to this atrocity, but that's my autopilot driving again. What's the point?

I check my watch. 12:12. Lunch. Do I have it in me to deal with lunch today? Again, I feel that indignant (and possibly stupid) resolve I felt this morning when my mother suggested I blow off school. It'll only be worse if I wait.

I hang out for another few minutes until the bell rings, having skipped gym completely, then I blend into the crowded hallway as if I am just like them and I head for the cafeteria. For a split second, I'm sure I hear the whispered words "razor" and "that's her" and "scars," but I turn toward the sounds and no one is looking in my direction. Regardless, I keep my eyes focused straight ahead of me, just like in my dream. If anyone cares enough to stare and whisper, I won't see it. I choose not to.

Casually, I get in line and pretend to be concerned about the day's menu. I'm not the least bit hungry. I am only doing this to prove to myself that I can. It is not a meal. It is a quest.

"You did not! With her?"

"Why not?"

"She's five hundred pounds."

"She's not that fat."

"Dude, she's a hippo."

"Well, she's a pretty tight hippo, then."

Derek Miller and Jason Chung. Dipshits. I back away to create some space between me and them, hoping someone will take the hint and jump ahead of me in line. It doesn't work.

"What happened to Jamie?"

"Tired of psycho-bitch drama."

I do my best to tune them out. The line slinks forward. I try to recall a particular melody. That little tune I came up with the other day. I can only think of the first three notes. It's so frustrating. I love the days when a song just presents itself to me, like a little gift. But I have such trouble remembering it if I don't write it down. And as soon as I start to write it down, it doesn't feel like a gift anymore. Mom once suggested I study music composition. She meant well, but come on. It's like, let's take the one thing I enjoy and make it as boring as everything else.

Derek and I make eye contact. He turns away from me as fast as he can, but not before twisting his face in revulsion. Feeling is mutual, degenerate.

The choices seem to be meat loaf or meat loaf. One of those things is probably not meat loaf, but I don't dare ask. Instead I take a prepared salad and sandwich from the counter and pay.

I walk back into the cafeteria and scan the room for a safe place. I am fully prepared to run the hell out of here if I have to, but by some miracle, I spot Jackie and Tracy. I haven't seen either of them since June, but I did speak to Jackie on the phone once or twice over the summer and Tracy sent me a card.

"They never pay attention to student input, but I think competitive rugby would be great for the school. Even if it's just intramural at first." Jackie saws her meat loaf or meat loaf as she says this. Before she can continue, Tracy gently nudges her and they both look up at me.

"Hi," I say, barely above a whisper. Where has my voice gone?

They're quiet for a moment. Then Jackie stands and hugs me. I can't hug her back because I am still holding my tray, so it's a sloppy hug. When she finally releases me, she just stands there and looks at me for a second.

"You look great, sweetie," she says. Jackie is one of those girls who has been calling her friends "sweetie" and "honey" since she was about eight. For some reason, I don't mind so much today.

"Thanks. Is it okay if I—"

"Of course! Sit down."

I sit.

"It's good to see you, Lily," Tracy says, but her face disagrees.

"How are you doing?" Jackie asks with parental concern.

"Fine. Thanks." I start to eat my salad, which tastes like paper.

"Well, you look terrific," Jackie says, and she nods vigorously with encouragement, and although I was relieved to conquer my first lunch without being annihilated, Jackie's decision to treat me like a brave cancer survivor suggests that I may have made an error.

"How was the summer for you guys?" I ask, shifting the focus.

"It was good," Tracy says, glancing around. She won't meet my eyes.

"It was better than good. Tell her," Jackie goads.

Tracy blushes. "I met a guy."

"A lifeguard. He looks like he belongs on the cover of *GQ*," Jackie squeals.

"That's awesome," I say, hoping I sound enthusiastic.

Jackie gushes about Tracy's new dude. I smile and nod at the right intervals, but internally I'm wondering if I will have to stay and listen to this for my entire lunch period. And will I have to tomorrow and the day after that and the day after that? While Jackie summarizes the pool party where she met Tracy's man candy (another party I wasn't invited to, but who's keeping track?), Marie Diaz joins our table. She politely nods in my direction, but then ignores my presence. They all do. We weren't always the best of friends, but we had been close. Really close. The three of us. Always the three of us. From seventh grade on up, it was me and Jackie and Tracy. I picture the card Tracy sent me over the summer: Van Gogh's *Irises*. The message inside was simple and sweet. *This too shall pass.* Her mother probably picked it out and forced her to sign it.

I barely know Marie, but apparently they'd all had quite a summer without me. Perhaps Marie has taken my place. Trade in one curly brunette for another. I pick at my soggy chicken sandwich, feeling angry with myself for the tears threatening to escape my eyes and embarrass me.

"Oh my God, Tracy, you're such a ho." Marie snorts.

"Just because I'm not ashamed of my needs does not make me a ho, beeyotch," she teases back. It's like they've always been friends. Maybe they have been and I just didn't notice. I sip my milk, which is white and wet but somehow doesn't taste enough like milk to be convincing. Who are these people? Were they always like this? Am I like this too when I'm not depressed? They're so annoying. And yet I still want them to want me here. Why?

"What school did you say he goes to?" Marie asks.

"He's at SUNY New Paltz."

"A college man. Nice," I pipe in. They all glance at me for a second, puzzled. But then Tracy sort of half smiles and says, "Yeah. Thanks," though she still won't meet my eyes. Then they all go right back to gabbing again, as though I weren't there.

I turn and look at all the tables. All the excitement. All the friends rehashing summer parties, passing around phones with beach photos, making new memories as they speak. I hate them.

The trio says nothing as I leave to dump my tray and the remains of my disappointing lunch. I'm contemplating getting back on line for a brownie to drown my sadness in fat when I notice a table next to the wall by the doors with a single occupant. I have never seen him before; I would remember if I had. He's black, pretty dark, with sharp cheek-bones, a faint beard growing in, and long dreadlocks. I inch just a bit closer and squint. He doesn't have any food or a tray at his table. Just a large sketch pad. He's drawing. I can't see what from this distance. He is completely engaged in his work. His left eyebrow is raised. Or perhaps his right eyebrow is furrowed. Hard to tell. He does not seem to be the least bit interested in anything going on around him, and definitely doesn't seem to care about the fact that he is alone.

Jesus. He's beautiful.

I decide to go for the brownie.

"Do you guys know that new kid?" I ask when I return to the table, projecting my voice well above a whisper this time. For a moment, they all appear dumbstruck, as though they'd forgotten I was their lunch companion for the day.

"What new kid?" Jackie asks.

"The one by himself. The black guy." I hate doing that, describing somebody using just their race. I wouldn't do that if I were pointing out my mother in a crowd. I wouldn't say, "She's that white woman over by the salad." In this case, my description works because our school isn't exactly overflowing with black kids. (It's so bad there was a *New York Times* article about it.)

They all look in his direction.

"I don't know him," Tracy mumbles.

"Me either," Marie offers.

Jackie nods dubiously. "Yeah. He's in my homeroom. And history. He has a weird name. Dariomitochondria? Dunno. Something with way too many syllables, if you ask me."

I didn't ask you.

"Think he might've been kicked out of his old school. That's what I heard anyway," Jackie says. "Why?"

"Just wondering."

The bell rings, and we all start to go our separate ways. With no warning, Jackie attacks me with another hug. In the midst of this embrace, I assure her that I'm fine and that she shouldn't worry.

She releases me.

"Let's get together and talk soon, okay? Like really talk."

I nod.

"Promise me, Lily," she says.

"I promise," I lie.

She smiles and walks away. We were just at the same table for forty-five minutes, and she had no interest in talking to me then. Probably just keeping up appearances.

As I grab my backpack, I look toward the table next to the wall by the doors, but he's already gone. I didn't see Tara McKenzie in the cafeteria at all.

The wind has picked up, and instead of kissing me all over, it whips my hair in my face and tries to lift my shirt like a kite. The ferry rocks back and forth and I feel slightly queasy. I know it will pass. It always does.

My phone vibrates. I don't need to check it to see who's calling me. To be fair, I am late. A good two hours late. But today, the beautiful part of today, passed with me indoors and unable to be a part of it. I also needed some time. All summer (not counting the bad days), my time belonged to me. Mom was always in her office, ostensibly writing, or attending luncheons and giving talks to disheartened but hopeful women. I could walk all over the city if I wanted to. I could sit in my room and stare at the hardwood floor if I wanted to. I got accustomed to the quiet of my mind. Now I'm back to the regiment. Now I'm back with the people.

A text. I read the screen: *Where r u? Pizza, Chinese, or Indian?* I sigh and text her back: *Indian. Home soon.* The ferry is heading back to the city from Staten Island. I have already ridden back and forth twice, but it's time to get off the boat and go home. Maybe Mom had a good day. Maybe she's finally had a breakthrough on the book that she's been writing for nine years. It's possible.

When I get home, I turn my key and open the door, and there she is: right where I left her, as though she's been standing in this spot all day.

"How was it?" she barks at me, and I jump out of my skin. After I recover from my mild heart attack, I tell her it was fine.

"Where were you?" she asks with more intensity than she probably intends.

"Nowhere, Mom. I just needed some time. Everything's cool."

She exhales a little.

I get out some plates and put the vegetable korma on the coffee table. I spoon out some fish curry while she searches through the Netflix options.

"Documentary? Movie? TV show? Look. *Nine to Five*! Have you ever seen this? It's a great flick." She chatters on about the brilliance that is Lily Tomlin as an evil Snow White, and I look at my fish and my papadums and my pakora and I pick up my fork and it feels so cold and familiar and nothing. And I just start sobbing like an idiot.

"Oh, Jesus," my mom cries, and she throws her arms around me. "Baby, what's wrong? What's wrong?"

Through hiccups comes "I don't know." Those three stupid words. I've said them so many times.

But I do know. For a minute, I felt content. Satisfied with my delivery food, the prospect of watching *Nine to Five*, and the thought that this was the best I could ever expect from life.

And I lost my shit.

2

SECRETS OF THE BOURGEOISIE

Dariomauritius Raphael Gray is bored as fuck. High school sucks. He hates it. He hates anything that is a waste of his time. This is supposed to be AP History, and he already knows half of this stuff from the History Channel, and the History Channel is "edutainment."

I can feel myself getting dumber every day. He raises his hand because he's feeling ornery. The teacher sees him and rolls his eyes.

"Yeah," he answers, ready to do battle.

"Are we ever gonna get more than just facts in this class?" Dari asks. Sweetly.

"Can you be more specific?"

"Who were the native tribes at Jamestown? Did any settlers protest the whole barge-in-and-seize mentality?"

He narrows his eyes at his least-favorite pupil.

He has hated me since day one, Dari thinks, *and I don't blame him. I'm smarter than he is. Fat bastard.*

"We only know so much from the evidence we have available."

"We have brains, though, right?"

"If you're interested in fiction, perhaps you should take AP Lit. In the meantime, I'd love to do my glamorous job, if that's all right with you." The ass-kissers laugh at this excuse for humor. Dari slumps down in his seat. That's his reward for taking an active role in his education. He's been here two whole weeks, and he's certain that his mind is shrinking. So much for bourgie schools and their bullshit reps.

He patiently waits for the bell to ring like all the other sheep, then he grabs his essentials from his locker and leaves.

No one notices.

The 1 train is a carnival of freaks this morning. A woman dressed as Michael Jackson—loafers, white socks, and glitter glove—moonwalks to the song blasting out of her boom box. Dari's 99 percent sure that it is a Billy Ocean song and the incongruence of this choice bugs him. He has half a mind to tell her so, but no one wants to hear from the peanut gallery. She also could be packing heat. Who knows? This is America. An elderly man in a fairy princess costume about two sizes too small sucks on a lollipop and winks at him. A younger man in a heavy winter coat (unnecessary in balmy September) warns an invisible person about the dangers of crack because, in his head, it's probably still 1991. There are two youngish women who seem normal, but Dari knows better than to assume that. One reads a book; the other a Kindle or something. You always have to watch out for the quiet ones.

He gets off the train and walks up to the movie theater.

"One," he says at the ticket window. The girl eyes him for a minute. *Really? You really got nothing better to do than worry about how old I am?*

But she says nothing. She takes his money and he walks in and remembers that the popcorn here tastes like feet.

No one is in the theater other than Dari. No one. It's cool, but it's a little spooky, too.

He makes himself comfortable, taking up a few seats with his stuff, and propping his feet up on the one in front of him. He's ready for some education.

Dari likes to think of Godard as a mentor. Not that he's interested in filmmaking. Just the images. His stories. The commentary. He prefers secret mentors from afar. Dead ones are his absolute favorites.

The lights go down and the film begins. No previews. Even though the popcorn here is offensive (dry and wrong), he grins, thinking about the suckers still sitting in class being crammed full of mediocrity. How can anyone live in this city and honestly believe that more education happens inside a school as opposed to outside of one? If somebody lives in the middle of nowhere, then yes, in that case, they'd better go to school. For real. What choice do they have?

Watching the silhouettes on the screen, he looks around again to see if anyone has joined him in the theater. Nope. Not even noon and this weird, barely lit scene about a threesome and an egg breaking in an unconventional place is giving him a monster erection. To avoid stroking something else, he takes out his sketch pad and makes some broad strokes in the dark. He attempts to render Mireille Darc in all her chilly French beauty and as the movie leaves this moment, he remains toiling on his drawing. Freezing her in time. Her head bowed down, knees bent into her chest, describing her unusual sexual escapade to her husband who wasn't invited.

His phone rings. He always forgets to turn the damn thing off at the movies. He gives it a glance to see who's called. It's Kendra. Two missed calls. Dari's baffled by her definition of "space." When he requests space from someone, he expects to get it. This is a difficult concept for Kendra. Apparently.

As the lights come up, he's still alone in the theater sketching. It's been a while since he's gotten this hooked. At the new school, he has yet to find a worthy subject—known or unknown. Back at his old school, he had several. Kendra was one until she became boring. Unknown subjects are the best ones. He's sure it isn't an invasion of privacy or a stop on the road to stalkerville. It's a compliment and a challenge. He looks around his classes, the halls, and all he sees are different versions of the same person. Nothing special.

His favorite subject ever was an old homeless chess player in Washington Square Park. He eventually told the old dude about the series he was doing and the guy asked to see one of the drawings. He was not impressed. He said, "You made me look like a duck."

A young woman with frosty blond hair and deep laugh lines enters and sweeps. He reaches a stopping place and leaves. Outside he turns his phone on again and it rings.

"What is it, Kendra?" he asks.

"Coffee. That's all. I just wanna see you."

"Why aren't you in school?"

"I don't have class today." Oh, yeah. She's in college now. "Why aren't *you*?" *Well played, Kendra.*

Ten minutes later, the two are sitting in Caffe Reggio waiting for their drinks. Double espresso for Dari and a latte for Kendra. The usual.

"What's the new school like?" she asks.

"It's school. How's college life?"

"All right, I guess. Overwhelming. It's so different," she says, and she shakes her head as if she couldn't possibly make him understand the difference. "How's your sister?"

"I don't feel like doing that. Just tell me what you need to tell me." It sounds harsh. He has a problem with that. Often his words sound much nicer in his head. Something corrupts them during their trip to his mouth.

She looks down at the table and fiddles with her napkin. "Did I do something to you?"

The waitress brings their drinks. He starts to add some cream to his when Kendra grabs his hand.

"Can you answer me first?"

Dari glances out the window toward the park. Still under construction.

Seems like it'll never be finished.

"No. You didn't do anything," he says.

"Then what happened?"

"It didn't seem fair. To you."

She takes this in as he creams and sugars his espresso.

"Why?"

"It's just . . . how you are. Calling every day. Several times a day. Making me gifts. Saying *I love you* all the time. I'm not like that," he tells her.

"So?"

"Don't you think you deserve to be with someone who is?" Now, that sounds amazing. Saintly even.

Kendra sips her latte thoughtfully.

Is he being completely honest with her? Not exactly.

Let's be real. Kendra is stunning. Short, dark curly hair. Mocha skin. Black eyes that shine like onyx stones, and a body to kill for. How hot is she? So hot that random men on the street—white men, Asian men, business men, homeless men—sometimes call her Beyoncé. She doesn't actually look like Beyoncé, though. That's their liberal racism. She's softer, more curious, more intelligent. She's also sweet and smart. But sometime during their ten-month relationship, Kendra stopped being Kendra and started becoming the girl version of Dari. His interests became her interests. She wouldn't read a book without his approval. She started drawing. She started to become cynical. He loathed the effect he was having on her. And it made her a whole lot less attractive. She became a bore.

"Dari?"

"Yeah?"

"Are you with someone else now?"

He shakes his head, annoyed that she asked. "It's not about that." He briefly wonders if he should've lied and said he was with someone. Would that make it easier?

Kendra raises her cup to her lips slowly. *Please don't start crying. Please, please, please don't start crying. . . .*

"All right," she says. She drops some money on the table and walks toward the door.

"Hey," he calls.

"Hey what?" An edge to her voice.

"Nothing. Just . . . bye."

And she's gone. She's never left Dari's presence without a long hug or more. Perhaps she finally got the message.

He thought he'd feel relieved. Instead, he just feels like an asshole.

Home by 5:45. Reluctantly. The Führer will come in the door at six on the dot. On. The. Dot.

Dari washes his hands and grabs some vegetables to chop for the salad.

Izzy stirs her mashed potatoes and takes the meat out of the oven.

"Thanks," she says absently.

"It's my job. Sorry I didn't get here earlier."

She waves that off, disinterested.

"What's wrong?" Dari asks, not really wanting to know.

"Had another interview."

"That's good, right?"

She gives him the thumbs-down.

"How do you know it went badly?"

"I find it hard to answer stupid questions like *where do you see yourself in five years?* from these little white boys that barely look older than you."

He tosses the salad with her homemade vinaigrette. "So? What did you say?"

"I said, 'Hopefully not in this company.' I just have a big mouth, Dari."

"No, you don't," Dari says. She doesn't. Not really. But she has no patience for bullshit. Her aversion to dishonesty is how she lost her job at Deutsche. She was there seven years, too (if you count her internship when she was still in college). Things went south when she discovered a huge discrepancy in the area of foreign exchange—something she was sure had to be an error. She was told that "price manipulation" was both normal and legal. She didn't buy it and talked to a couple of reporters from *Democracy Now!* because investors have a right to know what's being done with their money. It was pretty badass at the time, but forget landing another job in finance once you've been labeled "whistle-blower." She was lucky multimonth unemployment was her only punishment for bucking the system.

"Maybe you should imagine the interviewers are old," he suggests.

"Maybe."

"Or imagine them naked. With droopy balls."

She laughs. "You are a fool."

Izzy opens the kitchen window, sneaking in a quick smoke before six. She smoked in high school and claims she quit when she went to college and didn't pick up another cigarette until five months ago. That's when she moved back home.

"How was your day?" She already seems less tense as she blows a cloud of smoke out into the atmosphere.

"Fine, I guess. School is stupid. I went to Film Forum. They're showing *Weekend*. Have you ever seen it? It's insane."

"When did you see this?"

"Why?"

Izzy sucks her teeth and shakes her head. "You can't be cutting school like last year, Dari."

He sits in a chair and checks the microwave clock. 5:56.

"I mean it. I don't want you to become a slouch."

"Come on, I have perfect posture," he quips. Of course that pisses her off, but he hates how she can talk to him like a full-on adult and then change him back to kid brother over something as asinine as skipping class.

"It might not feel like it, but if you can stick it out and do well, you'll have a lot more freedom in the long run. I know what I'm talking about." She runs her cigarette under the faucet, fully extinguishing it, and once it's limp and soggy, tosses it in the trash can. She then sprays some air freshener.

"I was there every day for the past two weeks. Nobody wants to reward me for that."

"You don't get rewards for doing what you're supposed to do. A tragic fact of life you better get used to."

And then the door opens and he's home.

"Good evening," he greets. Izzy says, "Hi," and Dari nods at him as he walks past, hangs his jacket in the closet, and sets down his briefcase. Always in the same spot: due north of the bookshelf.

He sits in his chair and watches the *BBC World News* while the siblings finish arranging the food on the table. At six fifteen, he switches the television off and joins them, his plate already waiting for him. They sit quietly as he says grace in his head. Despite all his rules, he's long given up on trying to force God into his heathen offspring.

When he begins to eat, so do they.

"Ismene?" Izzy winces just a little. She has always hated that name. She legally changed it to Isabel when she turned twenty-one. If their father is aware of this, he pretends otherwise.

"Yes?"

"How was the interview?" He asks this between bites of beef. He chews it with some difficulty, as though it might be a touch overcooked. A message for Izzy.

"Not great. I'm pretty sure I didn't get it," she mutters into her mashed potatoes. Dari stares at her, imagining how confident she must appear at her job interviews. Arrogant. But not here. Never here.

"That makes no sense to me. Someone with your credentials. Did you thoroughly research the company to prepare?"

"Yes."

"Then what do you suppose went wrong?"

Izzy plays with the food on her plate as if she were seven instead of twenty-seven.

"I misspoke," she breathes.

"Can you speak up, please?" he asks.

You know you heard her.

"I spoke out of turn. Said something I shouldn't have."

Their dad eats his dinner quietly for a few minutes as if he actually hasn't heard anything she's said. But he has. He hears everything.

"Maybe you don't want to work. Maybe you'd rather I support you until my death. Is that what you want?"

"No."

"Then I suspect you had better learn how to speak properly to your superiors. If this conduct continues, I'll have to tutor you in the area of workplace decorum. And I do not have the time for that."

"Yes, Dad." She looks up at her little brother and smiles sadly. Dari can't stand it. He wants her to be angry. He wants her to challenge him. Cuss him out. Why can't she—

"Dariomauritius?"

Shit.

"Yes?"

"How was school today?"

"Fine."

"Trigonometry? Had a quiz today, yes?"

Whoops. He totally forgot about that.

"How did you do?" he asks. He holds his water glass up to the light, looking for something to criticize. Maybe Dari didn't pour it correctly.

"Fine."

"Just fine?"

"*Spectacular!*" This little outburst comes and it's now out there. He glances at Izzy, her eyes the size of softballs. Their dad turns to his son, an unfamiliar expression on his face. More confusion than anything else. Before he can say anything, Izzy bursts out laughing. That kind of laughter that hurts because you've been holding it in forever.

"You are a fool, Dari." Izzy shakes her head, trying hard to calm herself.

"A fool. Yes," their father agrees. He does not laugh.

The meal proceeds in silence. When they all finish, Dari helps Izzy clear the table and load the dishwasher. She turns the kettle on.

"Dariomauritius?"

Jesus Christ, just call me Dari!

He sighs. "Yes?"

"How was history class?"

"All right. I'm not impressed with the curriculum." Sometimes Dari attempts to speak to him as if he were a human being. Just to see what will happen.

"That's not for you to judge."

Dari doesn't respond and arranges the silverware in the grate. Their father's quiet again, but Dari can feel him staring, studying him.

The kettle whistles, and Izzy makes their father's evening cup of tea. Oolong. She places it in front of him and he nods to her, the closest he ever comes to saying thank you, and sips the steaming liquid. Why doesn't it burn his tongue? Is he immune to physical pain?

Izzy makes herself a cup. Dari washes his hands.

"What about English? What are you working on?"

What is he talking about?

"Why do you ask?"

For the first time tonight, Dari catches his father's eyes lurking behind his horn-rimmed glasses. Dark and beady and mean. A specific kind of mean he only trots out for special occasions.

"I don't need a reason to ask you anything. What did you do in English today?" he persists.

"Well," Dari begins, trying to imagine what he missed. "We read the first chapter of *Slaughterhouse-Five* and discussed it."

"Oh, Vonnegut. Very good. Sit down. Tell me: where do you think the book is headed?"

Izzy looks with longing toward the window. Wishing she were anywhere else. Dari does as he's told and sits down next to his father at the table, but makes sure to sit up straight as a reminder that he is now a good five inches taller than dear old Dad. (Six one and still growing. *What what!*)

"Well, it's hard to say, but I think that the book is . . . I think it's going to be about the futility of war. All war. I think it's going to be universal in that way. But with Vonnegut, who knows, right?" Not a syllable of that came out sounding as intelligent as it had in Dari's mind.

Dear old Dad picks up his cup and throws the contents into his son's face.

Tea bag and all.

Izzy gasps.

Tea in his nose, eyes, dripping off his chin, down his neck. At least it has cooled. Somewhat.

"How dare you lie to me in my house after eating my food. They called me. I know you weren't there today."

"They called you?"

He nods slowly, trying to suppress a grin. So proud of himself.

"Thought you were slick, didn't you? I explained your problem with attendance to your vice principal, and he agreed to let me know of each and every single one of your absences."

Oh my God.

"Well? Have you nothing to say for yourself?"

He wants an apology.

"Yes, I have something to say for myself. I *was* there today. I just left after first period." Dari is not sorry. Izzy rubs her eyes in worry and frustration. So what? He's ready for him. Whatever he's got. Open hand. Closed fist. It could be anything with him. Instead, he just stares at Dari in disbelief.

"Get out of my sight. You disgust me. Ismene, dear, another cup?"

Dari leaves the room as Izzy, no doubt, has jumped up to refill the kettle.

He can't help but smile. *Really? Is that all you got, old man?* Maybe he's getting soft.

In the shower he scrubs away the stink of oolong and imagines Mireille Darc in the shadows, talking about breaking eggs in inappropriate places and violent car accident pileups and car fires and bourgie idiots worrying about their junk instead of their souls. He tries to imagine his dad in the movie and can't. He can't see him in any situation beyond his control. He tries to picture him on his deathbed wishing he'd been nicer to his family, and this works. At first. In the next frame, he sees his frail father tearing at the sheets on said deathbed to find the label—wondering if they cheapskated him out of designer sheets for his finale. Trinidad must be a hellscape on a par with Guantanamo to create someone like Dari's old man. No wonder his mother drank so much. It's not an excuse for her, there are no excuses, but he can't imagine being married to Maynard Gray and being sober at the same time. Whatever. Dari is getting out of here. Izzy can stay forever if she wants to. But Dari is not Izzy.

Next morning, after his father has left for work and Izzy heads out for another round of interviews, Dari pokily eats his cereal. He will go to school today. He will do his best to stay there the whole day.

He washes his bowl, puts it away, and hops online to search for a phone number. Once he has it, he takes a drink of water, clears his throat, and dials.

"Good morning, this is Vice Principal Monaroy's office. How may I direct your call?" a cheerful-sounding receptionist asks.

"Good morning, Madam. May I please speak with the vice principal? It is important."

"One moment."

"Thank you." Since Dari's voice changed when he was thirteen, he has been able to effect a spot-on impression of his father's voice, accent and all. He used to do this to entertain Izzy, but he got so good at it, it frightened her. He stopped.

"Yes, Monaroy speaking."

"Hello, Mr. Monaroy. This is Mr. Maynard Gray, Dariomauritius's father."

"Oh. Yes. How are you?"

"I'm well. But, you see, after speaking at length to my son last night, it occurs to me that perhaps I was being . . . a bit overprotective. I'd like to retract my request. Please don't feel the need to contact me unless Dariomauritius's behavior gets out of line. If I have any further concerns, I'll call you directly."

"Fine. No more eyes on your son." He sounds relieved and indifferent. "Anything else I can do for you?"

"No, that will be all. And thank you for your understanding. Good-bye." Dari hangs up.

Who's slick now, bitch?

He attempts to eat the cafeteria offerings for the day, guessing what he has in front of him is stew, though it tastes more like a failed paella. It's food, so he eats it until he can't take it anymore. With no interesting subjects anywhere in sight, Dari draws a fictitious woman—a bald Vietnamese woman, specifically—standing on the edge of an active volcano. She has an important decision to make.

A shadow clouds his light.

"Excuse me." He says this though he's not the one that needs excusing.

"I'm sorry. Was I . . ." She trails off. She's a little confused. He waits. He has no intention of helping her finish her thought, whatever that thought might be.

"You're always drawing," she says. She sits down without an invitation.

"Yeah. I can't stop." It's true.

"Can I see?"

He hands her the sketch pad. She could be a lunatic, but he just hands it over like a zombie, and she starts flipping through all of his work. "These are amazing."

"Thanks."

She takes her time, concentrating on each one as though she needs to imprint them permanently on her brain. If her behavior weren't so strange and interesting, it would be rude. When she's finally satisfied, she delicately closes the pad and slides it back across the table.

"May I ask what your name is?" Her voice hovers just above a whisper. So timid.

"You can call me Dari, but my name is Dariomauritius."

"Wow."

"No, it's not 'wow,' it's terrible. Some pretentious, nonsensical Greek shit my dad invented." She's a little startled by this. Maybe cursing was a bad idea. She's like a rabbit. One misstep and she'll disappear.

"I like it," she says.

"And you are?" Dari ventures.

"Doesn't matter."

"Why?"

"Because I'm nobody you wanna know." She asserts this with sudden confidence.

The bell rings, and she jumps as if it had been a gunshot.

"Bye," she whispers and vanishes before he can respond. She is practically a specter, and Dari truly wonders, for almost a full minute, if he hallucinated her.

He smiles.

He has found a subject.

3

NEW CANDY

ecause I'm nobody you wanna know." I figure I should be honest. The bell rings, and I run away. I race down the hall to French and I can't believe my nerve. Walking up to strange boys and talking to them about their art is not in my repertoire. But then again, I don't even have a repertoire. Either way, it was an impulse. An impulse I followed because I didn't much like the alternative.

Before feeling so bold, I got a taste of the alternative.

About nine and a half minutes earlier.

"Nobody joins AFS anymore, Marie. Not unless they're planning to go abroad and you are not. Joining just to join went out with Timberlands and V-neck sweaters." Jackie can easily equate any number of life choices with current or past fashion trends.

"I want something easy. I can't join anything that's going to take up my time," Marie whines. I have been enduring lunch with Jackie, Tracy, and Marie for about two weeks, and I know and they know that this is not an ideal situation. As soon as I greet them and sit down, Jackie always smiles as though she's proud of me for successfully dressing myself, and the others pretend not to notice my entrance. My intrusion.

I know they don't want me here, and I don't want to be here, but I don't have the courage to flip everyone the bird and sit all alone. Like him.

Tracy mumbles a suggestion.

"What?" both Marie and Jackie say.

"*The Folio*. We need staffers. No big deal." She says it quietly, staring down at her carrot sticks. Marie glances at me out of the corner of her eye. Jackie looks like she might vomit.

"No offense," Tracy says, looking at me head-on for the first time since June. Before June, actually. May.

"Tracy," Jackie snaps. "What is wrong with you?"

"It's fine," I offer.

"Don't make excuses, Lily. Tracy, you are so insensitive."

"All I said was we need staffers. Christ, can't I even mention it? It's not like I'm blaming anyone for running the journal into the ground or screwing up my shot at a first publication or anything. Life doesn't just stop because someone had a nervous breakdown!"

The table falls silent. Truthfully, though, I'm glad she said it. I hate being handled with kid gloves. I'm not a flower. It's useful to know what people really think. Tracy is really, really mad at me. She has a right to be.

"Yeah. It was shitty. I'm sorry." Then there's this horrific pause and, because I can't stand it, I stupidly try to fill it. "If you guys have any, like, questions or anything, I can try to answer them."

"You're not a sideshow act, Lily," Jackie says.

"I didn't say I was. But I went through some things that, uh, a lot of people don't ever want to talk about. What I'm saying is . . . I can talk about them if you want."

"I don't mean to be rude or anything, but before you sat down this conversation was about extracurriculars, which are kind of important," Marie says. "And I think you should probably not spread all your pain around so easily like that."

Neither Jackie nor Tracy says anything to challenge Marie's opinion. I swallow. Okay. Well. I tried my best.

"I'm gonna go." I stand.

"You don't have to leave," Jackie says.

"I think I do. Thanks anyway." I take my tray and dump it, knowing there are still about five minutes left in the period. Knowing I no longer have a safe haven. But I don't much care. And since I'm not caring much about anything, I decide to talk to the beautiful boy who always sits alone.

I wait in the ferry station on the bench, watching the hordes of people file over to the gate. I ride this boat just about every day after school, but the light drizzle steadily increases in power, and I'm not quite feeling it today. I decide to just sit for a little while to watch the ferries dock and depart. Dock and depart. If I squint, I think I can see Staten Island from here. I think about all the people living there. One in particular. I wish I didn't, but I can't help myself. I wonder what their schools are like, if they have bowling alleys, bookstores, coffeehouses like we do. That's stupid. Of course they do. I can't believe I'm imaging SI as a tiny foreign nation with its own language and customs, so different from what I'm used to. In a weird way, I guess it kind of is: It is so close to me, so accessible. And I will never go there.

"Do you have any idea how much I love you?"

"Liar," I say aloud, responding to a shadow of a memory, not caring who hears me. Staten Islanders. They make terrible boyfriends. Pretty subpar teachers, too.

Back at home, I lounge on the sofa flipping through TV stations as Mom finishes her yoga routine.

"Are you sure you don't wanna come with me? I know they can work it out." She says this in child's pose, so I only make out about 75 percent of it. The rest I guess from the context. My mother intellectually understands that an important aspect to yoga practice is silence, but talking is like oxygen for her. She stops, she dies.

"I'll be fine, Mom. It's only three days." I have no intention of join-ing my mother on a "wellness retreat." Besides, imagine the looks on those poor fools' faces if they saw their guru's basket-case daughter. They would certainly want their deposits back.

She slides into cobra.

"Might be good for you."

"No, it wouldn't."

Camel pose. Her yoga clothes for the day consist of a sports bra and formfitting capris. While her head reaches for her heels, I briefly imagine flinging a nickel onto her exposed solid abs just to see the ugli-ness, the disorder of her reaction to such a violation. My mother is very beautiful. As far as I know, she always has been.

"What would you do all by yourself?" she asks.

"The same thing I do when you're here. Nothing." A music video comes on one of the cable access stations. Chris Brown. I mute him and study his stupid face. I fantasize about gathering a posse of all the toughest women I can find, knocking on his door, dragging him outside by his toes, and drawing and quartering the son of a bitch, Elizabethan style, in the middle of Times Square. This will serve as an eternal lesson for any guy who wants to beat the shit out of his girlfriend. The world will be a better place. But then again: violence to punish violence? Is that a good message to send the world? I think it over for a second. Yes. In this case, yes it is.

"Lily? Why are you smiling like that?" She seems genuinely alarmed. I must be wearing quite the expression.

"Uh, I don't know. Maybe I can try to write a new song. If I have the apartment to myself." She looks uncertain. "Mom, come on. It's not like I'm gonna have a party. You know that could never happen."

"Now, that I would actually find far healthier than you sitting here alone, staring at the walls." Sun salutations. She breathes into her asanas for a minute, so I think she's done with the subject. She is not.

"You could stay with Grandma."

"That would be punishment for me and her."

"Lily—"

"What? It's true."

She rolls her eyes as she slides into warrior two. I only see Grandma on important holidays and when she's sick. That's it. One of her hobbies is trying to guess which forms of cancer she'll get before she dies. Another is falling asleep with her stove on. The idea that she could be a passable chaperone for anyone is ridiculous.

I turn off the TV and head into the kitchen. In the cupboard is a giant bag of gummy bears. I stick my hand in without bothering to wash it first, and cram a bunch in my mouth. I hear the faintest hint of the song I've been trying to remember and hum a bit of it, then I beat out a rhythm. It's not only in 4/4 time. I feel 3/4 and 2/4 happening. This is complex. I drum the side of the cupboard lightly and the brown-and-white bottle hiding in the back falls to its side. Cymbalta. Only opened once. The song evaporates.

I go back and plop on the couch.

"New song?" She smiles at me expectantly.

"Not yet. I can't hold on to it."

"You gotta write it down, Lil. I keep telling you that. If you kept a journal, you could write down all your thoughts and your song ideas, lyrics. You'd know where to find everything. Not to sound like a broken record—"

"What's a broken record?" I mumble before I can stop myself. Mom shoots me a mean side eye and I grin sheepishly, hoping that'll count as an apology. She's not keen on age jokes even in her best moods.

"Lily, you have no idea how much better you'd feel if you gave yourself some type of creative outlet. Or an organized way to vent, if nothing else."

I stretch out on my back and count the unnecessary wooden slats in the ceiling. Twenty-one, twenty-two, twenty-three, twenty-four . . .

"Are you listening?"

"Yes. I will write the song down. It will be fine."

"When? By the time you do it, you'll forget again."

I massage my temples. "I won't forget," I say quietly, wishing she were at the gym instead of in my face.

"Yes, you will. You know you will."

If she's so certain of my inefficacy, what's the point of talking about it at all?

"I don't mean to be so hard on you. I just want you to be your best self. That's all I ever want," she claims defensively. I'm not even arguing with her. Why is she on my case?

Mercifully, she stops talking for a few seconds. I just hear her breathing as I close my eyes. If I'm lucky, maybe she'll forget I'm here and I can sneak in a nap.

"Could you stay with Jackie or Tracy?" she asks.

Nope. She hasn't forgotten I'm here.

"No."

"I know things have been weird, but honey, you have to at least try—"

"I said no."

She's silent and I can feel her staring at me, so I sit up on my elbows and stare right back. This continues for a few moments before she shakes her head in frustration and proceeds with her routine. This time she doesn't say anything more.

Mom works out usually four or five times a week. Mostly yoga at home, but sometimes she goes running. Sometimes to the gym. This started about a year ago. I asked her why and she said fear of looking old. Then she said, "*Getting* old, I mean." I think it's really the first one, though. This cute guy kept checking her out once at Urban Outfitters. He finally got brave enough to speak to her and asked if she was in his sociology lecture at Columbia. She giggled, but never answered him. She's shared this story with her friends more than once.

Later, I struggle with the chemistry assignment because chemistry is a dumb subject and no one like me belongs in such a class. I goof around online and briefly consider visiting my Facebook page, but then decide against it. It probably has cobwebs by now anyway. Or worse. Instead I visit Tracy's. Her relationship status is "complicated." Yeah, I bet. Her photo must be a new one: she's at the beach in sunglasses with her arm around Marie. I read her status: *I am so sick of certain people trying to soak up all the sympathy in the world. If you're supposed to be so depressed do something about it! Stop blaming everyone else for your problems.* She posted this at 12:49 p.m. today. Lunch. It is now 8:42 p.m. and this status has forty-eight likes and seventeen comments. My hands start to shake and I hear a loud sustained ringing in my ears. I close my eyes and breathe. She might not be talking about me. She might be talking in completely general terms. But then again, what if she is talking about me? So what? So fucking what? She obviously hates me just like most people, so what difference does it make? I open my eyes and quickly find my favorite YouTube video, "Mango loves Milkshake," and watch it over and over and over again.

There was a time when Tracy and I would discreetly roll our eyes at Jackie's bossiness. When Jackie's parents took us all camping in the Poconos in the eighth grade, Tracy and I made a secret pact that if we all went to the same college, she and I would be roommates. We decided we wouldn't tell Jackie until eleventh grade. Guess we won't be needing to break that news.

I hear a ding and look down at the corner of my screen. Tara McKenzie is attempting to chat with me. That has never happened before, and I have no idea why it's happening now.

Did u finish the HW? she asks.

Nope. Didn't get it. u?

Yes. Just a matter of following the equations.

Oh, God.

Can't follow what I don't get.

There is silence, and I wonder if she got bored and left. Then I see that she's typing.

I don't think it's so hard, but I've noticed that u have been struggling. I wasn't sure if it was the material or other stuff, she writes.

Now it's my turn to make her wait. She's noticed that I've been struggling? She hardly ever says more than two words to me, but she's been looking at my test scores?

No, I just suck at it, I reply.

I don't. If u want help ask for it. We are partners.

Is she just bragging or seriously trying to be helpful? It's hard to tell from words on a screen. Then again, Tara's so odd, I might not be able to tell if I was staring her in the face. I sigh and wonder why I didn't just hide myself. I hate chatting. It's invasive. I also don't like e-mails or talking on the phone. Or talking in person. To humans.

Thanks. But I think I'll b fine.

K, she writes. Seconds later, she signs off. Is it possible that Tara actually cares about me? Doubtful.

I watch little Mango kissing and slobbering all over Milkshake as he tries to sleep. I wonder if I'll ever feel that happy to see another living thing. I think about my hands and remember how they felt tearing up a drum kit, or to a lesser degree, picking on a bass. I haven't played music in a long time and I don't know if I ever will again. It's been tainted. Reminds me of last year, and him, and I don't need any more reminders.

I still have Tracy's Facebook up on my screen. The status now has fifty-four likes and twenty-one comments.

From my desk drawer, I dig out the books and papers and junk and pry up the board that serves as the false bottom. Beneath that is a treasure trove, and it will help me now. Junior Mints, candy corn, Mike and Ikes, Raisinets, Jelly Bellies. I'll have a little of each, thank you very much. As far as addictions go, mine could be far worse. I could be rolling on cough syrup. I'd try it too, if I didn't think it tasted disgusting.

Mr. Crenshaw drones on about the photoelectric effect, or some garbage that makes me want to dig up Einstein and punch him in the face. Tara steadily jots down notes. She seems rather enthusiastic, as though she's been waiting for this chemistry class all her life. Must be nice.

While he speaks, he smacks his desk without realizing it. As he moves, he bounces on the balls of his feet and his cheap dress shoes click on the ugly floor tiles. I hear a rhythm being tapped out and, in my mind, I add a high hat, then a bass, and now we got something cooking, and suddenly, I'm not about to fall into an irreversible coma.

"What are you doing?" Tara whispers, without looking up from her paper.

"Huh?" I ask.

"You're bobbing up and down like something's wrong with you."

Oh. Whoops.

I try to sit still after that. Dammit, Tara. She took my song from me. I can't remember a note.

"Lilith? Miss Rothstein?" Mr. Crenshaw calls.

Oh, no.

"Um, you can just call me Lily."

"Fine. Lily. Can you answer the question, please?"

Oh Jesus, Jesus, Jesus . . .

"I'm sorry, Mr. Crenshaw. Can you repeat the question?"

"The symbol for Planck's constant?"

My heart is pounding so hard, I really think I might have a heart attack. Right here in school. Just fall over on my face and get dragged out of here in an ambulance. That would be so embarrassing.

"I don't know," I struggle to say.

"Pardon?"

Louder, I repeat, "I don't know."

"Can someone help her, please?" He sighs in a way that I hate. It's not that he's disgusted with me. He pities me, like I'm some poor idiot that they all have to tolerate until they can get me the hell out of this school. I glance around to see if anyone's glaring or smirking, but no. No one looks at me. Yep. Still pretty invisible. I'm just relieved that I didn't vomit or faint or stroke out.

When the bell finally rings, I gather my things and I can feel Tara looking at me.

"Aren't you afraid of failing?"

I give it some thought. "No," I answer truthfully.

"Why?"

"Because I don't care." I almost end that sentence with a question mark. I didn't realize I felt that way until I said it.

"Then why bother? You should just quit," she offers, gathering her own books.

"That is a good point."

Lunch. Dammit. I still have to go to lunch.

I agonize over the choice of the day—some kind of pork sandwich or something yellowish. Polenta? What is that? Whatever it is, it looks like it's already been digested. I choose the pork knowing I won't eat a bite, but I feel like I have to choose something; I've been standing here too long to leave with an empty tray. I press play on my iPod and let Sleater-Kinney distort my hearing as I pretend not to care that I have no one to sit with today.

I peruse the room carefully, checking out all my nonexistent options. I can't go back to Tracy/Jackie/Marie after yesterday. I can't ever.

And there he sits. Well. Fuck it.

Quite unceremoniously, quite uninvitedly, I join him. He keeps drawing. My hands shake. I don't say anything. Why am I not saying anything? *Say something!*

"Hey," I say.

He glances up at me and seems surprised and confused to see me sitting there. He just nods and goes back to his drawing. I turn off my music and pick at my food. He doesn't even have a tray. He did yesterday, but he wasn't really eating. Does he not eat? Does he have bulimia? Do guys get that? He is thin. But then again, he has nice muscle tone. I don't think bulimics have that kind of definition. He's pretty much ignoring my presence. I think I've made a grave mistake, but it's too late now. I have to commit. I have to pretend I don't feel like dying.

"I don't see you around much," I say.

He nods, I think. He does something with his head, but he keeps drawing. He is so focused. Without looking up, he asks, "Are you ever going to tell me your name?"

Oh, yeah.

"It's Lily."

He nods. Neither of us says anything for a few moments.

"Lilith. It's an odd name." I don't know why I add this.

"That's a female demon, right? In Jewish mythology. You Jewish?"

Wow.

"Yeah, I've heard that story, and I am Jewish, but—"

Dari's eyes spot that pork sandwich on my tray and then he glances back up at me in earnest confusion. What was I thinking?

"Uh, yeah. I know. Pork. I'm not that religious, but I'm not gonna eat it anyway. I'm not hungry. And even if I were more religious, we are allowed to—ya know?—*look* at it." He starts to nod, but then stops himself and frowns. Deeper confusion? I need to change the subject.

"My mom named me after some women's music festival that used to happen in the nineties. Lilith Fair. She was obsessed with that festival. She used to be a lesbian, I think." Why am I telling him this?

"She's not a lesbian anymore?" he asks. He's actually interested.

"Well, no. Not to my knowledge. I guess she was bisexual. Is? I don't know. I just know when she talks about Lilith Fair and her special girlfriends, she gets this dazed, dreamy look on her face. I don't know. I should ask her."

"Really?" he asks, glancing up at me. God. His eyes are so brown.

"What?"

"You can just come out and ask your mom if she used to be a lesbian?"

"Sure. She doesn't like secrets. They're damaging."

"Wow." He's no longer drawing. He's looking directly at me, with a little more intensity than I'm used to in the lunchroom.

"It gets annoying. She likes to talk about everything. Sometimes I just need my space and she doesn't like to give it." I hope I don't sound too whiny, but it's nice to talk to someone who isn't obligated to talk to me. Someone who doesn't know me.

"Why are you sitting here?" he asks. So direct.

I shrug. "I just wanted to."

He stares at me with unwavering regard. He reminds me of my cat. She crawls on my chest and just stares into my eyes forever without getting tired of me. I often wonder what she sees. I wonder what Dari sees.

"Why do you always sit alone?" I can be direct, too.

He breaks his gaze and looks around the room. "People here. They don't interest me."

I nod, feeling a bit ill again. I grip my tray, preparing to make my exit, and then he says, "Except you." I look at him, but his eyes are already back on his drawing. I can't explain it, but I feel like he wants me to stay, so I do. He draws, I play with my food, and we barely say anything. But it's somehow okay. I dump my tray and come back. He still draws. Then the bell rings.

"Where are you going?" he asks. I jump because he hasn't said anything for maybe twenty minutes.

"The bell. I have to get to class."

"Wanna split?"

I've never been one to leave school in the middle of school. Sure sometimes I just skip, but that's typically with my mother's permission. This is advanced bad behavior. Perhaps a little too advanced for boring Lily.

But then again . . .

4

LIKE A JUNGLE SOMETIMES

See that guy over there?" Dari indicates the stranger by tilting his head slightly. "The one in the Nickelback T-shirt?"

"Yeah."

"Go over there and ask him if you can borrow some deodorant."

"What?! No!"

Dari smiles. "Does that mean you'd prefer a double dare?"

She sighs. Their impromptu game of Truth or Dare has been getting increasingly stupid as the afternoon wears on. But once you start a game of T or D, you have to see it through.

"Fine."

Dari watches her walk over to this poor guy with terrible taste in music and an even worse haircut. He strains to hear their conversation, but it's too windy. By the expression on Nickelback dude's face, she isn't cheating. He shakes his head at her, trying to smile, but he mostly looks frightened. She runs back to Dari laughing.

"He said he thought I smelled fine!"

They both crack up. People are freaks.

"Okay, truth or dare? And you'd better pick dare," she warns.

"Yeah, yeah. Dare."

She looks around the park and then her eyes stop on a mom (or a white nanny?) and two kids, one about two or three and a baby in a stroller.

"Go over to that woman and ask her if you can change her baby's diaper."

"Hell no!"

"Come on!"

"You want me to go to prison and turn up on some pedophile list?"

"Oh." She's disappointed.

"I change my answer. Give me truth," Dari tells her. He notices people in the park noticing them. Giving them that look. He knows that look. Time to rein in the game.

"You can't change your answer," she protests.

"I think I can, because I just did."

After ditching school, they went to an Afghan place—Dari's favorite. He barely touches lunch at school because he's always waiting for a better opportunity to present itself. Practically the moment they freed themselves from scholastic hell, Lily came to life. He was pleasantly surprised. Now they're here. Testing each other's boundaries. Lightly.

"You gonna ask me somethin' or not?"

"Why did you transfer schools?"

"I was asked to leave my old school," he says.

"Really? What did you do?"

"That's a follow-up question. You only get to ask one question."

"I won't judge you," she pushes, but it's a gentle push. Dari fiddles with one of his dreads. *How much am I willing to share with this girl?*

"I'll tell you a secret," he whispers.

She leans in, riveted.

"I'm an asshole."

She laughs. He doesn't. She stops laughing. They are quiet for a moment. Long enough for Dari to return to his sketchbook and start drawing again.

"Well. At least you're honest about it."

Dari looks up and smiles at her. In front of them, a group of tiny kids play red light/green light, some of them too small to know the difference.

It's getting late-ish. Lily should probably get home soon. Dari is already quite late and definitely does not want to go home. It's a conundrum. An unpleasant puzzle Dari silently attempts to solve just before his phone rings.

"Damn." He reaches in his pocket and looks at it, but he knows who it is.

"Hey, Izzy."

Lily watches him for a moment before pulling out her own phone. Dari hopes she's texting someone and not tweeting their location or what they're doing right now.

"I know. I know. I just . . . I had to do research for this paper I'm working on, so . . . I'm NOT lying!" He sits on the curb and rubs his head in agony. While Izzy monolectures him, he reaches into his bag, takes out a lighter and a Parliament, lights it, and takes three drags before he's able to get a word in. His voice is much lower now, resigned.

"I'm sorry. I'm on my way. Bye." He hangs up and continues sitting on the curb, blowing smoke through his nostrils. Lily sits next to him.

"You in trouble?" she asks.

"I'm always in trouble." He shrugs. "I have to go. I hate it, but I have to."

"Was that your . . . uh . . . ?"

"Sister. My dad's giving her shit because I'm not there. Sometimes I just can't take it. Ya know?"

She nods. "Does . . . does your mom not live with you?"

Dari stares straight ahead, quietly inhaling and exhaling.

"Sorry. I don't mean to be nosy," Lily offers.

"No. My mom does not live with me. She lives in the ground."

Lily gasps a little, but then tries to cover it up.

"I'm really sorry, Dari."

"Why? Did you do it?"

Lily shakes her head and looks away in shame. He didn't mean to cause that.

"I'm sorry, Lily." He stamps the cigarette out on the ground. "My family brings out my worst. I did tell you I'm an asshole." He stands up and Lily remains seated for a few seconds. Dari reaches his hand out to her and she takes it and joins him.

They walk uptown. Along the way, Dari stops with no warning.

"What's wrong?" Lily asks.

Dari gapes at a wall. When she follows his eye, she sees what he sees: in the middle of a mess of random graffiti gibberish is a small, yet pristine etching of Josephine Baker in a silvery flapper dress. It stands out on this old ugly wall. It's perfect. He goes up to it and touches it.

"Somebody did this," he muses. "Somebody cared."

"Do you ever do things like that?"

"Hmm?" He's still tracing the image in awe.

"Like tagging or whatever it's called? Do you do that?"

Dari sharply turns to Lily. "What does that mean?"

"You know? Like your name or your signature or something? I don't know. You know what I mean."

"Because I draw and I'm black, I must be a tagger?"

"NO! I didn't mean it like that at all!"

"Then why did you ask?"

"Because you were so into the Josephine Baker, I thought maybe you did stuff out in public too! I don't know."

"What's the problem?" A police officer appears out of nowhere, startling them both. Dari sighs.

"Someone gonna answer me?"

"N-no problem," Lily stutters. Regardless, the officer decides to search Dari. Hands against the wall, waiting for it to end, Dari just stares at the ground. *I am an artist, I am a thinker, I am a* person, *you goddamn pig.* When he's done, the officer backs away, satisfied (unsatisfied?) to find Dari clean. He makes a note on a clipboard.

"Where you supposed to be?" he asks Dari.

Dari's jaw tightens.

"He was just walking me home," Lily explains.

The cop gives Dari yet another once-over and then walks away without saying another word.

"That was awful," Lily cries.

Dari shrugs. "Happens."

"Why? You weren't doing anything."

Dari rolls his eyes. "For real? Didn't you know I was born guilty?"

"I'm sorry. I can be dumb sometimes. I just wasn't thinking," she says.

"Not something you have to think about, is it?"

Lily just stares at him. Fear and confusion clouding her face. He looks back at Josephine, wishing she could pop off the wall and provide some guidance. She doesn't.

"I have trouble trusting people," he finally says.

"Me too."

"I'd like to trust you."

"So trust me."

He looks back at Lily, uncertainty in his eyes.

"Truth," she blurts.

"What?"

"Come on! Pretend you just asked me and I picked truth. Ask me anything you want. I won't lie to you. You can trust me." Her voice sounds a hair higher than before, as though she's working hard to sound natural.

Dari stares at her for a moment, his expression of doubt melting into one of slight concern.

"Why don't you have any friends?"

Her whole being freezes up and her already pallid skin turns an unnatural shade of white. He asked the wrong question. He has to take it back. Now. In the blink of an eye, before he can apologize or say anything to reverse the situation, he notices the light dusting of freckles on Lily's nose. The tiny flecks of amber in her dark brown eyes, and a stray spiral of her hair that stubbornly falls in her face no matter how many times she pulls it behind her ear. And he has to catch his breath in that eye blink of time. What an inconvenient moment to suddenly see how fucking pretty this girl is.

"I slit my wrists and went to a hospital. But just for a little while. I didn't die. Obviously."

Dari is stunned. He had no idea.

"There was other stuff too, that I'm not ready . . . that I'd rather not go into right now. But I feel like the suicide attempt was the big one. I mean, that kind of thing can really strain a friendship," Lily finishes.

Dari smiles and then laughs a little, but tries to mask that with a cough, which only makes it worse. Then Lily laughs and they both laugh and neither of them can believe that just a few seconds ago they were this close to missing out on such a good laugh.

Dari trudges up the four flights of stairs, dreading the hell waiting for him on the other side of the door. No matter what it will be, it will be bad, but he feels okay. He feels kind of nice. Lily is okay. She's kind of nice. He wasn't expecting that. He wasn't expecting much of anything, but he likes her. She's something to look forward to where before there was nothing.

He turns the key and walks in. His father sits on the sofa watching a PBS documentary. Dari stands by the door, not moving far beyond the threshold. He knows better than to simply go to his room. It will be best if he just waits, playing his role in this game.

The program is about the migratory patterns of hawks—something Dari knows damn well his father couldn't give two shits about. But he waits as the old man watches the hawks taking flight with rapt attention.

"Where have you been?" he finally asks without turning away from the TV.

"I was out. I had to do research for a paper."

"Why do you lie to me?"

For a moment, Dari actually asks himself the same question. *Why do I lie? Won't make any difference.*

"I'm not lying," he lies.

His father stares at the television again in silence. Dari has to pee. He's had to pee for about forty minutes. Is it worth going to the bathroom now and coming back to face the fight, or is it easier to stand here and let his bladder burn his insides? His father continues to watch the documentary and time passes. A small bead of sweat slides down Dari's forehead.

"Dad," he moans.

Dad pays him no attention. He chuckles as a baby hawk stumbles and bumps into its mother.

"Dad? I'm sorry. I really have to go to the bathroom."

He turns and inspects Dari. He smiles and glances at his watch.

"Well, that is interesting. According to my count, you are two hours and twenty-six minutes late. In two hours and twenty-six minutes, a young man should have many opportunities to urinate. Many. I wonder how many. Are you curious? I'm curious." He pulls out his smartphone and starts typing on it. Dari swallows as tears well up in his eyes. He will not cry. He will NOT cry.

His father references something on his phone. "Hmm. Well, it says here that the average person does not urinate more than two cups every two hours. So if you need to go more than that, perhaps we should take you to a urologist. What do you think? Let's see if there are some good urologists in the area. Perhaps—"

Dari runs down the hall, into the bathroom, and slams the door. Whatever is coming, it can't be worse than this. And worse than letting his father see him cry would be wetting himself like an infant.

Sweet, sweet release. He allows himself a moment to enjoy this feeling. Thank God. Or thank whatever entity out in the universe has allowed him to survive this long.

And then that moment is gone.

He returns to the living room. The documentary has been replaced by a fund-raiser.

"Sit down, Dariomauritius." Dari heads for an armchair, but his father shakes his head and indicates that he should sit next to him. Dari does as he's told with serious anxiety. He literally can't remember the last time he and his father sat next to each other on the sofa.

"I understand the urge to behave recklessly. I also know that at your age it makes sense to defy me just for the fun of it. But it can't go on. I give you rules because rules help you to excel in life. If I didn't punish you, you would have no sense of structure or even right and wrong. I care too much about you and your sister to turn you out into the world unprepared for its challenges. It is how I was raised and my father was raised and someday, it will be how you raise your children. Like it or not, I'm right."

Dari stares straight ahead and remains still. He refuses to confirm or deny anything his father says.

"Unfortunately, your mother was not raised this way. When they weren't neglecting her, her family indulged her. Instability was all she knew. You don't want to end up like her, do you?"

Dari clenches his fist and imagines it smashing his father's jaw.

"I just want what is best for you. Do you hear me? Dariomauritius, answer me."

"Yes, I hear you, Dad."

"Do you care?"

No, Dad. Quite frankly, I don't give a flying fuck. You're a hypocrite and the second I turn eighteen, I am leaving this crazy house and I'm never coming back.

"I care." It oozes out of Dari's face, barely words.

"Good."

Maynard Gray touches his son's head. Dari winces, expecting a blow, but instead, receives a pat. His father grips one of his son's dreadlocks delicately. Then he reaches over with his other hand. In it is a pair of scissors.

Snip.

Dari sucks in his breath. His father holds the lock in his hand. Ten inches of hair. In memoriam. He opens the drawer in the coffee table and drops the lock inside.

"Tomorrow you won't miss curfew."

Dari stands and goes to his room.

In the mirror, he decides that he can adjust his hair. He decides that if he's careful to hold his head a certain way, no one will notice the absence. He tells himself this so he will not cry. Even in private, crying is not an option.

He traces his image in the mirror. He doesn't understand why things must be the way they are. He imagines Lily at her house having some delicious family meal. During a dessert of strawberries and whipped cream, someone pulls out Scrabble and—uh-oh!—it's family game night! He laughs to himself. This isn't exactly what he wants. He just wants something else.

Izzy knocks lightly then opens the door a crack.

"You okay?" she asks.

He shrugs.

"Sorry I went a little ballistic earlier."

Dari shoots her a puzzled glance.

"On the phone. When I called."

He'd already forgotten about that.

"You, I forgive."

She enters and sits down on the bed. Then she sees his hair.

"Coulda been worse." She's right.

"Has he always been like this?" Dari asks her.

Izzy thinks about it. "I don't know. I guess he's gotten worse as he's gotten older. And after Mom. But he's never been happy. Not as long as I've known him.

"Got good news, though. I finally got a job. Less money than before, but enough."

"Congratulations!"

"Thanks, Dari."

"Sorry I wasn't here earlier to celebrate."

Izzy moves to her brother and looks at the empty spot where his lock once was.

"It'll grow. But, either way, you have to really concentrate to notice it." He knows she's just trying to make him feel better, but he appreciates the effort.

"You're so good-looking anyway. A few flaws couldn't possibly hurt you."

Dari looks back at the mirror. They don't share a lot of compliments in their family, so he's not sure what to make of this one. His impulse is to assume she's mocking him. But this is Izzy. Izzy isn't Dad.

"You think so?"

"I know you know so."

"I do. But I didn't know you did," he teases. She hits him with a pillow.

"You have to stop testing him, Dari. I don't want you to get hurt."

"So it would be my fault?"

She sits on his bed and lets her head fall into her hands. It's a gesture that comes from living nearly three decades with Dad.

"Dari? I'm gonna be leaving."

He shuts his eyes and nods. He didn't want to hear it, but of course he knew this was coming. Get a job, get some money, get the hell out.

"I don't want to worry about you pissing him off every day of my life. You're old enough to know better. If you live here, you gotta deal with his rules. Nothing is gonna change that."

"All right."

She stands and reaches her arms out to him. *What is this? A hug? What is going on?*

"What?"

"Come on. Give me a hug."

"Why?"

"Because I'm a good sister and I want a hug, dammit!"

Bewildered, Dari gives his sister the hug she so badly wants. She squeezes him tightly. Twice he tries to disengage, but she doesn't allow him to. He has no idea when this hug will end.

"Be good, okay?"

"Wait a minute." He pulls away and her eyes are misty. "You're not leaving this minute, are you?"

"No. I'm leaving tomorrow."

"What?" *It makes no sense! How can she have an apartment lined up already?* She just found a job. She's supposed to save, look around, reject the first choices that come her way until she finds the perfect place. It's supposed to be a whole process.

"I, uh . . . Trisha and I got back together. Happened about a week ago.

Are you kidding me?

"Why didn't you tell me?"

"Because I know how you feel about her. You have a right to feel however you want, but I love her and I'm an adult and I'm moving in with her. Tomorrow."

"Get out."

"Dari? Don't be a baby."

"Fine. I'm a baby. Leave my room. Go be with your psycho girlfriend."

Izzy wipes away for-real tears that are streaming down her face, but she obeys his command and leaves.

Dari puts on his headphones and blasts Grandmaster Flash in his ears. His family sucks. Everybody leaves. Only one that stays is Big Papa. Damn them all.

Don't push me cuz I'm close to the edge
I'm trying not to lose my head
ah huh-huh-huh-huh

Boop.

He looks down and sees someone trying to chat.

Hey, is all it says.

Hey yourself, he writes.

Truth or dare?

He smiles.

Dare.

There is a pause and he waits as she types.

I dare u 2 eat dinner w/me at my house tomorrow.

Lily wins the cuteness award.

That's an odd dare, he types.

Nothing for a moment.

Scared?

He chuckles. He's about to start typing a response when he catches a glimpse of himself smiling in the mirror. He never sees himself smiling, and it's a strange picture. He looks much younger. Like a little kid. Taking in the picture of this strange new person that he didn't recognize for a second, he has time to assess and agree wholeheartedly with Izzy: *This is a good-looking dude staring back at me.* Then his eye wanders over to the dread stump. He touches it and wonders in horror what he'd look like if his father attacked the rest of his locks with those damn scissors.

Boop.

He forgot to reply.

U still there?

Yeah, he replies, still touching his hair. Would he be as handsome without the locks? Possibly.

Dare accepted. And on an impulse, he presses the less than sign and the number three, and then he hits return. A heart. But he panics. Before she can reply, he quickly signs off.

Hopefully, it wasn't too much.

5

TO SOCIALIZE LIKE
NORMAL HUMAN BEINGS

Too effing much! A heart? Did he just send a heart?
He's gone.
Wow.

I collapse on my bed and stare at the ceiling. Who am I becoming? Where'd I find the guts to leave school with my manic pixie dream guy, spend all evening with him, and now?

That. Was. A. Heart. He couldn't have done that by accident. Those two keys are nowhere near each other on the keyboard. And what else could he have been trying to say? *>2??* That makes no sense. He meant it.

Don't read too much into it, Rothstein. This is how things go badly. I get excited. I let my fantasies get the best of me and then I'm—

Knocking.

"Come in."

Mom bursts in with Mexican hot cocoa in two deformed mugs from her pottery class. I would normally roll my eyes, and that's probably what I should do, but instead I smile like the giddy dork I am right now.

She hands me one and sits on the edge of my bed, beaming so hard I think her face is going to explode.

"What did he say?"

"He said he'll come over."

She squeals. This is getting out of control.

"Mom, seriously, though: We're just friends. Don't make a big thing outta this," I plead, imagining her grinning like a demented cartoon character the whole time Dari's here tomorrow.

"I know, I promise I won't, but please let me be excited! I haven't seen you like this since . . . Well. I'm just glad you're happy, honey. You deserve to feel like this." She clinks her mug against mine. "What did you guys do?"

"Nothing really. We talked. Played Truth or Dare. Walked. It was . . . it was nice."

"Yeah? What else?"

"I don't know. We ate. We joked around—"

"What kind of jokes? Be specific, Lily."

"Mom, please." I laugh it off, but she's being way too intense.

"What?"

"Nothing. I just . . . I don't feel like sharing every detail right now, okay? I want it to be just mine for now. Do you know what I mean?"

Mom tilts her head and frowns at me.

"I think I do. But, um, do you think I don't let you have things just for you?"

I repress the urge to sigh; that would only worsen matters.

"I don't think that, Mom. I don't know. This might sound crazy, but sometimes the line where you end and I begin gets a little fuzzy."

She goes stone silent. Oh, no. I may have just mortally wounded her feelings.

"Never mind, never mind, never mind. I'm exhausted. I'm just gonna go to sleep. I didn't mean anything weird."

She plays with her hair, looking at the floor, the neurons churning in her brain.

"Seriously, don't worry. Thanks for the cocoa," I say and kiss her on the cheek.

"No. This is good. I want you to always be honest with me. You're probably right. I need to let you have your experiences without feeling the need to . . . monitor you all the time. I'm proud of you for speaking up." I smile and mouth the words *love you*. And then she relaxes. She whispers the words back to me before leaving. As she closes the door behind her, I notice that her face seems softer today. No deep worry lines interfering with her beauty. She's my beautiful mom as I remember her before I became a living PSA.

"Lily? Lily!"

"Huh?"

I look up to see the mess I've made of our experiment. Tara sighs and grabs a handful of paper towels. Epsom salt and honey all over the place. No crystals for us.

"You never pay attention. I don't know why you come to class at all."

"Me either," I agree.

Tara scribbles something down in her notebook angrily and continues working. I finish cleaning the mess. I should apologize. She is doing all the work and I'm just in the way. But then again, come on! She hasn't exactly been the most fun lab partner imaginable. When I ask questions, she answers me, but not before sucking her teeth, rolling her eyes, and/or asking if I ever do any of my assignments. She treats me like I'm a complete idiot, and I am far from being an idiot. The truth is I do sometimes do my assignments. But mostly I don't. Because mostly I don't care. And I certainly don't plan on becoming a chemist when I grow up.

"You used to be a goody-goody," Tara mumbles.

"I haven't heard anybody say 'goody-goody' since about third grade."

"I want a new lab partner," she announces, and before I can say anything she marches to the front of the room and starts talking animatedly to Mr. Crenshaw. My heart starts pounding, and I wonder what fresh humiliation is waiting for me thanks to Tara's complaints. I hate her.

Mr. Crenshaw listens, but looks really tired and annoyed, which is generally how he looks all the time, so it's hard to tell if she's having any impact. He glances at me a couple of times, but doesn't quite make eye contact. Then he heaves this big, gigantic bear sigh.

"Class? Apparently there is some disharmony. Is anyone willing to exchange lab partners so Tara will be happy?"

The room is shocked into silence. There are some weird, muffled giggles, but nobody says anything. Nobody raises a hand, and nobody walks forward. Tara's face is redder than I've ever seen a face get. I wonder if she should go to the hospital.

"Fine. Thank you, class. Get back to work." He then talks to Tara for a few more minutes before she slowly walks back to our table.

"What did he—"

"Just leave me alone," she hisses. Her hands shake as she returns to her work, and though her jaw is locked in rage, tears pool at the corners of her eyes. I look at the clock. God, this period always feels endless. It's awful. She has every right to want a new lab partner.

"Sorry," I whisper. "I'll try to be better."

She shakes her head, a sad yet still angry smirk on her lips. She knows I'm lying. I'm not going to be any better. I think she even knows I'm not sorry. I just said it because I know I should be.

I sit in the cafeteria with Dari, and he draws while I eat. We discuss possible menus for our dinner tonight at my house. I warn him that it will most likely be served in takeout containers, but this seems to delight him.

If I'm careful—and super quiet—I can smell him and he doesn't know I'm doing it. He smells amazing. I don't know how to describe it. It's spicy and sweet and there's a roughness to it too. Maybe he wears Old Spice? Not sure. My granddad used to wear that and I remember liking it, but then again maybe that's something only old people wear. Whatever it is, it's nice.

"Do you know everyone here?" he asks me.

I stop smelling him and focus.

"In this school?"

"No. Just in the lunchroom."

I look around. Yeah. I know most of these losers. A few since I was five or six. Sad.

"Pretty much."

He looks around the cafeteria and points to a random guy. Jason Chung.

"That guy. He seems like a dick. Is he?"

"Completely. He's on the rowing team and supposedly he was really drunk at this party last year and he peed in every glass in the house."

"Oh my God!"

"Yeah. He's disgusting."

"What about her?" Dari points out Megan Parsons.

"I don't know her that well. She's in band."

He nods, but seems disappointed by this answer. So I add to it.

"I did hear once that she's a serious sleepwalker. In the middle of the night, she left her apartment, got on the subway, and ended up out on the beach at Coney Island before she woke up."

"Holy shit."

"I know. Creepy, right?"

Did I hear that Megan was a sleepwalker? Yes. But the story I heard was that she got out of bed, left her apartment, and woke up at the twenty-four-hour Gristedes across the street. I like my version better.

He looks around again and his eyes stop.

"What about her?" I follow his gaze and see Tara McKenzie standing in line for lunch and looking lost. Why did he pick her?

"That's my lab partner. Tara. I'd rather not talk about her."

"Why?"

"Not worth it," I say, choosing not to go into any more detail. Tara may get on my last nerve, but I don't want to be the one to start that god-awful rumor rolling around again.

When the bell rings, I gather my things, and only then do I realize that we've made no concrete plans for later.

"Uh? Should I meet you after school somewhere or . . . ?"

He blinks then nods his head. I try not to feel crushed, but I do. If

I hadn't just mentioned it, would he have forgotten about it entirely?

"Yeah. Do you walk home or take the train?"

"Why?" I sound far more defensive than I meant to. I didn't mean to sound defensive at all.

"No reason. I'll just meet you at the front entrance."

"Cool," I say and then leave before I can say anything else weird.

As I walk down the hall to class, someone grabs my sleeve and I jump.

"Is everything all right?" Jackie asks with severe emphasis, suggesting that she's sure it isn't.

"Oh. Yeah. I'm fine, Jackie."

"Are you sure? You haven't joined us for lunch in a while."

I thought it was pretty clear that I'd never be joining them for lunch again, but I guess it wasn't to Jackie.

"No, nothing's wrong. I, um, I met a guy."

"I can see that." Uh-oh. Jackie is using her grown-up, parental voice. "I certainly won't tell you who you can or can't socialize with, but I can warn you as a friend that you might not know as much about him as you think you do."

My head swims a little. She obviously thinks she knows something about Dari. I'm not in the mood for this. We're about to be late for class. I have to remember to meet him at the front entrance, text Mom about dinner. What is she talking about?

"Jackie, he's a nice guy. What's the problem?"

Jackie frowns. "I've heard some things, Lily. He was kicked out of his old school. I've even heard he has a record. Like"—and for this, she whispers—"a criminal record. Haven't you been through enough?"

Two things happen to me simultaneously.

1) I am instantly terrified that Dari might be a serial killer.

2) I am furious that Jackie thinks she has the right to talk to me this way.

"Jackie. I'm fine."

"That's what you said last year, Lily. You weren't fine. At no point is intimacy with your teacher fine. It's abnormal. I don't mean to hurt your feelings, but how many disastrous choices are you gonna make?"

My fists clench, my jaw tightens, I hear blood pumping in my ears. If I do not get away from her, I am going to do her harm.

"Good-bye, Jackie."

"Lily, I'm worried about you."

"Then where were you this summer?" Jackie's mouth falls open, like she really wants to say something, but can't. "Exactly."

I leave her gaping at me in the hall. I never planned to confront Jackie about abandoning me, but what difference does it make now? I feel my hands shaking and tiny beads of sweat on my forehead, but at least I don't feel angry anymore. Honesty isn't easy. Or comfortable.

The final bell of the day rings, and I head to my locker, drop off everything, and then go downstairs to wait by the entrance. For a few brief seconds, the halls are so crowded, I can't imagine ever finding anyone here. But it only lasts for those few seconds, and then it's fairly dead.

There are a few seniors goofing off out front. Two guys and a girl. One of the guys throws the girl over his shoulder and she punches him to let her down, but she's laughing the whole time. I don't know them. They look like burnouts.

While I wait, I strain to remember the song I've been trying to create. I finally wrote a little bit down, but I know there's more, and it's a tricky one. It might be my perfect song. That's quite a high bar to reach, but then again no one knows I'm making it but me, so nobody can tell me if I've failed or not. I'm the only judge. My anxiousness is too distracting, and I can't think of more than another two measures. Lame.

I glance at my watch. I've been waiting for almost ten minutes. I decide to think about what I'll do if he doesn't show. Will I play it off and pretend it meant nothing to me at all? Will I act like I forgot about it too? I don't know. But I won't cry. It never solves anything. In any case, if he doesn't show up soon, I will be getting on the ferry today. I will ride out to Staten Island. I will only get off the boat long enough to reboard the one returning to Manhattan. And I might do it once or twice more before going home. HE can't control me. HE can live out the whole rest of his life in his beautiful home on Staten Island with his beautiful sons and his beautiful wife and his beautiful Irish setter, Annabel Leigh (what a stupid name for a dog). But I still exist. I matter, motherfucker! I—

"Hey! Sorry it took me so long," Dari runs up to me, out of breath.

I shake myself out of my momentary psychosis.

"I had to run back up to the art room to return a book to Ms. Spangler, and she ended up showing me some other ones. I kept saying, 'I have to meet somebody.' Sorry about that."

I smile. He's here. It's going to be okay now.

"What does your mom do?"

"She's a writer. Self-help. She wrote a book years ago that sold like five million copies or something. Her author name is 'Price,' though, if you look her up. She's been trying to write a follow-up book forever, but, well, she can't seem to finish it." He nods. I guess this is interesting. We're still walking on Broadway, but we're not too far from my block.

"She also does a lot of lectures and workshops. Some call her a guru, but she hates that word."

"What does she teach?" he asks.

I think. My mind's gone blank. It's been a part of my life so long that I can't distinguish her self-helping from her mothering.

"Well, I've never gone to a workshop, so I don't know how she does it exactly, but she has these things called the five Cs. Consciousness, compassion, consistency, control, and creation. I don't really know what you're supposed to do with them, but that's like the core of what she teaches." I feel bad. I'd be a terrible agent for my mother. I'm making her sound like a total flake.

"Is her book any good?"

He asks this just as we arrive at my building, and I stop.

"I've never read it," I tell him honestly. He's astonished, but tries to conceal it. I walk us past Marcus, who still makes sure to look down whenever I go by. We're silent in the elevator, and I feel like the crappiest daughter. Why haven't I read her book? It doesn't make any sense. She's never mentioned it either. The only logical reason I can think of is that I was too little to understand it when it first came out, and by the time I could . . . well, I guess I just never thought about it.

We enter and Mom is nowhere to be found, but sounds come from the kitchen and the Buena Vista Social Club is blasting. Her housework music.

"Mom?" It's sort of a half yell.

She pops in from the kitchen, looking a little frazzled. Her curls are roughly tied in a knot at the back of her head, but some of them have escaped.

"I know what you're thinking, but don't panic: I'm not cooking. I'm baking. More or less. Hello! I'm Savannah." She offers her hand to Dari. He shyly shakes it, averting his eyes, which I find strange until I notice something.

"Uh, Mom?"

"What sweetie?"

I shake my head and turn to Dari. "Have a seat. Do you want a drink or anything?"

"No, I'm good," he says and sits as I try to gently yet aggressively pull my mother into the kitchen.

"What's the matter?"

"I think you forgot something," I say, eyeing her chest.

"What?" she looks down. Her tight cotton tank top is clinging to her by the sheerest layer of perspiration, and then she, too, notices that she somehow neglected to wear a bra. This is quite normal for her, but having a guest is not.

"Oops! Well, I didn't know you guys would be coming straight from school. I thought I had some time to prepare." She checks the oven and turns the music down.

"Be back," she says and then scurries off to her room. Not the best start to the evening.

In the living room, Dari studies the photos on the bookshelf. There aren't a lot.

"Is that your dad?" he asks about the one photo we have of a man on display.

"No. That's my uncle Raymond. That's an old picture. I think he's in Uganda now. He's a Doctor Without Borders, so we don't get to see him much."

"Wow. I bet he's seen some shit," Dari says. He sounds low-key, but I can tell he's seriously impressed.

"Yeah." I hope he doesn't ask any follow-up questions because I know very little about what Uncle Raymond does. He sends e-blasts and a quarterly e-newsletter to the family about his work, and I usually just skim them, if I open them at all. Uncle Ray is a really cool, righteous guy and I've always liked him, but you can only read about children with HIV and malaria and filthy drinking water for so long before you start to lose hope for all of humanity.

We sit for a bit in an awkward silence. Typically our silences aren't that awkward, but this one is and I don't understand why.

"Are you sure it's okay for me to be here?" he asks.

"Of course!" I say it a little too fast and perhaps a little too earnestly, but it's true. If I'm completely honest with him, which I will not be, I think Mom might be more excited about his visit than I am. Finally, she gets some tangible proof that her daughter is capable of socializing like a normal human being.

"Okay," he says, "You get along well with your mom, huh?"

"I don't know."

"You do," he insists. He picks up a photo of my mom and me that was taken when I was twelve. She looks radiant in it, her long chestnut curls all wisped away from her face neatly, but not too neatly. Her turquoise eyes shining. I remember that she cried in the parking lot that day before our photo appointment. She used to cry a lot more back then, when she was dating Adam. She was either ecstatically happy with him or horribly depressed. It was good when he finally moved to Seattle.

That day, we went out to Elizabeth to sit for this photographer. I can't remember why we would've done something as random as that unless Grandma put her up to it. We pulled into the lot and she cried really hard for two or three minutes, clutching the steering wheel. The engine was still running and "The Hook" by Blues Traveler played on the radio. A corny song, but I kind of like it. I just sat there and watched her knuckles tighten on the wheel, wishing I knew what to do. Then she wiped her eyes, laughed, and said, "Let's go make a goddamn memory." The next day, she put our car on Craigslist, and a week later, it was gone.

I look terrible in the photo. Bad skin, braces, and dark circles under my eyes because I was going through a long bout of insomnia. I hate that picture so much. I wish I could cut myself out of it, but Mom won't let me.

Dari studies the photo for a while. A long while. It's agony. What is he looking at? Is he trying to decide if I'm still that gross? I keep thinking he'll either put it back or say something. When neither of those things happens, after the longest minute of my life, I try to pull the photo from his hands. He actually holds on to it tighter, so I snatch it away from him and shove it back on the shelf where he found it. Except I turn it toward the book spines so I'm safely hidden. Like it matters now.

"What's wrong?" he asks. Jesus, he has pretty eyes.

I shrug and prepare to change the subject, but I don't have to because Mom comes back. She's now wearing a bra accompanied by a tight black blouse with a modest neckline and one of her famous, flowing gypsy skirts. It's adorned with a colorful Mexican print, and I'm pretty certain she got it as a gringo tourist in Tijuana. I rarely think about what I wear, but Mom takes ensembles very seriously. A few times she's attempted to dress me up like a little doll, but I've never been into it. Before she finally gave up, she said by the time I'm ready to attract attention, it'll be too late. I have no idea what that means; guys are attracted to you or they aren't. But I think the "too late" part scares the crap out of Mom.

"Food will be here in less than an hour. Heard you like Mexican, Darian. There should be plenty to choose from, so you can mix and match, make it whatever you want." Oh my God, why is she trying so hard? And is her outfit part of a Mexican theme? It's like she's never met another living person before.

"That sounds great," he says.

"Dari, Mom. Not Darian," I correct.

"Oh, I'm sorry. Dari. Like milk. Got it."

Oh my God!

"What is that short for?" she asks.

"Dariomauritius," Dari mumbles.

She tilts her head to the side like a puppy hearing a new whistle for the first time.

"That name is like a work of art," she declares. Dari kind of looks down bashfully. This is definitely a side of him I have not seen before.

Mom sits across from us and sips from her ever-full water bottle.

"So? Dari? What is your favorite subject in school?" Did she just do a Google search called *appropriate conversation topics for your teenager's guests*?

"Art, I guess. I don't really like school," Dari answers.

"I don't blame you. The idea that everyone should be taught the same way because it saves time and resources is ludicrous. And it's the main reason American children will always trail behind their Asian counterparts," Mom finishes, punctuating the thought with a large gulp of water. I can't believe she's talking about this.

Oh, no. She isn't finished.

"Well," she begins, "not all of Asia, of course. Things aren't so great in East Timor. China and Japan are really the ones. These days." She finally stops talking. She has this weird expression on her face, like the time when she felt forced to lead the Passover seder. By now, Dari looks rather stricken. I can't tell if he's bored or scared, but he's clearly not enjoying himself.

For the first time in my stupid brain, I wonder if inviting Dari over to my house after hanging out with him once was such a good idea. Maybe I shouldn't have gotten so excited. Now we're all uncomfortable and I don't know what to do and it's my fault.

"Savannah," Dari says so suddenly and casually, I jump.

"Uh, yeah?" I can tell Mom is a little thrown by his ease with her name too. She did offer it to him, though.

"Lily told me you're writing another book. What's it about?" My mother's eyes light up as if some sparklers just went off in her skull.

"You really want to talk about that?"

"Yeah," he says, and he means it. I sink a little in my seat. *I* don't even know what my mom's book is about.

"It's different from my first book. I consider it more of a . . . a philosophical conversation then a self-help guide. It's actually sort of the opposite of self-help in some ways. Using some research from my brother Raymond's work in Africa, my experiences in South America, and recent work I've encountered detailing the cycles of poverty and violence in this country, this book is about how healing the self isn't enough to heal the world. My first book was called *Heal Your Beautiful Self, Grow Your Beautiful World*. This book is intended as a response, and it keeps evolving. I try to give logical and intuitive arguments for how we can reach beyond ourselves to literally end the widespread suffering in the world. If we want to."

We are quiet after she finishes. She inspects the nails on her left hand. She does this when she feels especially vulnerable.

"I didn't know that," I say quietly.

"That sounds revolutionary," Dari says.

My mother smiles at Dari, a surprised smile, and her cheeks turn a little red. Maybe she doesn't receive compliments often enough.

"Well, that's sweet. I appreciate that. But the problem is I'm struggling to finish it and my publisher isn't very happy with me right now."

The oven timer dings, and Mom takes the brownies out. I'm sure they're Duncan Hines or Toll House or something, but they smell delicious anyway. So much so that the aroma lures me into the kitchen to soak up as much of it as I can. For some reason in this moment, as Mom places the brownies on the counter to cool and then shakes her hand in pain because the cloth she used as a pot holder wasn't thick enough to keep her from burning herself, I almost want to cry because I'm struck by how much I love her. I don't even know why.

She looks up at me then.

"What's up?"

"Nothing," I say.

She nods toward the counter. "Ghirardelli. Only the best!"

I kind of half hug her. It's stiff and she's totally confused, but it's the best I can do.

Dinner was delish. Nobody beats Casa Verde. The conversation wasn't bad either. We talked more about Mom's book, and she asked Dari about his artwork. He didn't say too much, but seemed pleased that she asked. Mom brought up my relatively dormant songwriting. It's not much of anything these days. I think she just didn't want me to feel left out.

Then we started playing Scrabble. When I brought it out, Dari giggled to himself for some reason. He was mostly bad until he got a triple word score on "redux," which I found impressive and which made me jealous (or envious, whichever one makes more sense). But then he quickly thanked us and got up to leave. He said he'd see me tomorrow and he hoped we could do this again sometime and he was gone. Mom and I kept playing because it seemed odd to just stop.

"I like him, Lily. He's such an interesting person," Mom says this as she lays down an *O*, an *X*, a *G*, an *E*, and an *N*. I already had the *Y* out there. Damn. Only my mother would find that word.

"How did you do that?"

"Did you hear what I said? I really like him. He's a catch."

"I know. I like him too."

"Duh," she says playfully.

"We're just friends, though, Mom." This is true enough, but it's not the whole truth. The whole truth would include the fact that he has the body of an Adonis and I've imagined him without a stitch of clothing on more than once this evening. But he's officially only my friend. I have to be cool with that.

"He seems very wise for someone so young," she says. "He is your age, right?"

"Yeah," I answer, though I hadn't thought about it before. He's in my grade. How different can our ages be?

"Does he ever talk about his family?"

"Not much. He doesn't like to."

She nods, a slight wrinkle of concern developing on her forehead.

"Well, he's welcome here anytime. Make sure he knows that," she says, as I grapple with three *A*s, an *O*, two *I*s, and an *R*.

"Thanks, Mom," I tell her. Instead of taking my turn, I go into the kitchen and grab my third brownie. I consider doing some homework before going to bed.

"Lil? You think I'm a cool mom. Right?"

I come back into the room and try to deduce where this line of questioning is headed before I answer.

"Uh, yeah. Why?"

"Well. I was just thinking. I know you really don't want to come with me to the wellness retreat—"

"Mom. I swear to you: I will be fine by myself. I'm not gonna . . . try anything. You seriously don't have to worry."

"I believe you. But I might feel a little more at ease if . . . maybe your new friend stayed over that weekend."

I just about choke on a brownie chunk. "Wait. You want me to ask Dari to spend the weekend here? Nights included?" I ask in the most obvious way possible to make sure I'm not hallucinating and she didn't just enter a momentary fugue state.

She fiddles with her Scrabble tiles for a few seconds. "Mm-hmm. Lily, I trust you, but I don't want you to be alone. And I don't mean to boast, but you may have noticed that my intuition about people is nearly impeccable."

Except the ones that impregnate you and disappear.

"I feel nothing but good vibes from Dari. He's genuine. Thoughts?"

"I'm just surprised. I can ask him. I guess."

"Good. Do it and tell him his folks can call me and I'll explain everything."

"Like . . . you'll tell them you want Dari to babysit me for a weekend?

She presses her lips together, knowing she misspoke and unsure of how to proceed. "No. Just that this is a safe environment for their son and he's invited with my full support." She lets out a little sigh and glances up at me, looking for some sign of approval.

"Cool-ish?"

"Coolish," I tell her, though I have no idea if this will be cool or not. I just hope Dari isn't frightened by the invitation.

"It's nice to see you happy," she says.

I think about that for a second. Happy? Yeah. Right now, I'd say I am happy. I smile and nod in agreement.

"Do you think you might want to try talking to a therapist?"

My smile vanishes. Why would she bring that up now?

"I know it hasn't been that successful in the past, but if we do some serious research this time to find the right fit—"

"Where is this coming from?" I remain calm.

"I just think you're in a good place right now and I want you to stay there. I'm not pressuring you."

That's funny, because this feels distinctly like pressure. I say nothing. I hate the idea of talking to some judgmental "doctor" about all my problems when I know they don't give a shit and they just want to make as much money from me as they possibly can. Then they'll just give me more pills that make me feel tired and tired of life. They never fix anything.

"Can you try it? For a month. Four weeks. And if you absolutely hate it and see no good that can come of it, you can quit. But you have to promise me that if you don't absolutely hate it, you'll give it a chance. What do you think?"

The last time we had this discussion was about a week before school started. It ended up with tears and yelling and me punching the cement wall in the basement laundry room hard enough to leave marks. On the wall. But then again . . . it's possible that she's right. Possible. I guess I am in a "good place," because I don't feel angry now. I feel resistant and annoyed. But not angry. I don't feel the need to punch anything. Her deal actually sounds doable.

"All right, Mom. But only if I can leave after a month."

"If you"—and at the same time we both say—"absolutely hate it."

Somehow I manage to make "axe" on the board, and then I go into the kitchen to load the dishwasher.

"I can do that," Mom says, joining me.

"It's fine, Mom."

"Is it?" She watches me anxiously, fidgeting with her fingers.

"I'm not mad. I'll do it. I'm not mad," I assure her. She then smiles and kisses my hair. It must be exhausting for her. Any time she has an idea, she has to prepare for whatever crazy reaction I might have. It's not just about me, though. Mom could use a friend too. Or someone she trusts enough to talk to who isn't me.

6

SPANISH FLY

The light in the hallway is fluorescent and indescribably ugly. What's worse is its insistent brightness. There is no spot on earth that needs this much light. It is not a hospitable atmosphere. Dariomauritius has been sitting on the floor outside his apartment for the better part of an hour, waiting for his father to shut off the television and go to sleep. Once he is asleep, few things can awaken him. Dari has done this before, though it's been a while. He just has to wait it out.

Propped against his knees is his sketch pad. He practices contour drawing, which he doesn't love. But under the circumstances, this method is ideal: the pencil must stay on the paper until the line has found its end. A human figure, for example, only requires about seven solid lines in total. The less the pencil moves, the less noise it makes. He barely breathes, and he certainly doesn't move anything but his wrist. The only sounds that can be heard are the maddening hum of the light and the occasional footsteps on the stairs. No footsteps come near him. No danger of anyone saying hello. Though he usually isn't in danger of pleasantries from strangers.

Izzy is a bitch, he thinks to himself. He immediately feels guilty. Of course she had to leave. Nobody wants to stay here. And now he's on his own with the old man.

He can handle himself, but it takes a lot of energy. A lot of patience. Will he always have enough?

After a few moments of working on the hands, he hears the faint white noise of the television from inside cease. He looks up, stops drawing, stops breathing. For a few seconds. He hears the kitchen sink. His father's ritual: glass of water before bed. The faucet shuts off, and there is a moment of quiet. Then he hears his father's footsteps as they head toward the back bedroom. Dari smiles and starts to breathe softly. The homestretch. At last.

And then his phone rings. Dari drops his sketch pad with a clatter and fumbles nervously through his pockets, trying to grab it and silence it. Why the fuck didn't he turn it off before? He's able to stop it after three rings. He stands perfectly still, not breathing, not blinking. Until the door opens.

"Dariomauritius. Nice to see you this evening." The old man smirks. Pure evil. Dari slumps inside. So close. So close.

"Thought you would just sneak to bed?"

Dari says nothing.

His father leads him into the kitchen and gestures for him to take a seat. Dari remains standing.

"Well? I'm waiting for an answer."

"I need more freedom."

His father is briefly perplexed. Then that man laughs like he just watched Key and Peele's "I Said Bitch" sketch.

"You want me to give you more freedom? I suppose you see yourself as a slave." He barely gets the words out, he's laughing so hard.

Dari sighs, trying his best to draw from the patience well within himself. He decides to try reasoning.

"Would it be possible to at least discuss my curfew?" Dari carefully asks.

"I don't see why," his father answers. "You'll just defy whatever I say. It's your nature."

"No, I won't," Dari unconsciously touches the dreadlock that got maimed the last time he tried to talk to his father.

"When you start obeying me consistently, I will consider altering the rules. You have not proven to me that you deserve such consideration."

"What time did Izzy leave?"

"If you'd cared about that, you'd have come home earlier."

"Do *you* care?" Dari asks, feeling bold.

"I beg your pardon?"

"Do you care that everyone leaves you?"

The freezer door. A little blood, but not much. His father is fast. Dari didn't see the rise of the arm nor did he feel the impact of the punch. He did feel his face bash into the freezer door. And he now feels the blood seeping out of his lower lip where his teeth ripped into his flesh.

"Apologize to me."

Dari wipes at his mouth, still seeing the proverbial stars. In his momentary haze, he wonders what freezer doors are made from. Is it hard plastic? Can't be. Magnets can stick to it. Does that mean it's metal? What the hell kind of metal looks like that?

"Son? Apologize to me." He says it softer this time. Dari stares at him.

"You should apologize to *me*." He says it quietly, but with authority. He is not proud. He does not feel defiant. He feels tired. So tired he can't help but be honest. The old man is astounded and something else. He tries to cover it up, but it's there. For a millisecond, maybe a nanosecond, he is afraid of his son.

"I swear I don't know where you came from." But then he quickly shakes his head, eager to contradict himself. "No. I do. This is your mother's influence. You are her son," he says as though it were the worst, most despicable thing a person could be. "She had the devil in her and now you have it in you."

Dari almost laughs. The devil? For real? But he maintains his seriousness and stares at his father. His father stares at him. Neither of them willing to budge or back down. It is a staring contest in hell. Time slows. Dari imagines the moon moving all over the sky at this moment, the second hand on the clock spinning around and around, hours passing. Days. The men have reached an impasse.

"Go to bed," his father finally stammers.

"I'm not tired. You go to bed." Dari does not stammer. He has found his deep reserve of patience. He is prepared to stand here all night. The longer he looks into his father's eyes, the more he sees. The more anger and resentment and confusion and heartbreak. His father is a dreadfully unhappy man, and no one likes him. This is no major surprise to Dari, but looking into his eyes something does surprise him: His father knows no one likes him. Dari begins to feel sorry for him for the first time in his life. Not sorry enough to back down. Never that sorry.

Resisting defeat with all his might, his father finally just shakes his head.

"You are a great disappointment to me," he proclaims and then skulks off to his bedroom and closes the door.

Dari swishes some water around his mouth and spits blood out in the sink. He feels calm. Not shaking from terror or euphoria. He just feels calm. He feels like he can handle whatever he needs to handle. He feels like the baddest ass that ever lived. Not in a puffed-up, arrogant way. It just feels like a fact. Like discovering that water is wet.

He checks his phone and sees one missed call. It's from Lily. She also sent a text.

Hope u don't get in trouble. Had an awesome time tonight. My mom digs u. He laughs quietly. He's glad she called. No more hiding in hallways. Like a pussy.

A new face peers at him.

Alone in the art room, Dari works on a large piece that Ms. Spangler is allowing him to store there. Drawing comes naturally to Dari. He generally gives it as much thought as he gives breathing. Painting is different. It asks more of his hands. It's more mysterious. It makes him work harder. At nine feet tall and six feet wide, this is the largest canvas Dari's ever painted. He built it from objects he found all over the city. Two broken window frames, several stray plywood platforms, and some two-by-fours he found in a Dumpster. Took him almost two months to build the damn thing, and then his super caught him with it in the basement and had a piss fit. He still can't believe Ms. Spangler had no problem with him keeping it in the art room, considering he's a new student and all. Most folks are scared of tracking in bedbugs.

But here is this face. He follows the brush instead of leading it. Sometimes images sneak up on him like this. He badly wants to Picasso the nose and ears, but the face demands symmetry. Thus far, it is the most normal-looking addition to his painting, which he hoped would stay abstract. Not this face. She becomes clearer as he goes. His mother. Why must her shadow loom over everything?

"That looks so cool."

Dari jumps and turns to see Lily watching him and his brushwork. He didn't hear the door open or close. The final bell rang over half an hour ago. Most people are gone. Dari just stayed late to get some work done.

"Thanks. What are you doing up here?" he asks.

"Nothing. You need privacy?"

"I don't know. Maybe not." He doesn't *need* privacy, but he does desire it. He can sketch and draw with others around, even in the midst of heavy conversations, but painting requires his focus and makes him feel more exposed.

"Well, I don't wanna bug you. I just . . ." She laughs a little anxiously. "I wanted to ask you something. I was gonna ask earlier, but I didn't." She shoves her hands in her pockets and eyes the painting for several seconds. Dari awkwardly moves closer to the canvas as if protecting it from premature criticism.

"So, the weekend of the thirtieth, my mom's going out of town. Did I tell you about that?"

Dari shakes his head. As much as he enjoys talking to Lily, he is really impatient to get back to work. He's about to clash with his mother via oils, and he's ready.

"She's a guest speaker at this wellness retreat thing. She thought I should—I mean, we were wondering . . . Want to come over and spend the weekend with me?"

"Huh?"

"Want to come over that Friday night and stay until Sunday? It's totally fine if you don't want—"

"Your mom wants me to do that?"

"Yeah. I mean. Mostly, *I* do. But she thinks it would be nice." She nods and looks down at the floor, nodding as if continuing her thought process silently.

"I'm not sure I understand what you're asking," Dari says. "Like? Why would . . . I mean . . . *what?*"

Lily then looks up at him and shrugs with this goofy expression on her face, and they both bust out laughing.

"I don't understand," Dari says through his laughter.

"Me either!"

They keep going until the laugh tears start coming and their sides start to ache.

"Okay," Lily starts, calming herself down. "My mother doesn't want me to be all alone, and I don't want a babysitter. She decided we're both mature enough to handle a weekend together. Well, at least she thinks *you're* mature enough."

"Just a hang? Like a weekend hangout session?"

"Totally."

Dari nods, thinking. He's thinking there's no way in holy hell he'll be able to get away with staying at Lily's for a full weekend, but he can't say it. He can't accept it.

"I have to see. I mean, it sounds fun, but—"

"Yeah I know your dad's super strict. Mom said she'd talk to him if you want, but no pressure. Seriously."

"Okay."

"Okay, what?"

"The weekend of the thirtieth sounds good to me," Dari tells her. It feels good too. His de-pussification plan is taking effect.

"Awesome! You still have to ask your dad, though, right?"

"I'll discuss it with him. And then I'll come."

Time passes in the usual way. He does his best to stick to his curfew. He experimented with giving the old man the silent treatment for a few days, but instead he accidentally instituted a new silence rule that they both follow when in each other's presence. Same difference, ultimately. It helps having things to want outside of his walls. His drawing, his painting. Lily.

Another Friday. He seriously makes every effort to go to school. He's been doing well for nearly three weeks. An 89 percent attendance rate is not bad at all. But the sun is shining and late October is gorgeous, so . . . he doesn't make it there today.

He decides to walk uptown until he's tired and then he'll see if he feels like going back to school. He passes a small group of preschoolers all holding hands together in a long buddy chain. Cute. A twentysome-thing couple riding unicycles. Pretentious. And then he's accosted by a drunk/high/mentally ill man who truly believes Dari is his long-lost baby brother.

"Why you never visit me? Huh? Why you never visit me?" the man yells in Dari's face.

"Look, man, I don't know you."

The guy grabs at his sleeve a few times, trying to hold him there, but eventually Dari wrestles away from him and sprints for a few blocks, putting distance between himself and his fictional brother.

Dari pauses just north of Union Square for a smoke. A woman in a purple sweat suit asks to bum one. Reluctantly, he gives it to her. She smokes next to him for a few minutes. Then, with no warning at all, she vomits all over the sidewalk. Dari thinks it might be time to head indoors.

He quickly walks over a few blocks to an older movie theater he never goes to. He's intrigued by a poster for a film called *Sister My Sister*. Looks foreign. He puts his money down.

Dari sits in the dimly lit theater and works on two drawings simultaneously before it starts. They're similar but different. He likes challenging his hand to find the intersections and disconnects of drawing more than one figure at the same time. He doesn't know what this skill will lead to, or if it's even a good thing to know how to do, but it keeps his mind occupied in a peaceful way.

He feels slight pangs of guilt. Lily. She will be expecting him to be at their lunch table, and she will be disappointed. Not to mention that this is the weekend her mom's going away. He stops drawing for a moment. He tries to identify the Muzak version of the classical piece pumping through the speakers. Mahler? He isn't sure. He considers returning to school, just in time for lunch, for her sake. He'll decide after the movie.

This is not the type of film that will allow Dari to casually sketch while watching it. It is horrifying. Much more so than *Weekend*. And hot. And he feels filthy for finding it hot, but he does nonetheless. He tries to focus on the carnage: a brutal double homicide based on a real case that happened back in the 1930s. But the fact that one attractive woman is eating out another attractive woman in a closet is difficult for him to ignore.

His phone buzzes. He looks down, and it's a text. From Kendra. How does she always know when he's at the movies? Does she work for the NSA?

Found 1 of yr old shirts. You want it? If not I'm throwin it out.

Dari writes, *Why aren't you in school?*

Kendra writes, *Why aren't YOU?* She knows him well.

Dari stares at the big screen, transfixed and repulsed, excited and nauseous. He checks the time. There's still about a half hour left in the film.

He texts, *u home?*

She texts, *Yep*.

He texts, *B there in 20*.

Kendra pours club soda for both of them. Then she goes in her bedroom, comes back out, and throws the shirt at him.

"Thanks," he says.

"Whatever, Dari."

He inspects the shirt. It's from M.I.A.'s "People vs. Money" Tour. He has never seen an M.I.A. concert. He doesn't much care for M.I.A.

"This isn't my shirt, Kendra."

"Yes, it is."

"No. It's not."

He hands it back to her. She turns it over and over in her hands as if some clue will emerge.

"Well, it's not mine. You want it?"

"Nope," he says. "Maybe it's Donovan's."

For some cruel reason they laugh. It's not funny. The shirt certainly doesn't belong to the simpleton that once pined over Kendra.

Kendra stares at him strangely.

"What?"

She touches his head, his hair, and finds the lock stump.

"What happened to this one?"

Dari pulls away.

"The old man happened." He downs his drink. "If you don't start goin' to class, you're gonna turn into an idiot."

"What about you? You already a genius?" she throws back at him. He smiles to himself, feeling like the jerk he is. He puts his glass down, grabs Kendra, and kisses her. He presses her as close to him as she can go and realizes how much he's missed this. He moves to her neck and he can hear her saying something, but barely, then she gets louder.

"What?"

"Get off," she repeats. He does. He doesn't want to, but he does.

"What happened?"

"You're messing with me. That's not right," she tells him. Of course he knows this is true, but in his lizard brain he thought maybe she'd want to use him too. So gross. So pathetic.

"I guess . . . I just miss you," he mumbles.

Kendra sighs. "No. I think you miss something else. I can't compartmentalize like you," she says softly. He knows exactly what she means, and the devil on his shoulder (his dick) wants him so badly to say, *I'm not compartmentalizing! I love you*, but his heart knows that isn't true anymore.

"I'm sorry. I'm an asshole," he says.

"I'm sorry you're an asshole too," she replies.

He laughs bitterly.

"You really were kind of a lousy boyfriend," she muses.

"Thanks."

"You give and give and give and once you get love back, you can't wait to cut yourself free."

"Are you taking Psych 101?" Dari asks.

Kendra sips her club soda, thinking. "Do you ever think about how similar you are . . . to your mother?"

He does not have a sharp quip ready to respond to this one. Instead he feels a cold chill and a sudden wave of nausea.

"Good-bye, Kendra." Before she can say anything else, he quickly exits the apartment and runs down the stairs. Why did he tell her so much? It's none of her business. Yeah, his mother could've done a better job with him and Izzy, and she was possibly the most unreliable human he's ever met, but that was her problem. Not Dari's. He is not like his mother or his father. He is his own person and always will be. He does NOT have to become his parents.

Out on the street, he's calmer. So what if he needs to cut himself free from time to time? Is that such a crime? Doesn't everyone want freedom?

He sneaks back into school. There are still fifteen minutes left of lunch. He races upstairs and into the lunchroom, but Lily isn't there. He sits down anyway and begins to draw. After a moment, he texts her.

At lunch now if u wanna join.

He sends it and then realizes that she might be the type to keep her phone turned off during school hours. He admires that. He draws for a bit until he feels prying eyes. He turns around and that bossy Asian chick from history stands there, glaring at him.

"Where is she?" she wants to know.

"Excuse me . . . what?"

"I saw you slipping in. Did you take Lily somewhere off campus again?"

Jackie. That's her name.

"No. I haven't seen her today."

"She is a good girl. I just want you to know that. She's been having a tough year, but she's got a great heart and a bright future ahead of her if she watches her step."

Dari frowns at Jackie. He honestly doesn't know what she's talking about.

"I know all that. We're friends. Are you her friend? She's never mentioned you," he informs her. Jackie scowls.

"I don't like troublemakers. Do not get her into trouble," she warns and stomps away.

Dari is amused. Her approach may have been wrongheaded and obnoxious, but he had no idea there was anyone in this school who would try to protect Lily like that. It's kinda cool.

Later, Dari's back where he feels most comfortable: in the art room, painting. Technically, he should be in study hall last period, but lately he's been hanging out here. Nobody seems to care. He is in the building, after all. While lying on the floor doing detail work on the bottom right corner, his phone vibrates. Spangler is close enough to hear it.

"Phone should be off, Dari." It's a warning, but completely perfunctory. She couldn't care less about his rule breaking, but she has to play the role.

"Sorry, Ms. Spangler," he says, but looks down to read his message anyway.

Yr dad give you permission to stay the weekend? It's Lily. And no, his father certainly did not give him permission to stay at Lily's place for the entire weekend unsupervised. To be fair to his father, Dari never asked because there would've been no point.

Think it'll be cool. Everything okay?

Just come over. Pls.

The "please" is kind of intense.

Of course I'll come over. Meet u downstairs after the bell.

K.

Dari shuts off his phone and tries not to worry. Lily is depressed. She tried to kill herself. He hopes that standing her up at lunch didn't upset her too much. Then he takes a deep breath and remembers that he is not responsible for her happiness or her sadness and that he has a pattern of being drawn to fragile girls. This is probably a bad thing, and he should think about what this says about him. Satisfied with his own self-therapy, he resolves not to worry and goes back to working on his corner.

"That's nice," Ms. Spangler says, admiring Dari's work.

He shrugs.

"It's not too obvious?" he asks.

She smiles and shakes her head at him. From where he is on the floor, she is an upside-down pear with glasses.

"When that happens, I'll be the first to tell you," she says and walks away. He looks at the whole painting from his vantage point for a minute, forcing himself not to touch the canvas. He closes his eyes and tries to imagine he is someone else. He chooses an identity: a seventy-year-old Austrian jeweler. With a knee injury. From the war. His name is Klaus. No, Fritz. He then opens his eyes and tries his hardest to imagine what Fritz sees when he looks at the painting. Sometimes this actually works, opening his mind to other possibilities he wouldn't have thought of just as himself. Other times, he just feels crazy. This is one of the crazy times. He sits up and two girls at the back table stare. He turns to them and they look away and giggle. Freshmen.

Before the bell, he cleans up his workstation, and the second it rings, he rushes downstairs.

"Hi." She says it, but it sure doesn't sound like she means it. Before he can respond, she heads for the doors and exits, walking so fast Dari has to run a little to keep up.

"Uh, hi. What's goin' on?"

"Nothing."

"Why are we walking so fast?"

Lily doesn't answer. A deep frown on her face. Dari thinks she slows down a hair. Either that, or he's just found the right rhythm to keep up with her. Not knowing what else to do, he takes a cigarette from his bag but soon realizes they're moving too fast for him to light it. He struggles for about two blocks before grabbing her.

"Stop!" He takes a breath and when he's convinced she won't run away, he lets go of her and lights his cigarette. He takes a few puffs while deciding on a tactic. For better or worse, he does have experience dealing with unstable women.

"I'm sorry I wasn't at lunch," he says. Lily frowns again and then laughs. It's not the kind of laugh that puts one at ease.

"Do whatever you want," she says.

Dari nods, still trying to strategize. He wonders for a second if it's even worth his time. Maybe he should just go home. Better than starting something with a possible nut.

"You want to get coffee? Caffe Reggio?"

She shakes her head. She reaches for his cigarette pack, but he won't give it to her.

"Why not?"

"Because it's a vile habit," he lectures, taking another drag. "What do you wanna do, Lily?"

She stares down Broadway.

"The 1 train."

They ride in silence. After several stops, they get off at South Ferry, end of the line. Once they are back aboveground, Lily slows down and then stops.

"What?" he asks.

"You can leave if you want. I would totally understand." She's doing everything in her power not to cry. He isn't leaving.

She heads right for the Staten Island Ferry terminal, and Dari follows her. They wait with the crowd for the next ferry. Lily stares at the snack stalls.

"You want something?" he asks. She shakes her head. On an impulse, Dari heads over to one of them just as the boat is pulling in.

"Dari," she yells.

"Don't worry! I'm coming," he says, but then notices a bit of a line. Shit. In a panic, he howls.

"OHHH! My leg!"

"What's wrong?" A middle-aged Indian woman on line with her chubby son looks at Dari, who has fallen on the floor.

"Oh, it's nothing. I just have this old injury and I'm trying to get home." Dari gestures at the mob moving toward the exit and then winces in pain.

"You poor thing," the woman helps him up and rushes him to the front of the line, despite complaints behind her. She even offers to pay for Dari's two hot pretzels, but he won't hear of it: Her kindness is more than enough.

"That's a sweet boy," she tells her chubby son as Dari hobbles into the crowd, before breaking into a sprint, practically pushing an elderly Korean couple into the water.

Once on the boat, he catches his breath and somehow manages to dial Lily while juggling the two hot pretzels in his hands. He finds her at the ship's bow, mysteriously alone. He hands one to her.

"No mustard?"

Dari's whole being deflates for the three seconds she can maintain a straight face.

"Kidding. Thanks," she says, flashing a genuine, if sad, smile.

"You're welcome."

They eat, and apparently Lily was more than a little bit hungry, because she puts that thing away like it's the last pretzel she's ever gonna get in her life. This is a good thing. If she were really on the brink of anything drastic, she wouldn't be able to eat a bite, and even if she could, she'd just vomit it into the Hudson a few minutes later.

"So what's on Staten Island? Batting cages? Minigolf?"

"My ex," she says. She shields her eyes, looking at the approaching Statue of Liberty.

Ahhhh. Suddenly this all makes sense.

"Gotcha. Piece of work, huh?"

She nods.

"You gonna talk to 'im? I'll back ya up," he tells her.

"I don't talk to him ever," she says matter-of-factly.

"Might be useful. I dunno." Dari knows better than to be pushy. People need to come to Jesus when they're ready.

"I saw my ex today." Right after he says it, he regrets it. Lily turns to him and gives him the death stare to chill all death stares. He shrugs. "Sometimes it's healthy. Closure and all."

Lily continues staring at him. Her dark eyes seem to drop several shades to a midnight hue.

"So?" she asks.

"What?"

"Did you fuck her?"

Christ.

He shakes his head. "She's my ex. I have no interest in being anything more than friends with her." In this moment, it is 100 percent true.

"That doesn't work for everyone," she says.

"What did he do?"

Lily shakes her head and stares at the water smashing into the boat. Then she takes her iPod out from her book bag and sticks her earbuds in her ears. Not cool.

Dari removes them from her ears, shocking her.

"I got you a pretzel. If you don't wanna talk to me, that's fine. But you don't need to be rude."

"I'm sorry. It's a mess."

"It always is."

"Really? Is your ex married with two kids?"

Whoa. Dari has no idea how to respond to this. The wind whips Lily's hair around her face, and she squints.

"It's a mess," she repeats.

"How did that . . . happen?"

Lily shrugs. "Thanks for the pretzel. I appreciate your thoughtfulness."

Dari nods. "No big deal."

"Thank you for, um, hanging out this weekend. I mean, I would be fine alone and everything, but . . . thank you."

Dari stares at the floor of the bow, slowly becoming aware of how important his presence might be to Lily this weekend.

"Let's maybe start with tonight and see how that goes."

Lily's eyes drift back out over the water. "Up to you."

Man up, Dari.

"Lily?" Something in his voice forces her to look him directly in the eye. "I'll make it happen. Okay?"

Lily nods and the right half of her mouth curls into a grateful smile. It's pretty adorable.

Carefully, she slips her earbuds back into her ears and Dari understands and turns his attention to the water and the fast-approaching island. He assumes Lily has some kind of plan, and he decides to trust her enough not to ask about it.

As the boat slows, just about everyone has already made their way toward the exit, filling up the stairways as though waiting the thirty extra seconds it might take if they stayed in their seats until the boat docks would mean the weekend is that much further away. Once it comes to a full stop, the mob clamors to get out. Dari makes Lily go ahead of him so he can keep an eye on her while they navigate the crowd. They get into the station and it's basically the same as the one on the Manhattan side—pretzels and all—except for two large, mesmerizing aquariums with an assortment of tropical fish right in the middle of the giant room. No one seems to notice them. Not even children. Dari walks right up to one of them and peers inside. He wonders how often they eat, if they're neglected, if he could maybe feed them if he asks an attendant. But then he remembers that he'd have to ask an MTA worker for assistance and they generally don't like to assist anyone for any reason. That's about when he remembers that he doesn't know why they're on Staten Island. He turns to Lily. She is now wearing sunglasses. Strange because she wasn't wearing them when they were on the ferry shielding their eyes from the late-afternoon sun.

"You don't have to tell me what's wrong, and I probably can't do anything to help, but you might feel better if you talk," Dari attempts.

Lily stares. At what, he doesn't know, because of the sunglasses. He is pretty sure he sees a few tears slip down the left side of her nose, but could it be sweat? Probably not. She inhales and exhales hard and then unzips her book bag and reaches in with shaky hands. She pulls out a folder and hands it to Dari. He opens the folder and gasps.

"Holy shit! Is this some Photoshop prank?"

Lily slowly shakes her head.

"People were giggling and looking at me today. I tried to ignore them. Then my stupid lab partner told me I should visit the lit office. This is the proof for the cover . . . of *The Folio*." Lily stops herself. Her quickened breathing has advanced to hyperventilating and Dari grabs her to prevent her from fainting. He pulls her to a bench and they sit. Her breathing gradually slows.

"Stupid," she mumbles. "I already fainted once today. Maybe I should see a doctor." She tries to laugh. She fails.

Dari rubs her back delicately and tries to piece the puzzle together. Staten Island, tears, literary magazine, explicit photo of Lily with music notes hiding her nips and a frowny emoji covering her pubes. He's coming up blank.

"Well, they can't print it. There's no way the faculty will let 'em." He knows it's a pitiful consolation, but it's something.

"I know, but it doesn't even matter. Somebody thought this was funny and the literary staff agreed. It's like . . . they went to all this trouble. Just to hurt me."

"You have to report this," he tells her. He feels her back muscles tighten under his palm. "I can go with you, if you want. It's horrible that they did this, Lily."

"Yeah. So the VP can see me like this? And call my mom?"

"Better him than everyone else. I mean, there's no way of knowing how many people have already seen it." He wishes he could take back that last statement, because all the color fades from Lily's cheeks and he's certain that she's going to barf all over him. But the moment passes and he decides to shut up and just let her breathe for a while. After about ten minutes or so, she takes the folder back and stuffs it in her bag.

"We should go," she says.

"Where are we going?"

"Home," she says, as if only an idiot would not know this.

"But aren't we gonna go to your ex's place and confront the bastard?" Dari's suddenly in the mood for a good old-fashioned fight.

Lily smiles. "No, I can't do that. I come over here just to remind myself that he's stuck here and he deserves what he gets, and after I do that once or twice, I feel better and I go home." She already seems more relaxed and stands, passing the aquarium.

"What? Is this like a ritual or something? Come on! Don't you wanna get in that jerk's face? I mean? How old is this pervert?"

"He'll be thirty-five in February."

"Lily! He's an old man!"

Lily stops for a moment. She removes her sunglasses.

"I can't legally be within one hundred feet of his house. I broke the rule once and it was bad and I can't break it again."

She leads the way as they walk back toward the ferry entrance. In a little over an hour, Dari has learned more things about Lily than he would've dreamed possible. He isn't the type to scare easily, but he must admit, he's a bit anxious. This young woman has a restraining order against her—or at a minimum, an order of protection—which suggests violent tendencies. She has posed for a minimum of one explicit sexual photograph. Her last relationship was with a Staten Island man old enough to be her dad. And Dari has agreed to do his damnedest to spend the whole weekend with her.

As they pull out and head back to the city, Dari discovers something about himself: Danger is his Spanish fly.

7

LISTEN

I text him. And I wait.
He replies. He'll meet me. Maybe I'm gonna be all right.
Maybe.
I didn't think so a little while ago.

The door is closed. I peek through the window just in case. Mrs. Bayer isn't inside and neither are any students. The lights are off. I try the door. Unlocked. I slip inside as quietly as I can. Since meeting Dari, I've become adept at sneaking in and out of classes, but I am not the least bit relaxed about it. I quietly walk over to my desk. I mean Tracy's desk. Since she's now the editor, I assume anything I should know about would be found here. Some old, ratty notebooks, a bunch of old copies of the magazine, Strunk and White's *Elements of Style*, blah, blah, blah—nothing here. I will kill Tara if she's messing with my head.

I look at Mrs. Bayer's desk. It's ridiculously neat with hardly anything on it, which suggests to me that she doesn't care about *The Folio* at all and is a crappy faculty adviser. I shake my head in disgust. Nothing I can do about it now.

I have no idea what I'm supposed to be looking for, and clearly I haven't found it. I'm about to give up when I hear the doorknob turn. Do I hide or do I play it cool? I opt for the former and duck under Tracy's desk.

I hear feet walking toward me. I really hope they are Mrs. Bayer's ugly brown pumps. Since they don't have class in here this period, she might just be grabbing a tampon or something. Please, please, please . . . but no. The closer they get, the more certain I am that I'm not hearing pumps. Clogs. These are Tracy's shoes, and she walks right over to her desk and sits. I have to scrunch way back so she doesn't knee me in the face. She logs on to her computer, and I wonder just how long this will take. It's last period, so school will end in . . . forty minutes? But what if she plans on working past the bell?? Oh no, oh no, oh no . . .

"Oh my God." I hear her gasp and then laugh and then gasp again. I can't help but miss her. She always used to do that. Someone would tell a dirty joke and she would be horrified by it, but laugh just the same. And then go back to being horrified.

She hits some keys, and then I hear the printer. That same old broke-down printer. I swore it only worked when it was sunny out. If you had a deadline during a rainstorm, you better hope the admin office liked you, cuz if not, you were screwed.

Wait. She's getting up to go to the printer. The printer is against the wall, three tables behind her desk. That would mean I'd have about twenty-five seconds of time when her back would be turned. I have already lost precious fractions of a second doing the math, but I decide I can make it and so I edge out from under her desk and I take a step and—having REALLY long, thick, curly hair can suck when it can get stuck just about anywhere without me knowing it. In part of this desk, for instance. My fast movement rips several hairs out at the root, and I scream.

Tracy turns to me, stunned.

"What are you doing here?" she asks, her eyes about to pop completely out of her head.

"I was just looking for . . . I don't know."

"You're not supposed to be here." She says it with no authority whatsoever. Like she's the one that's been caught.

"Sorry."

Tracy regards me with terror. This seems extreme. What does she think I was doing under there?

"I didn't mean to. Someone told me something about . . . I don't even know. I guess when enough people hate you, you start to get paranoid. Sorry."

"Fine. Just . . . don't creep around like that. It's weird," she clutches the page she just picked up from the printer to her chest.

"I said I was sorry."

"Then why are you still here?"

I feel a huge lump in my throat. I will seriously strangle myself if I start crying in front of her.

"I heard you laugh. It reminded me of when we were younger."

Tracy nods.

"That's all." I turn to leave.

"Lily?" I'm amazed she's calling me, so I stop. "You should see something."

She takes the page she's holding against her chest and shows it to me. I look at the photo and I can't breathe.

"Someone submitted this to me as a cover idea, which is disgusting. It's a fake, though, isn't it? Somebody's playing a prank, right?"

I move my mouth, but no words come. Where are my words?

"Lily," Tracy begs. "Please say you didn't do this."

I can't find my words. I can't breathe. I can't see. I can't hear. I can't stand.

A second later, Tracy is screaming my name and some kids must have come in from elsewhere because several random faces now stare at me. I'm gaping up at them, which tells me that I'm on the floor and my arm hurts. Apparently, I passed out. How femme of me.

"Lily, are you okay?"

I somehow pull myself back up to standing.

"Someone can take you to the nurse," she says, but I don't need a nurse. I need to get the hell away from here. I snatch the page from Tracy's hands, run from the room, down the hall, and into the girls' room, where I puke up the disgusting tacos that supposedly counted as lunch. Where the fuck was Dari?

I text him. And I wait.

He replies. He'll meet me. Maybe I'm gonna be all right.

Last night, I kept Mom company while she packed her turquoise rolling suitcase and a burlap shoulder bag a faithful follower made for her a few years back. It's dyed all the colors of the rainbow, and in tedious, black and charcoal cross-stitched letters is the word "Gratitude." It's shockingly not tacky.

"Oh, dammit!"

"What?"

"I wasn't thinking. We should've gone to the gynecologist this week."

"Why?"

She opened her top dresser drawer. "Don't read too much into this," she said and handed me a large pack of condoms. "I just want to embrace whatever happens with intelligence and caution."

"We're just friends."

"That could change at any time. Trust me."

Ick! It was like the conversation when she asked if I wanted to go on birth control and I told her my vagina was closed for renovations. I hate talking about this stuff.

"Are you like hoping I'll have sex with him?"

"Jesus, Lily!"

"Jesus what?" It was a genuine, honest-to-God question. It's hard to tell with my mother what she's decided in her modern, new age brain might be best for me.

"I want you to be happy. I want you to do what feels . . . right while taking proper precautions. But at the same time, I don't want you to just rush into a potential quagmire of emotions."

That's when I fell backward on her bed laughing. Did she seriously just use the word "quagmire?" Is she talking about my life or *Syria*?

"Lily, it's not funny!"

I covered my face with one of her lavender-scented pillows. God, my mother loves lavender. The suffocating, purple sweetness dampened my laughter.

"You're lucky, you know? It's nice to be fifteen and have everything to look forward to. I envy you."

I stopped laughing then and shot her a you-gotta-be-kidding look.

"I do, Lily. Bad things happen to everyone. Some of us more than others. But you can't just give up."

"I haven't."

"Good. Then please don't mock me when I'm trying to help you. Yes, I want you to be careful with your body and your soul, but I want you to enjoy your life too. So you can't . . . only be careful. Get it?"

"Got it," I said. But then again, do I get it? How do I know I have everything to look forward to? I could be pushed in front of an oncoming train, fall asleep in the bathtub and drown. I could get my heart trampled on again before it's had a chance to properly heal. Under normal circumstances, I'd bring all this up to her. But last night I was too tired to fight.

"Promise me you'll keep those handy," she reiterated, referring once again to the condoms. I was strangely flattered that my beautiful mom thought she and I might be desired in remotely the same way. Weirded out overall, but flattered.

"I promise."

Dari flips through the Netflix options. He's fascinated, but I'm bored as a rock.

"Wanna see my room?" I barely get the words out before wishing I'd thought that through. My room is kind of messy, and I don't think I've asked someone that question in those words since I was about seven years old.

"Sure." I don't think he's judging my inadvertent childishness. Hard to tell with him. But right now, I appreciate his ambiguity.

I sit on the floor with my back against my bed and feign interest in Angry Birds, though I'm far more interested in Dari slowly, methodically scrolling through my iTunes. His face is so hard to read. If he's disgusted by any of my music choices, I have no idea. If he's impressed by any of my music choices, I have no idea.

"You can play something if you want," I say. He turns to me briefly and then he nods. At least, it looks like he nods. The movement is so subtle it could've just as easily been a muscle spasm.

"You have decent taste," he decides.

"Thanks."

"I was afraid you'd be into that pop crap."

"Really?"

"Hey. You never know. Somebody can seem cool and then you look in their music library and there's Katy Perry."

I mock gag myself with my finger.

"As a musician, I take offense to that."

He smiles at me. "Never heard you describe yourself that way before."

I can feel my cheeks going red, so I turn away from him, but not before sharing his smile. Why I feel embarrassed, I don't know. But he's right. I haven't even thought of myself as a musician in months. Especially considering how little I play these days. Like . . . neverish. It's funny that I just said that to him like it was nothing. Like it's just a natural part of who I am. No big deal.

"Cool," he says, still smiling. It's like he just read my mind. That's an unnerving thought.

"That's why I like a lot of old stuff," I say. "Some new stuff too, but you have to really seek it out. The radio is such a joke."

"I know, right? It's like every song that gets played is the music equivalent of a Big Mac. Mass appeal. Mass marketing." He shakes his head and keeps scrolling. "Not into hip-hop?"

Oh, no. Is that bad? "Some," I claim.

"I'll send you some tunes. Good stuff. Old and new. Talib Kweli. Eric B. and Rakim. Some Childish. Not the corporate shit. I'll set ya up."

You can set me up anytime. Oh, man. He *better* not be able to read my mind.

"You're into Radiohead," he says. This is a statement, not a question. And I can't tell if he thinks this is a good thing or not. Well. Whatevs. I'm such a devoted Radiohead fan I refuse to be all sphinxy about it.

"Yep. Seen them in concert four times." I may be cramming my foot right in my mouth, but I ask, "Do you like them?"

"I do. I'm not in love with them, but I like them a lot," he says. Then he starts typing. Apparently, he's now in another program. He's beautiful and awesome, but I do feel a tad uncomfortable with his easy commandeering of my space. If a stranger walked in right now, they'd surely assume that this is his room and I'm his semiwelcome guest.

"Have you heard this?" he asks and then plays a song that he must have just found. It's clearly "Climbing Up the Walls," but not the version I know. A woman sings lead, and it has some kind of reggae arrangement.

"No." I'm kinda loving it, but I'm not sure if I should admit that. Is he suggesting this cover is better than the original? Because he would be wrong about that.

"Badass, right?"

"Yeah. I mean, I'm still partial, but it's an interesting take. To make a reggae version of this song."

He turns to me, and I see a flash of something in his eyes. Something I don't like.

"What do you mean 'interesting'?"

"Nothing. Just . . . interesting."

"Is there something wrong with a black artist singing a Radiohead song?"

Where the hell did that come from?

"NO! Why would you think that was what I meant?"

"Because you can't seem to tell me what you meant."

Why does he get so defensive?

"I just never imagined it like this. I think of that song as sexy and tense. But I always associate reggae music with easygoingness. I'm sorry! Clearly I was wrong." At this moment, I decide to take back my space. I shove Dari out of the chair; he doesn't even bother to protest. Hands shaking, I scroll through my songs until I find Radiohead's "Climbing Up the Walls." I blast it loud enough for the neighbors to call 311 to report me if they're feeling bitchy. Then I run to the bathroom and slam the door. I kick said door a few times, leaving a dent, and I grab a vase. I'm about to smash it when I stop myself. What is wrong with me?

Fuck, shit, fuck. What am I doing? This is the one person I never ever wanted to scare away. And now I've done this. Over a goddamn song?!

I pace back and forth and try to catch my breath. Today has been a day. One of those days. I am so sick of having those days. I just want to have a normal freakin' day with no disasters and no outbursts and no humiliations. Doesn't have to be every day. Just one whole day without that triad of terror would be nice. It might even be heavenly. After a few seconds, the volume goes back down. I decide to stay in the bathroom. Once I hear the apartment door close and know that he's safely gone, I'll come out. But not before then. I cannot be humiliated again today. Enough is enough.

I sit waiting, and I don't hear a sound. Now I'm getting kind of annoyed. He needs to go. I don't want to hide all night.

My phone vibrates. I look down. It's a large file. I'm about to delete it, assuming it's another ad for Viagra, when I see the sender. The message simply says: "Listen." I open it. It's a song. "This Woman's Work" sung by Maxwell. I play it and I'm transported. I lie on the bathroom floor and close my eyes, my head against the phone, absorbing this beautiful song. So beautiful I can't believe anybody would be willing to share it with me. I start thumping the rhythm out on the floor, feeling tingly, but I stop myself. I ignore my urge to play along. No. It's best to just listen. When the song ends, I open my eyes so I can replay the whole thing again, but when I do, I see that Dari is now lying next to me on the floor.

"Nice, isn't it?" he quietly asks.

Why is he here? Why is he wasting his time on a mess like me? I think about telling him to leave. I think I should chase him away so he doesn't get wrapped up in my problems. But I don't. I guess I'm just too selfish. I don't want him to leave. Ever.

"Let's go somewhere," he says, and he pulls me up gently.

"I thought you would've left," I say, trying to conceal my shame.

"Why? I just learned that you have quite a passion for music. That's a good thing."

We climb the stairs and I feel giddy. Like I'm getting away with something naughty when we're really only walking up to a renovated train track that is now the High Line.

At the top, Dari moves fast, like he's searching for one specific spot. I don't complain, though I've never been up here before and it's a little weird and the people here right now are a little weird as well. But I trust him and I do my best to keep up as he trucks through. It's like when I was little and Mom and I would go to F.A.O. Schwarz, except right now Dari is the kid and I'm the mom. I'd pull her arm, dragging her along, as I ran through the clusters of tourists, dodging baby carriages until we reached my favorite spot: the giant piano dance mat. On a good day, you might catch an associate giving a live demo. On a bad day, it would be powered off and lifeless. There was a movie in the eighties or nineties where this guy got to dance on it long enough to play most of a song, but they wouldn't let you do it that long in reality, because I tried. The last time I went there was a few years ago, and I was by myself. They'd replaced the piano mat with a miniature version of Hogwarts Castle. I left, got an ice-cream cone from Mister Softee, and sat in the park for a while, needing the sugar to soak up my sadness. I heard that the store is now closed for good. Oldest toy store in the world and they couldn't pay their rent anymore. New York City real estate. Nothing good can stay.

Dari stops abruptly. There's a large glass wall in front of us. Below you can see the busy traffic of Tenth Avenue whizzing by.

"Watch this," he says and he jumps up as high as he can, like he's trying to reach the top of the glass, and he yells something. I couldn't understand a word of it.

"What?"

"Exactly! You couldn't hear it!"

"Okay."

"I made a wish. I threw it out into the universe. Well . . . out to Tenth Avenue. Your turn."

"Are you serious?"

"Yes!"

"I don't like yelling. It makes me feel stupid."

"You're not stupid! Just do it!"

I start shaking. What is he trying to do to me?

"What is the worst that can happen?"

I try to think, but my mind is blank and I can't breathe.

"Lily, let yourself feel free for two fucking seconds!"

I inhale and exhale and then I scream at the top of my lungs:

"I WISH I WAS TWENTY-ONE YEARS OLD AND LIVING IN ROME!"

Unfortunately, at the moment I decided to yell my wish, I forgot to jump, traffic had briefly stopped, and there wasn't any wind at all. So everyone within a mile radius probably heard me. Dari stares at me with this goofy look on his face: shock and amusement. A handful of people down on the street look up at us. Am I gonna vomit? Am I gonna pass out? Again? This day is just the worst.

"Hey!"

Oh my God, some weirdo on a bike is yelling up at me.

"Why Rome?"

Did he really just ask me that?

I look at Dari. He just shrugs.

"Why not Rome?" I shout down at the weirdo.

"Of all the places in the world, you couldn't pick something more exotic?"

"How do you define 'exotic'?" Dari yells down at him. "Third world? Bad plumbing? Black or brown folks workin' at fancy resorts?"

"I wasn't talkin' to you!"

Dari's jaw tightens. I know he wants to keep arguing, but instead he just turns away.

"How old are you right now?" the weirdo asks.

"No more questions," I shoot back.

Dari has moved up to a higher point and stands on a bench. I follow him as I hear my weirdo yelling up at me one more time, "Where ya goin'? I can take you to Rome, if ya want. You're eighteen, right?"

I join Dari up on the bench.

"You know what I've noticed?" I ask him.

"What's that?"

"We both freak out super easy."

He laughs.

"Look there. Can you see where I'm pointing?" He directs my attention east, through a few buildings. I realize then that up on the bench, we're pretty high up above the ground.

"Yeah, I think so."

"Can you see the mark?"

I squint and then I think I see what he means. Someone's tagged it, but I can't make out what it says.

"Yeah. How'd they get up so high?"

"I hate that guy." He sits down. I try to squint once more to make out what it says, but I can't so I sit with him.

"Who did it?"

"This asshat from my old school. Goes around stickin' his mark everywhere. Link168. So original. Like anybody cares. Like 'Link' will ever be famous."

"What was your old school like?"

"It was school. Like any other. Well, not as fancy as yours. Ours. But it wasn't a bad school." He watches me from the corner of his eye. "Can I ask you something?"

Uh-oh. "Yes." My voice creaks, and I take yet another deep breath.

"Is that photo of you connected to your old-ass ex-boyfriend?"

Of all the questions in the known universe that Dari could've asked me at that moment, he picked the worst one.

"Yes."

Dari nods. Sometimes when he nods, it means he's satisfied and you're off the hook. But not now. His right eyebrow is raised. He's getting warmed up.

"He took that picture?"

I stare back over at the glass wall, longing for my conversation with the bike weirdo to resume. Anything but this.

"Sometimes you do things that seem fine at the time because of . . . love, or something." I hate myself, I hate myself, I hate myself . . .

"You loved him?"

"I did. I was stupid." So stupid, so stupid, so stupid . . .

"Not to sound like a parent or anything, but he seriously took advantage of you. He's a piece of shit. Another thing. I don't want you to call yourself stupid anymore. You're the smartest person I've met in a long time. My standards are quite high."

I swallow hard and try to concentrate on the air, the smelly garbage from below, the loud clatter of cargo trucks speeding by. Anything to not go back into that painful place. It's like this tiny room in my head that I've locked up tight. Dead bolt and chain. But I walk by it, try to run by it, and no matter what I do it's still there. It could open at any second.

"If you could take back one thing you've done in your life, do you know what it would be?" I ask him, desperate to shift the focus from me.

"Is that yours? Being with that pervert?"

Why are we still talking about my life? "I don't know exactly. I think it's too hard to narrow down to just one single thing. And what if some of the bad choices have led to good things by accident? It's kind of a hard question to answer."

"Not for me," he says.

"No? What's yours, then?"

A tired-looking middle-aged man walks toward us.

"Kids, park's closing in five minutes. Better make your way out."

"Thanks," I say. Dari says nothing. I stand and make a show of gathering my bag and my jacket though this only needs a few seconds of my time. I hope this will encourage Dari to get up and join me. It does not.

"I—I think we have to leave now, Dari."

He sighs and rubs his head. I keep expecting the park guard to come back and yell at us. After another minute or two, he finally stands.

"The last time I saw my mother, I told her she was a selfish bitch."

It's about two a.m. Dari sleeps soundly in the guest room. I am on the computer, unable to sleep. I hate insomnia, and I hate it even more tonight because I know what it means. I hope I'm wrong, but I'm usually not. Dammit. I do not want to be obsessed with Dari. That is the last thing I want to be feeling right now. I just can't help thinking about it. Being with him. The possibility of it. The beautiful unknowability of it. He's so mysterious and beautiful and sexy and weird and sometimes volatile, but so am I. At least I'm those last two things. But to be in a relationship with him, to be his girlfriend? That would be so . . . normal. I didn't realize how much I've been craving a normal bond with a guy.

I just wish I could calm myself down and stop imagining what might not be real at all. I'm just setting myself up for pain, and I'm sick of it. But I can't help myself. I can't stop thinking about the diner after the High Line, and his smile, and how he insisted that he pay the check. Oh my God, how can I be a feminist—and I am definitely a feminist!—when something so old-fashioned totally turns me on? I'm such an embarrassment. He said I'm smart. But maybe he doesn't think I'm pretty. Or not pretty enough. What is pretty enough? Are pop stars pretty enough? Supermodels? I don't even know what his type is or if he has one. I should ask what his ex-girlfriend's name is so I can look her up on Facebook. No, that's creepy. Besides, she's probably gorgeous, and I'll just hate myself even more. And I'll hate her. And I might hate him. I hate this I hate this I hate this!

I have an overwhelming urge to go into the guest room and watch him sleep. No. No, no, no, no, no. I'm not going to be a nutball stalker. Never again. I have to let him be. If he wants to come to me, he will. I hope.

7:37. I open my eyes and I'm exhausted, but I can't sleep anymore. I wonder how late he sleeps in. Should I wake him? No, that's crazy! Maybe I should read for a while. Watch TV? Oh, man. I feel just as nutty as when I went to sleep.

What was that? A tiny *click*. Did I hear? Yes. I did.

I bolt upright, throw on my robe, and run down the hall to the guest room, and he's already gone. I open the door to our apartment, which I know I just heard close, but I don't see him.

I flop on the couch and turn on the TV, not seeing anything. So I figured he probably wasn't actually into me, but I didn't expect him to just leave. No good-bye. Nothing. Did I offend him? Probably any number of things I did yesterday could've offended him. But then again, he could've left before. He could've left before we got on the damn ferry. But he didn't. Why now? I love his strangeness, but right now, I wish he could be just a little bit predictable.

Megan McCormick sits in mouthwatering anticipation of the Peking duck she's about to eat on *Globe Trekker*. I've seen this episode about sixty times, and I'm learning nothing new from yet another viewing, but it makes me feel less alone.

I briefly think about calling Mom, but that would be about as sad as it gets. And she's probably leading a morning meditation or something else I would hate, anyway. She might not be allowed to use her phone there at all. Some of them have rules like that. Whatever. It's fine. I shouldn't complain. I like being solitary. Sometimes I actually like loneliness. That's the problem with getting your heart wrapped up in things. The dumbest stuff starts to carry way too much significance. You think about things way too much. You imagine a hole being filled that rarely bothered you at all when it was empty.

My phone buzzes.

Sorry I vanished this morning. Had to get home to deal with the old man. I'll come by later on?

As soon as I read these words, I smile and the whole world feels fifty shades brighter. Dammit. I do not want to be in love.

8

YES PEOPLE

He dunks his head in. Opens his eyes. The cold burns at first, but then he adjusts. How long can he hold his breath in ice-cold water? He stares at the bottom of the bowl. Scratches and scorch marks. He wonders what Izzy may have done to burn the bottom of a bowl.

He comes up for air. Didn't last too long. Maybe thirty seconds. Maybe forty.

The ice has melted. This water hasn't been ice for a few hours now. Dari hasn't moved from this spot. Not to smoke. Not to pee. If he moves, he is afraid of what his hands might do.

He lets the droplets of water slide down his face onto his neck. Things changed this morning. He changed them.

8:10 a.m. Dari comes home knowing he will walk into hell, but not knowing which circle of the inferno he'll be on. How deep his hell will go.

He doesn't bother with deception. No pretense of sneaking in. Too late for that. He opens the door and his father sits on the sofa drinking his oolong tea and reading the *New York Times*.

Dari stands in the foyer, waiting.

Without looking up, of course, his father says, "You might as well come in."

But Dari just stands where he is, staring at him.

"Scared?" he sneers. This is too much.

"Is it possible for us to ever find a middle ground?" Dari asks this in his lowest, most composed and intelligent-sounding voice. His father puts down the newspaper, removes his glasses, and rubs his eyes.

"You're not stupid, Dariomauritius. Far from it. So how can you expect me to compromise with someone who treats me with nothing but contempt? Would you be willing to work with a person like that?"

Dari walks over to his father and stands in front of him.

"What kind of person do you want me to be?" he asks.

His father shakes his head. "I don't like your tone."

"I'm serious."

"Sit down."

"No."

"Can't you do anything I ask?"

"You never ask me to do anything. You only give orders."

His father sips his tea and rubs his temple. It's hard to know if he's ever really listening or merely strategizing. Chess on steroids.

"Will you please be so good as to sit down and talk with your father?" he sweetly asks. Sweetness coming from him is like a love poem courtesy of Edgar Allan Poe. "That was a question, wasn't it?"

Dari sighs. He sits on the far end of the couch safely out of reach.

"What were you doing out there all night?"

"I was with a friend. I slept at her place. Nothing happened. We weren't even in the same room."

"If nothing happened, why didn't you just come home?"

To this, Dari has no response. At the same time, both men sigh deeply. *I'm so tired of this. So fucking tired.*

"Why don't you make us some breakfast?" he suggests. It's sort of close to being civil.

Reluctantly, Dari goes into the kitchen and heats up a pan to make eggs. He's stuck. Stuck here with the old man and no one else. The butter slides around the pan, and Dari wonders how long he can stand this. Each day worse than the day before.

They eat their eggs in silence. This is a game. Whoever speaks first is the loser. Dari does not intend to lose. Nor does his father. To distract himself from the tension and his growing anger, Dari thinks about Lily and hopes she's all right. He thinks that maybe they should go to a movie tonight. Someplace where there's no pressure to talk. Not that he minds talking to her. He remembers how mad she got yesterday when she stormed out of her room and he nearly laughs. He knows she was upset, but it was kind of funny. He still can't believe she knocked him out of that chair.

Crash! The old man has thrown his plate against the wall and it has smashed into pieces.

Dari flinches, but only slightly. He looks at the mess of broken IKEA-grade dishware and suppresses the urge to instantly start cleaning. It bugs him, all the pieces, the grease from the eggs slithering down the wall and onto the floor. It is not aesthetically pleasing.

The old man quietly sips his tea. He's not going to get up. He's not going to speak. Dari finds himself impressed. His father really intends to win this game.

But he won't.

Dari unhurriedly finishes his food, takes his plate to the sink, washes it, and sets it in the rack to dry. For a moment he leans against the kitchen counter. He considers asking his father if he'd like anything else. Toast? Pancakes? Just to taunt him. But that would require speaking, and he isn't about to do that. He decides to make some coffee. As he fills the filter, the old man huffs sharply, but still he says nothing. Dari pours the water in and remains standing as he waits for his pot to brew. While he stands there, he thinks—though he can't be positive—that his father's hand is shaking. Which would mean he is really angry or really scared. Or both.

Coffee's done. Dari pours himself a cup—milk, no sugar. Not in the mood for sweetness. He walks toward the kitchen table, and then decides instead to adjourn to the living room. He sits on the sofa and turns on the television. He can feel his father's eyes burning holes in his head, but he doesn't care. Honestly, he's kind of enjoying it.

Saturday-morning cartoons sure aren't what they used to be. The animation is lazy. Too clean. He misses being able to detect pencil lines and paint strokes in his favorite cartoon characters, his mind never quite separating the creatures from the art that brought them to life. He finally chooses a raunchy reality show. Not because he likes it. On the contrary: He finds it idiotic. But because his father detests vulgarity with an irrational zest, this is his choice. He turns up the volume a little bit too high. He takes a luxurious gulp of coffee, savoring what he imagines Colombia must smell like, and then he glances over at his father.

He remains alone in the kitchen, white-knuckling his teacup, eyes glaring though his dorky glasses. Dari stares into those angry eyes and it takes all his strength to keep from laughing. This little man with the pride of a goddamn lion? This is who has scared Dariomauritius all these years? He doesn't laugh. He knows that would be cruel. No. Instead he keeps his eyes on his father as he lifts one filthy combat boot and then the other and crosses them comfortably on his father's antique coffee table. Then . . . he smiles.

A victory.

The old man moves with the speed of a panther and punches Dari three times in a row in his face. Then he grabs his hair and knocks his head into the coffee table, where there were probably a few traces of dirt left from his boots. When he sees blood, the old man backs down, but he's still got hold of Dari's precious locks.

"Do you have anything to say to me?" he growls, breathing hard.

Dari's face burns from the pain, his vision is blurry, and he wants his father to let go of him, so he thinks, *Yes, I do. I'm sorry, Dad. I'm sorry you hate me. I'm sorry I remind you of Mom. I'm sorry you're a bitter old man.* He thinks these words and he thinks he's saying them for a moment, but he is not. He isn't speaking at all.

Dari shakes himself from a brief leave of his senses to find his hands around his father's neck and his father slowly turning a color he didn't know humans could turn. He lets go and the old man collapses on the floor.

Dari can't believe his eyes. He can't believe his hands. He has no memory of reaching out and attempting to end his father's life.

A chilling thought crosses his mind. *It would've been so easy to do it. Too easy.*

He can't look at him. He can't watch him pant on the floor like that. So he fills a bowl with ice and tends to his injuries alone in his room.

Time has passed. Not a single word has been said in that time. A while ago, he heard the apartment door open and slam shut, but no repeat of those sounds. His father is out there somewhere. Licking his wounds. Dari glances at his hands again. Since he was young, he's feared his father's wrath. Now he fears his own.

They share a crazy-strong pot of French press coffee.

"What about a raw steak? They do that in boxing movies. Would that help?" Lily asks, referring to the purple bruise forming just under Dari's left eye.

"Doesn't hurt much. Does it look awful?"

"It's not so bad," Lily assures him. But he knows it's not so good, either.

Dari opens a *Daily News*. "We could do a movie. There's a Kenneth Anger fest happening nearby."

"Describe Kenneth Anger in two words."

Dari thinks for a moment. "Gay Satanist."

Lily crinkles her nose. "I don't know if I'm in the mood for that."

"Comedy? Foreign? What're you feeling?"

"Why don't we just head east and see what's playing? I'm also fine just walking around," she says, still frowning at his bruise.

"Sounds good."

"He shouldn't treat you this way."

Dari continues drinking. He knows this, but so what? Knowledge is not always power.

"I feel like maybe I should report it or something. I dunno."

"No authorities. They just make things worse."

She squints a little, giving him a perplexing expression. "Can I ask you something?" she starts.

Oh, Jesus.

"Go ahead," he says.

"What went down at your old school?"

He snorts and stares out the window.

"You don't have to tell me if you don't want to," Lily offers.

"I know that," he replies. "This dumbass senior couldn't stop messing with me because he was obsessed with my girlfriend." At the word "girlfriend," Lily stiffens.

"*Ex*-girlfriend," Dari clarifies, not that he needs to. "He was always runnin' his mouth, trying to get under my skin, and I mostly ignored him like you would a fly that keeps buzzin' in your face. I eventually had to deal with him. He got ahold of a painting I was working on and painted over it. Painted the whole thing goddamn puke green. And the fool made sure I knew he did it too! So I beat his ass pretty bad. Broke his nose and one of his ribs. Not one of my prouder moments." He pauses to pour more coffee into his cup. This time he stirs some sugar in it. "They, uh . . . they called the cops. I got pulled outta class in handcuffs."

Lily covers her mouth in shock. Then tries to casually lift her cup to her lips, but her hands are clearly trembling.

"It was all a big show, ya know? Just to scare me or embarrass me, I guess. I was held overnight and then released. Doesn't matter. My record gets expunged soon as I turn eighteen. Man. You shoulda seen my old man's face. I was lucky. Day before the fight, he found out he's got high blood pressure, so his doctor put him on Lozol and told him to control his anger. She said one more outburst could give him a stroke. So I was grounded and that was it. I was so lucky."

"Wow."

"Should I keep going?"

"There's more?" Lily practically shrieks.

"After I was released, I snuck into school after hours, went into the girls' locker room, and spray-painted 'Donovan Washington is a cunt' in big letters across the windows. It was like I was still so mad that sending him to the hospital wasn't enough. I got notified the next day that I was officially expelled. Shocking, right? The irony is that by the time he destroyed my painting, I'd already broken up with Kendra. I was no longer an obstacle to his dream girl. If he'd just asked me about it, I coulda told him and the whole thing might've been avoided. Course she had no interest in him anyway," he says, shaking his head. "Stupid."

Dari sips his coffee as Lily stares at him in silence.

"He *is* a cunt, though," Dari adds thoughtfully.

"How'd you get into our school with . . . that kinda background?"

"My dad knows how to pull strings. Plus I add much-needed diversity. And my art. Bullshit like that."

Lily nods. Mildly shell-shocked.

Dari fiddles with one of his locks and clears his throat. Maybe he's revealed too much. "You sorry you asked?"

"No," she breathes. "I just hope I never piss you off."

"Ditto." He winks.

While walking east, Dari notices something and stops.

"Come here for a sec," he tells Lily. He leads her into a small alley and she watches as he scales a few feet up a brick building like he's Spider-Man. He then hoists himself up onto the fire escape.

"What are you doing?" she calls.

He shushes her and takes some things from his bag. He cautiously looks around, does some quick maneuvering with a can of black spray paint, a brush, and a sharp, knifelike tool. He's fast as hell, but always precise. Before Lily can inspect what he's done, he's back on the ground and running.

"What—"

"Come on! Now!"

Lily races after him until they get to the next avenue. Only then does he stop and check behind him to make sure she's there.

"What was that?" she shouts, gasping for air.

"My tag," he says, not quite as out of breath as she is.

"Wait a minute! I asked you weeks ago if you were a tagger and you said I was being racist!"

"I never said you were being racist. I *implied* you were."

"*What?*"

"I don't like being profiled. Doesn't matter what the truth is."

Dari continues walking, heading toward the first movie theater on their list.

"I don't know what to say to you," Lily mumbles.

"Then don't say anything," Dari replies, with a sly grin.

They check out the movie choices. None appeal.

"What is your tag? I couldn't see it."

"I'll show you later," he teases.

"When?"

"When the time is right."

On the way to the next theater over another block, they pass a long line of wannabe punk kids way too twee to be anything approaching edgy.

"What is this place?" Lily asks.

Dari follows the line with his eyes and it seems like they're all waiting to get into a dark basement.

"I wonder what they're waiting for."

"Ask," Dari urges.

Lily sighs. She clearly doesn't want to ask. Dari considers stepping in and doing it for her, but she quickly summons her courage.

She spots a girl with long purple braids and a nose ring and gently taps her barbed-wire-tattooed arm. The girl jumps.

"Oh, sorry. I just wondered who are you guys waiting to see?" Lily cautiously asks.

Purple Braids seems confused for a second, but then her face breaks into a radiant smile.

"Bevvy Botswana. She's the truth."

Lily and Dari exchange looks.

"The truth?"

All at once, several heads of varying neon colors turn and echo: "The truth."

"When she plays, it's like . . . it's like she's giving you an all-access pass to the solar system," Purple Braids gushes.

"Bigger than that. It's like she's putting the universe in your hands. She is everything and more," a white guy with aqua dreadlocks and matching beard contributes.

A few of them argue about the size and scope of Bevvy Botswana's "truth." Solar system? Universe? Nature all-encompassing? They argue about how to label themselves in Bevvy Botswana nomenclature. Are they Bevvians or Botswanians? Or BevBots? This is more than enough for Lily and Dari. No movie could compete with this. They hop on the back of the line. Lily giggles.

"What?" Dari is dying to make fun of these clowns and hopes this is the moment.

"Nothing. I just never do stuff like this."

Dari considers what Lily has said. Generally, he doesn't either. But he does sometimes.

"Do you think you're a 'no' person?" he asks.

"I don't know. What does that mean?"

"Do you say 'no' to things automatically? Easily?"

"Yes."

"Let's try to say 'yes' to things tonight."

"Are you serious?"

"Totally. Let's do it. Let's be 'yes' people for"—he checks his watch—"at least the next three hours and change. As soon as Sunday starts, we can go back to 'no.' If we want. What do ya think?"

"I think you're awesome."

She says it and she means it. She's completely vulnerable, like she's not expecting this feeling to be reciprocated in any way. Dari takes in a breath. He likes to be prepared for these things, and he wasn't. They stare at each other for several seconds as the line begins to move forward.

"I—I think you're awesome too." He says it quietly, looking away slightly.

They follow the crowd inside. Lily is silent. Damn. He said the wrong thing, or maybe he said the right thing, but at the wrong time. He's not used to freely expressing his feelings. Not positive ones anyway.

Down inside the basement—it is a basement—chairs are strewn all over the room. There are no actual rows. A lot of people choose to stand or sit on the windowsills or the floor. The room is a mass of bodies. Lily's attention darts around the space as if trying to appraise everything she sees. Her eyes won't meet Dari's.

"What's wrong?" he asks.

"Nothing. It's just . . ." She pauses. Then she looks at him directly. "You don't ever have to tell me something if it isn't true." She swallows hard and then inspects the fingernails on her hand. She looks exactly like her mother right now, which isn't such a bad thing.

"It is true," he insists.

Lily shakes her head. "Really. It's okay. Don't worry about it."

Dari stares at her for a moment. Hesitantly, he pulls his sketch pad out of his backpack. He quickly flips to a page that he visits often. Now Lily seems to be counting people in the room to keep from looking at him. He taps her arm and she finally meets his eyes again. He nods toward the sketch pad. Lily stares at it for a few minutes. Then she pulls it onto her lap, delicately touching the soft lines.

"That's how awesome I think you are," Dari mutters.

It isn't complete yet. The legs barely have any detail, but the face . . . the face has been wrought with care, detail, and so much beauty.

"You made me look so beautiful." Her voice once again caught in her throat.

"That's just how you look," Dari says as if it's obvious, and takes the pad back, slipping it in his bag.

"Thank you," she says, with the timid voice she used when they first met. But she holds his gaze.

Dari smiles. Then the lights shift, the crowd starts chanting, "Truth!

Truth! Truth!" Dari and Lily smirk, and join in the chanting.

Two men jump out of the darkness and start beating on bongos, yelling, "Ha," in time with their beat. Then three women enter with harps and proceed to play them with their teeth. Someone from the audience screams in ecstasy. Dari looks toward the sound, and it clearly came from Purple Braids, who is already writhing around in pleasure. Finally, Bevvy Botswana enters. She is a dark-skinned, bald woman with black lipstick and a dress that seems to be made entirely from fish netting. She opens her mouth and lets out a howl. Not a scream, but a howl. Dari is so shocked, he begins laughing uncontrollably. A few of Bevvy's loyal Bevvians (or Botswanians or BevBots) glare at him and he could swear one of them hisses like a cat. Lily nudges him and he tries to stop, but without success. Unfortunately, Bevvy notices her laughing audience member. With razor-sharp focus, she leaps off her perch and gallops toward Dari and Lily. She does a snakelike movement, shouts something in another language (which sounds suspiciously like fake Swahili to Dari), then tips her head to the ceiling and releases a high C so loud, the room quakes and her loyal flock bows down to her, breathing the word "truth" over and over. This just makes Dari laugh even harder, and now Lily can't hold it back, either. The followers shout and throw things at these cynical brats. They run out of the room, up the stairs, and back out into the night, still laughing, but running for their lives just in case Purple Braids and her cohorts are armed.

They don't know where they're going, but these past several weeks, they've proven that they can have a good time doing just about anything at all.

If they're together.

9

THE MOON AND
YOU AND ME

I'm dying. I'm melting. But it's from happiness! Who would've thought that was possible? Not me. Certainly not me. Not after yesterday. Not after summer. Not after last year. But here I am. Here he is. And in this moment, I am happy. Then again, how present in this moment can I be if I'm stepping out of it to assess how happy I am? Screw it! Tired of second-guessing myself. Who cares? I feel fantastic!

"You good?" He's looking up over his milk shake at me. He's been making some kind of sculpture with his fries poking out of the shake at differing heights.

"Oh, yeah. I'm great."

"Where to next?"

I can't tell him that I would be overjoyed to just sit in this crappy diner and gaze at him all night. No. He'd get bored. Understandably. We have to do something.

"Remember: We're saying 'yes' tonight," he reminds me.

"I remember." "Yes" gets us up and out of the diner, down several blocks, and into the strangest karaoke bar I've ever seen. Not that I've seen many. I was in one once just long enough to use the bathroom, but it was nothing like this. It's packed. Tinsel and Christmas lights line the walls and ceiling, and the clientele is a mix of wildly gay and goth, though some of these people are probably dressed up for Halloween. Some of them are definitely not. On the back wall of the stage area are letters about five feet tall made up of tiny purple lightbulbs that spell out the words HAPPY ENDINGS. I'm amazed that we got in. No one seems to be manning the door, but when Dari walks up to the bar, I nearly run out of the place, knowing we're gonna be found out. Instead, I hide at a tiny table with swirls of red and gold glitter glued all over the surface.

He squeezes through the hordes and turns up at the table with two beers.

"How the hell did you manage that?" I yell over the music.

"What?"

"How did you get . . ." and I just point at the beers. He flashes me the license of Jeffrey Dean Stewart, who is currently twenty-two years old. I've never met anyone with a fake ID before.

On the stage, a glamorous drag queen in a glossy pink wig sings all the parts of "My Humps," complete with choreography, in stiletto boots. Holy crap, she's good!

Dari raises his glass to me and I clink. Cheers. Cheers to everything. Because "yes" is so much more fun than "no."

Cameras are flashin' while we're dirty dancin'
They keep watchin', keep watchin'—

Dari pulls me offstage before I can invite the crowd to "gimme more" again. Some of them boo. I boo too. *Boo!* I think I'm putting on a pretty good show here. Doesn't he know that this is just funny? It's a joke! It's hilarious! And the song isn't nearly over. Come on, man!

"Dari, it's a joke! I don't like this song really. I'm just singing it cuz it's funny. Get it?" I'm sure this is all coming out of my mouth, but I don't hear any response from Dari. He sits me down. I swear I blink and he's gone! Where'd he go? I blink again and he's back with a tall glass of water, pushing me to drink it.

"Come on. Just a little," he says raising the glass to my mouth. His eyebrows are frowning at me. Awww! He's so serious.

"What's wrong? Everything's fine. I feel fine!" I do! I have never been drunk before and I must say that it feels great! So much better than . . . not being drunk, because, I don't know. It just does!

"That's good. Just sip it."

I drink some water so he won't worry. He's the coolest guy ever!

"Hey, Dari?"

"Hey, what?"

"I think you are the coolest guy ever," I tell him. Right now, I can tell him anything. Who cares? I have no fear. Maybe I should tell him I love him. Right here at gay/goth karaoke, I should just scream *I love you* so everyone can hear me. It's good to be honest, right? I mean . . . honesty is the best policy. Isn't that what it says in the Bible? Or the Torah? Or the . . . Ohhhhhhhhhhh. I no longer feel fine. I don't know how I'm moving, but I am, and I make it to the bathroom just in time to puke in the toilet. Mostly in the toilet.

"Lily!" Dari throws the door open, looking like a frightened little boy.

"I got sick," I report as I lay my head on the floor.

He wets a paper towel and hands it to me. While I'm wiping my face, he gets another wet towel to wipe up the vomit that didn't quite hit the target. Wow. That's absurdly nice of him.

"I'm sorry, Lily." He says this as he's washing his hands.

"Why?"

"How are you feeling?"

I'm still on the floor. A few girls—women, I guess—come in and give Dari the what-the-fuck-are-you-doing-in-the-ladies'-room glare, but they eventually go into the other stalls, ignoring us.

"I think I'm okay now." I actually feel much better now than I did a few seconds ago. Well, I feel like myself again. Which isn't necessarily better.

"I shouldn't have let you drink more than one beer."

I had more than one beer?

"I just didn't know you hadn't . . . whatever. I'm just sorry. Let's get you home." He gently lifts me from the floor, but as soon as I'm up, I can totally walk on my own. I don't want to go home.

Outside, it's gotten chilly. I wrap myself in my scarf, realizing that winter isn't too far off. No more Indian summer teases. That's offensive. Is it offensive? Who comes up with these terms?

We walk in silence for a few minutes. Then I stop.

"What is it?" he asks.

"I'm having fun. I don't wanna go home."

"You got wasted. It's my fault. Told you I'm an asshole."

"No, you're not." I check my watch. "We still have fifty-eight minutes of 'yes.' I don't wanna lose 'em."

Dari shakes his head, concerned. He's taken on a pseudo-parental role. This I do not like.

"Dari? In case you haven't noticed, I rarely have spontaneous fun. I really, truly feel fine now. Can we please just forget it happened?"

Dari smiles, but it is a weary smile. My mother uses that smile with me a lot. God. No matter what happens, I don't want Dari to ever feel responsible for me.

"Truth or dare?"

He laughs. Now that is a genuine smile.

"Truth."

Oh. I was really expecting him to say "dare."

"If you could do anything in the world at this very moment, what would it be?"

He frowns again, but at least he's no longer worrying about me. We continue walking until he stops.

"I'd be at the Louvre. With my mother."

His mother. Shit.

"How long ago . . . ? I mean, how old were you—"

"It's not easy to talk about, Lily."

I nod, trying to think of what I could possibly say that might be helpful.

"I was twelve. I miss her a lot. I wish I could just get over it."

I hope I didn't get too personal. I didn't mean to. I've been through a lot, but I have no idea what Dari's been through.

Without thinking, I take hold of his hand. He doesn't let go.

"Special reading, five dollars" comes bellowing at us from a store-front. I turn and a short, olive-skinned woman smoking an electronic cigarette stares me dead in the eye.

"I don't believe in that stuff," I tell her.

"Normal price is ten. For you and your friend, five." She stares intently, calmly, while synthetic smoke oozes from her nostrils.

"It *is* 'yes' night," Dari reminds me once again.

This is dumb. I know this is dumb. I know that these people are total fakes because of this documentary I saw once. They just read your body language and your comfort level and that tells them which script to use. But I shrug. What the hell? And it's getting cold.

We go inside the storefront, but no farther. This is where she conducts business, it seems. She shows us where to sit, and then she sits in her seat so we're making a triangle. My drunk self would probably find this amusing and not be the least bit bothered by the fact that anyone walking by can look in the window and see us sitting here like a couple of suckers. My sober self is quite a different person.

She starts to look in my direction, but then turns to Dari instead. If I didn't already think this was stupid, I'd be insulted.

"You're old," she says to Dari.

"I . . . am?" He's trying to keep a poker face, but is instantly thrown off his game.

"I know you think you are a teenager, but you've lived many lives and you'll live many more. When you dream, do you always dream your own dreams?"

Dari shakes his head slowly. Is he saying "no" or just confused?

"Listen to your dreams. They are great teachers."

She takes his hand and runs her finger over his palm. Then she turns it over and runs her finger over the back. She sees a tiny spot or something on one of his knuckles and makes a circular motion on it. I would not like her taking such liberties with my hands, but Dari doesn't seem bothered. She gently releases his hand and inhales on her e-cig.

"Your libido is no match for your talent. Try not to let it run things. There's too much at stake."

"Like what?" Dari asks.

"Your freedom, of course."

I chuckle, but when both she and Dari shoot me a sharp look, I shut up. How can Dari be taken in by this crap? It's so general. It could apply to anyone.

"You've hit a crisis point, yes? You need answers and you're not gonna find 'em in the old places you once did. Don't even bother. You already know what you need to do. You're ready to be your own person. You just have to do it."

"How?" Dari asks her, enraptured.

"That I can't tell you, but you'll know when it's time. You can't live with him anymore, can you?"

That's when I start to listen. Dari doesn't respond, but he's so still now. Like he's stopped breathing.

"Pay attention to yourself. Pay attention to your dreams." For a second she looks at me. "Well. You have people in your life that might be allies. Anyone who is not an ally, cut off. This is not the time to give every loser the benefit of the doubt. If someone wrongs you, remove them from your life. Do not suffer bullshit. Got it?"

Dari nods solemnly. The woman takes a drink from a tall glass of ice water, signaling the end to Dari's "special" reading. He reaches in his pocket and pulls out a five. He attempts to hand it to her, but she gestures toward a small parlor table where there is a clay pot with lots of bills. Dari shoves his five in it.

She turns to me and she just stares for several seconds. Directly into my eyes. She reaches into her pocket and pulls out a stick of gum.

"What?"

"Take it. You need it," she says. And then I remember that I did puke not too long ago. I take the gum.

She does the whole running-her-finger-over-my-palm-and-the-back-of-my-hand routine. Thankfully, this is brief, and she releases my hand not long after grasping it.

"You're holding on to the past. It's eating you alive," she says indifferently.

Maybe. But I'll bet that's true for most people.

"Meditate. Take time to appreciate all that you have going for you in the present. Once you've done that, you can begin making future plans. But don't get stuck there either. You have a tendency to get lost in the horrors of the past and the worries of the future. You struggle to keep yourself planted and secure. Not everything is negative. You have to find the positive light you once had. It's still in there."

"How do you know?" I challenge. Dari glances at me.

"You're not a skeptic, but you want to be. You admire those who'd call me a hustler. But that fake exterior will make it harder for you to settle your problems."

"You didn't answer my question," I mumble.

She takes another drag.

"Everything about you is pasted on your face like an Internet banner. I know you're having the time of your life tonight, but tomorrow will be a different matter." She then turns to Dari and gestures to the door. "Go outside and wait. It'll only be a minute."

Dari looks uncertain, but follows instructions. He stands right outside the door and watches us through the glass.

"Why can't he be here?" I ask, trying to steady my voice and push away the anxiety creeping in.

"You're in love with him and he doesn't know it, yes?"

I don't move. I don't want her to know that she's right.

"I strongly encourage you to use caution. He's centuries old, maybe older. You're still quite young. He's wading through treacherous waters right now, but he'll never tell you that. He doesn't think you can handle it."

Ouch.

"Listen to yourself, your fears, your body. Your dreams.

"There's another. A man from your not-too-distant past. You've given him way too much power. He is a dark cloud. Visualize that dark cloud exploding into rain and vanishing. Do it until it's gone. You have to stop holding on. Let go."

She nods toward Dari, still peeking in through the window.

"You and him? You may meet again. Time is longer than you can imagine. Use it wisely." Again, she leans back and takes a long sip of ice water.

"What am I supposed to do with all of that?" I ask.

"Do with it what you like. That's all I can give you."

I fish out my five and toss it in her pot and walk out.

"What did she say?"

"More bullshit. I don't know. Something about wishing away a dark cloud and you being centuries old. Whatever. We said 'yes.' Guess that's what we get."

At that moment, she opens the door.

"One more thing. For both of you," she calls. "Forgiveness is a life-long endeavor. Be patient with yourselves." Then she goes back inside, locks up, and shuts off the neon PSYCHIC READINGS BY AMELIA sign.

"What do you think she meant?" Dari asks.

"I think she just wanted our money," I say.

"Maybe. Some of what she said was kinda on point, though. I know I have a hard time forgiving people."

"Doesn't everyone?"

He shrugs. I shake my head. Determined not to take it seriously. I refuse to be burned by yet another person.

As we walk through the cold, I start to think that maybe our night should wind down soon. I wouldn't be opposed to some Mexican hot cocoa and curling up on the couch in front of a popcorn movie right about now. I'm tasting the cocoa when some girl yells down from a fire escape in a faux-British accent.

"What's the password?"

Is she talking to us?

"'ello! Dreadlocks and curly top! What is the password?"

Dari looks at me. "We done for the night?" he asks. Normally, I would nod and ignore this loon, but it seems fitting that I don't, so I don't. We approach the building.

"Kumquat," I call up.

"No," she shouts, delighted.

"Lucifer," Dari attempts.

She laughs. "Nope."

"Uh. Porkbellies?"

"*What?* God, no!"

"It's fucking cold," Dari suddenly shouts. And at that moment, the door just ahead of us buzzes and we go inside.

"This is nuts! We don't know these people. We don't even know which apartment is theirs," I protest. That's when another girl pokes her head over the stairwell from the fourth floor.

"Come on in, guests," she calls. Dari looks at me. I check my watch: 11:53. Fine. Seven more minutes of "yes."

The apartment is huge but dingy. The music is loud. I think it's MGMT (a band I'm wholly on the fence about). There are people everywhere in really strange costumes, like it's the 1920s or something.

"What kind of party is this?" Dari mutters. I shrug and then our hostess from the fire escape appears to answer our question.

"This is a Prohibition-era speakeasy," she exclaims in that terrible accent again. She hands us two dainty teacups filled with a clear liquid. I take one sniff and my eyes start to water. It smells like paint thinner.

"Then why are you doing a British accent?" Dari asks.

She sighs. With no trace of the accent at all she says, "Dude. I'm just tryin' to have fun, okay?" And then she skates (Prohibition-era roller blades?) through the swarm of *Great Gatsby* fugitives back into the kitchen. Dari and I look at each other and crack up. How do these people find us? Or do we find them?

Dari takes my cup away—probably afraid of more regurgitation—and carefully sets both of our cups on the windowsill. That's when I see the moon. It is humongous and orange and glorious.

"Look!" No one notices when I open the latch to the window and climb out onto the fire escape. Dari follows.

We both look up. I've never seen a moon like this before. I close my eyes and it's still there. I feel like I can smell it. It's right here. Just for us.

"Hunter's Moon."

I turn to Dari. The moon is a glowing orb in his eyes.

"What?"

"That is a hunter's moon. Some people call it a blood moon, but that's inaccurate. For a blood moon, there has to be a lunar eclipse. This is just the first full moon after the harvest moon."

"Does it mean anything or is it just pretty?" I shiver a bit, but play it down. I don't want Dari to think he has to give me his jacket. No. He doesn't do that, but as he talks, he encircles me from behind. Now I'm warming up so fast I could melt.

"In Native American culture, it signals the beginning of hunting season. A time to start storing up for the coming winter. Wiccans call it the shedding moon because when it appears, the walls between worlds are the thinnest. Like you're shedding one life for another. If you believe that junk."

"How do you know all this stuff, Dariomauritius?"

He shrugs, his arms still around my midsection.

"Useless information gets me off. Lilith."

We laugh and soak in the big, beautiful hunter's moon or shedding moon or whatever the fuck it's called. Nothing else, none of it—not that weird psychic reading, not vomiting at gay/goth karaoke, not being chased out of Bevvy Botswana's show, not the photo, not stupid school, not Tara McKenzie, not Jackie, not Tracy, not Mom, not the summer, not the hospital, not even Mr. Wright . . . Bobby—none of it matters now. All that matters in the world is this moon. And Dari. And me.

I hear a bit of the song that's currently playing. It is "Evangeline" by the Cocteau Twins and I think I'm going to cry. It's one of my favorite songs, and if I were programming the sound track to my life, this is the song I would play at this very second.

"I love this song," I breathe.

"Wanna dance?" he says right behind my ear.

"On the fire escape?"

"Can you think of a better place?"

No. I can't.

He gently spins me around and we awkwardly attempt to dance on the fire escape. Before long, we hear some loud creaking and wonder if maybe we should axe the dance party.

As I'm giggling nervously, he kisses me. Just like that. It is not awkward. It is the truest kiss my lips have ever known. I feel his lips, his tongue, his skin in every pore. Everything. Everywhere. And now I do cry. Two single tears. He kisses my tears, and I laugh. This is a moment. I want to remember this moment. Every detail, every sense. It's one of those moments in life that makes everything else worth it. One of those moments that feels like an eternity of bliss in one tiny bite of time. It's one of those moments that falls from some heavenly plane to remind you that life can be wonderful.

Right before everything falls apart.

PART 2

10

IF WE WERE IN COLORADO

Dari gives two bucks to the beggar on the corner. The guy smiles big and God-blesses him and tells him of his recent misfortune, which includes being thrown out of his aunt's house on his birthday. Dari listens for a few seconds and then wishes him good luck. Usually, Dari pretends he doesn't see the homeless. Not out of callousness (he hopes), but mainly as a defense; he's seen them all through his childhood, and if he allowed his heart to bleed each time he's accosted, his heart would be bloodless by now. But it's a sweet Sunday evening, he's in a nice mood, and he felt like putting someone else in a nice mood too.

Lily is all right. Not his typical girl by any stretch, but he imagines he's not her typical boy, either, considering the fact that he isn't married with children. There's just something about her. He doesn't know what it is and doesn't particularly care. It just seems like they fit. It has been a while since he's felt that way.

When he gets to his door, he takes a deep breath, searching for that ever-depleting well of patience within himself. No idea what tonight's episode of *Father Knows Best* in Bizzarro World will bring.

Strange. Dari squints his eyes. Did he just do that wrong? He tries again. Same thing. He tries a third time. He considers trying a fourth, though he knows that would be useless. His keys no longer work. His father has changed the locks. After the initial panic, Dari laughs. *Really? You're scared of ME??* He can't believe it. He doesn't know if he should feel terrified, ecstatic, or relieved. Anger wins the day.

"Open the door," Dari spits as he pounds on it.

No footsteps.

He pounds again, and again no one comes. He crams his ear up against it to see if he can hear activity inside. Nothing.

He slides down the wall and sits there. He knows his father too well. This is a tactic. It's psychological warfare. He wants to establish Dari's dependence on him for his survival. Yes. That is what is happening. It's ugly. He closes his eyes and remembers being small and fantasizing that his dad was Michael Bluth from *Arrested Development*. The fun kind of dysfunctional.

He gets out his phone and starts to call Izzy, but stops himself. He can hear her sighing already, see her eyes getting red and glassy as she starts chain-smoking her Marlboros. He hates being a burden. Then there's Trisha. Trisha, who has never said a kind word to Dari and blames him for Izzy's permanent frown lines. He flips through his mental contact list for anyone who might owe him a favor, but honestly, there's only one person he trusts right now. He sends a text.

I hate to ask, but it's kind of an emergency. Can I crash at your place tonight? Again?

Marcus barely looks up now when Dari enters the building. He starts to sign into the guest book, but the doorman just waves him on. Not out of friendliness so much as annoyance.

Before he can knock, Lily opens the door.

"What happened?"

Dari hesitates. How much should he tell her?

"He changed the locks. Guess this means he kicked me out."

Lily gasps. Still in gasp mode, she pulls Dari inside the apartment.

Immediately, he sees the suitcase. Her mom's home. This could be weird.

"I don't wanna get you in trouble," Dari whispers.

"Don't worry. It's fine." But her face betrays her. She's nervous. Dari cautiously sits on a chair near the door in case he needs to make a quick exit. Savannah enters from the hallway.

"Hi, honey. What happened?" she asks.

Dari looks at both Lily and Savannah, both staring down at him with the exact same expression. Big eyes full of concern. One set blue, one set brown, and for an eerie second he almost can't tell them apart, they seem so alike. He tries to picture this scenario in reverse: What if Lily had been given the boot and she was sitting on his couch looking up at him and the old man? What a different situation that would be.

"My dad and I don't get along very well."

"I've heard."

"He changed the locks," Dari mumbles. He feels embarrassed. Like his stupid family problems are now spreading to this family.

"Jesus," Savannah breathes. "Stay here. As long as you want."

"Thank you, but—"

"No 'buts.' Your father, of course, can't legally do that, but until we figure this out, you stay here as long as you need to." Savannah smiles and gently touches Dari's cheek.

"Really?" Lily asks her mother, a bit surprised.

"Of course." Savannah rolls her suitcase into her bedroom. Lily sits next to Dari.

"She's never just invited someone to stay indefinitely. She seriously likes you," Lily says, giving him a little nudge. Then she lays her head on his shoulder. "I don't get your dad. I don't understand how anyone could be mean to you," she says quietly.

They sit in silence for a few moments before Savannah reenters the room in pajamas: a pair of cotton plaid capris and an ancient "Free Mumia" T-shirt.

"You know you can help yourself to anything around here. Don't be shy with us," Savannah assures him. He thanks her as she sits down on the end of the sofa under a lamp. Lily goes into the kitchen to find snacks. Savannah is most definitely a "cool mom" by anybody's standards, but more than cool, she seems genuinely kind and genuinely interested in other people. And happy. Not a small thing in a world where more adults are on antidepressants than aren't. (He has no data to back up this hypothesis, but he's sure it's true.) So it surprises him when he happens to glance over at her, leafing through a *New Yorker* with an expression on her face that is anything but happy. It's somewhere between sadness and rage. Maybe her overly generous offer to him wasn't so genuine after all.

"Uh? Dari?" She's startled. So is Lily, who stands in the kitchen doorway frowning and shaking Skittles into her hand. He didn't realize it, but he was staring at her mother for probably a good thirty seconds. Oh, God!

"Um, I'm sorry. I was just . . . I wasn't thinking. Spacing out," he mumbles, edging himself closer to the door.

"That's okay." Savannah looks uncomfortable and Dari feels like a creeper. "Did you guys have a nice weekend?" she asks.

Lily and Dari both nod.

"We had a blast," Dari says shyly. Lily smiles, one of those smiles that holds all the warmth of the sun.

"Good," she says, and with that she opens a drawer in the coffee table and pulls out a cigar box.

"Mom."

Savannah looks up at her daughter.

"Lily." She laughs a strange, exhausted laugh. "There really are worse things, and if we were in Colorado right now or Washington, this would not be the slightest issue."

"What's the matter?" Dari asks.

Savannah sighs. "Dari, do you mind if I smoke some cannabis? If you do, that is fine. I can go elsewhere."

For just a moment, Dari hears that lyric from *Annie* ringing in his ears: *I think I'm gonna like it here!*

"No. I don't mind. I don't mind at all," Dari answers, a bit too eagerly.

Lily ducks back into the kitchen. As Savannah fills the paper with leaves and starts rolling the joint, Dari follows Lily. She crams her face with gummy worms.

"Your mom is mad cool," Dari whispers.

Lily shakes her head. "She's in some kinda mood. I don't know. She almost never smokes anymore, especially in front of a guest. Can't be good." Lily continues stress-eating candy. Dari grabs a few.

"All I know is I wish my dad was this cool."

"Cool. Right." Lily tears open a box of Nerds and dumps them down her throat.

"You eat a lot of candy," Dari observes.

Lily freezes midchew.

"Just sometimes," she admits, mouth full.

"No judgment or anything. Do what you want."

"I just like candy. I dunno. I guess it's more than that. Calms me down," she says.

"Yep. That's why I can't seem to quit smoking," Dari commiserates.

Lily turns on music and goes back into the living room. Dari wonders if he sounded too judgy about the candy. He certainly didn't mean to imply that she should lose any weight. Lily has a nice shape. Actually, with just a few more pounds, she'd be a for-real smoke show. A modern-day Helen of Troy or some shit. Dari shakes himself out of that reverie and tries to focus on anything else.

Savannah lights up and takes a luxurious inhalation. She holds on to it for as long as she can, and when she finally exhales, something releases. She's lighter now. More present.

"How was the retreat?" Dari asks.

Savannah nods as she takes another hit and then blows smoke out through her lips. "Retreaty."

No one says anything for a moment after that. They just listen to the music. One of Lily's hipster bands. Harlem. You know gentrification is deep when a garage rock band made up of three white boys is called "Harlem." Dari shakes his head.

"A woman asked me to clarify the statement about humility I'd

133

made on page two-oh-three. I asked her if she could be more specific and she was shocked that I didn't automatically know what she was talking about. I said, 'Ma'am, I wrote the book over a decade ago. If I had those kind of memory powers, I could go on tour with David Blaine.' She didn't find it funny."

Dari laughs. Savannah smiles.

"Used to be better. Years ago, when I first started doing these things. Conferences, retreats. People were just more open in general. Now? It's different now. Now they want you to prove to them that you're worth their time. They like to cross-examine you now."

"What's changed?" Dari asks.

"Hard to say. One thing is me, I guess. I get older every year, but my words never age."

Lily stares at her mother as though she wants to say something, but she doesn't.

"Also, just life changes. You get these ideas and think things are going to go a certain way and then they don't."

"It's because of me, isn't it?" Lily asks.

"Huh?"

"If I were happy and normal, you might not have any doubts."

"Not true, my dear. And please cool it with the self-deprecating stuff. Look on the bright side for once. You got a cute bright side sitting right here in front of ya."

Whoa. Is she talking about me? Dari wonders if Lily's thinking the same thing, because her jaw just dropped a bit.

"Eh? Enough of this morose stuff. We should have a pleasant evening. Pretend we're enlightened or whatever. Oh, but really, Dari, if the smoke bothers you, please let me know. I don't want you to feel uncomfortable."

"No. Not at all. I . . ." Dari stops himself as he was perilously close to mentioning his own occasional herbal indulgences.

"What were you gonna say?"

"Nothing. Just believe me: I don't mind. I *really* don't mind."

Dari hopes his emphasis might convey his strong hankering to share Savannah's treat. And for one magical moment, a slight sparkle in her eyes suggests to him that she just might permit this, but then a new song comes on, killing the magic.

"Lily, I didn't know you liked this song! This was my jam," Savannah cries happily.

"How appropriate," Lily grumbles.

Savannah stands, swaying to the music, and then she starts to sing. She knows every word.

Breathe it in and breathe it out
And pass it on, it's almost out

She laughs and takes another hit. "Oh, that takes me back. Lilith Fair 1998. That was such a good time. You know? I named her after that festival. That's how much of a good time was had." Savannah laughs.

"All women performers, right?"

"Mm-hmm. It was a special time. I can't imagine something like that existing these days. Makes me sad." Her face floats far away. Perhaps to the days of Lilith Fair, or her disappointment in today's youth culture.

Tentatively, Dari reaches his hand out to her.

Savannah's eyes widen in amused disbelief. "Oh! Uh-uh. No way!"

"You said it yourself: It's legal in two states. If we were currently in Colorado, would my age matter to you?" he asks, quite reasonably.

"Yeah, I don't think that would really change—"

"If he smokes, I'm doing it too," Lily informs her.

Savannah laughs anxiously, shaking her head. "All right. I think that's enough for one evening." She extinguishes the j, which disappoints Dari, though he's not that surprised. Everyone has a limit.

But the damage is done. All of the people in this room are fairly toasted thanks to a little phenomenon known as the Contact High. This probably explains how Dari easily convinces them to play Pictionary. With three people. The compromise being that Dari must play on both teams.

"Uhhh? *Tree of Life? The Giving Tree?*" Lily squints and tries to guess what Dari's drawing in his sketchbook. The category is movies adapted from books. Lily has no idea what Dari's drawing, and he can't seem to help her. This is when he remembers that he actually sucks at Pictionary. He's too single-minded. He gets an idea of what he wants to draw and then he just does it. If he likes his idea, he won't scrap it to assist his guessing team partner. He's more interested in seeing the drawing through to its conclusion. He's also too detailed. Effective Pictionary sketches are simple. Not complex compositions done in forty-five seconds. But he can't do anything about it. Even when he consciously tries to amend his game techniques, he consistently falls into the same patterns.

"Time," Savannah yells.

"*A Tree Grows in Brooklyn,*" he sighs in frustration. He really thought she might be able to get this one. Other than the large, flawless Norway Maple he drew at the center of the page, in the background is clearly a skeletal version of the Brooklyn Bridge.

"My turn," Savannah says with glee. She dips into their homemade clues and Dari slides over to her side of the room. Him moving back and forth between "teams" had made them all laugh at the beginning. He sees that it is now getting old.

She looks at the scrap in her hand and cracks up. "Whoever did this is a mean person."

"Ready?" Lily asks.

"I suppose so. The category is musicians."

"Go." Lily starts her timer and Savannah just shakes her head in laughter.

"Come on! Do something," Dari pleads.

Savannah struggles to draw a stick figure man holding a guitar. Dari guesses Hendrix, Page, Cobain, and then she starts making weird teeth and the lack thereof. She concentrates on this musician's nightmare mouth. Dari runs out of guesses.

"Time!"

Savannah collapses in laughter. "Lily, you are in so much trouble," she cries, trying to catch her breath.

"What was that?"

Lily smiles mischievously. "Eddie Van Halen."

"Who?" Dari asks. Savannah slowly calms down, wiping tears from her cheeks.

"What's up with his teeth?" Dari eyes them with horror and fascination.

"I was trying to give him meth mouth," Savannah explains.

Lily laughs too, clearly proud of this curve ball. On their next turn, Lily draws for Dari. He gets it right away. The category was sixties bands and the clue was the Doors. Lily simply draws two doors. Easy.

Now it's Dari's turn to draw for her mother. First, he stuffs a handful of popcorn in his mouth. (The munchies led them to make several batches of popcorn in a variety of flavors. The grossest by far is blue Jell-O, and yet this is what he chooses.) Lily gives him a few seconds to chew and then asks if they're ready. Savannah giggles again and he says yes.

Dari begins to draw something that looks like a wild animal. A cat. Quickly, it evolves into a beautiful cheetah. Then, out of nowhere, Savannah yells: "Of course. *Mrs. Dalloway*!" Dari throws down the pencil and high-fives Savannah.

"WHAT," Lily screams.

They both look at each other and then they crack up.

"Just kidding," Dari winks.

"Sorry, baby. It was totally his idea." Savannah laughs.

"That's what you get for Eddie Van Halen," Dari informs her.

Lily laughs in spite of herself. As she should: It's hella funny! Dari hopes she isn't too bothered by the prank, though. He hopes she isn't bothered by pranks in general. He loves pranks.

Not long after the cheetah incident, Savannah yawns with exaggeration and Dari helps Lily clean up their little party. Without announcing it, Savannah reignites the joint and inhales quietly, her eyes far away searching for some point beyond the walls.

In the kitchen, Dari asks Lily if her Mom is okay. She nods, but then admits that she doesn't really know.

"Sometimes strange things come up at these retreats. Emotional things."

Dari ruminates on this for a moment before returning to the living room. What could be so strange and emotional about a wellness retreat? Isn't the whole point to leave that stuff at home?

"Um, Savannah? I just want to thank you for being so generous. I'll call my sister tomorrow and figure out what I should do. But thank you."

She smiles sadly. "I'm glad you're here."

"Mom? Is everything all right?" Lily asks.

"Everything is fine. I think it's totally fine. So what if it takes nine years to write one book? Maybe it'll take nine more. So what. Right?" She's looking for approval. Something bad happened this weekend.

"Of course, Mom," Lily assures her. "Your first book was such a massive success that the expectations people have for you just aren't fair. And you know there'll always be assholes." Though her intentions are clearly sincere, her response to her mother's despair sounds hackneyed. Like lines from a play they've both acted in before.

"Did someone suggest otherwise?" Dari asks and Lily whips her head around to him sharply. Did he say something inappropriate?

Savannah takes another luxurious hit and closes her eyes. When she exhales, her eyes remain closed. "It is very possible . . . probable that I will never finish another book again." Lily seems shocked and distressed to hear this.

"Yes, you will, Mom. You have to shut the critics out of your head. You know that," Lily explains.

"What if you don't finish the book? Or any other book? Would that be so terrible?" Dari throws out.

"She *will* finish it," Lily replies.

"But what if she doesn't?"

"But she will, so there's no point in asking that question." Lily is firm about this. Something unfamiliar dances in her eyes. The need to protect her mother, perhaps?

"All I'm saying is maybe there might be other amazing things out there for you that won't have anything to do with publishing a new book," Dari finishes, looking at Savannah.

"I guess it's possible," Savannah concedes.

"You might have talents you don't even know about."

Savannah smiles, but clearly she isn't convinced.

"You probably do, Mom, but that doesn't mean you won't finish the book." Lily eyes Dari, silently asking him to drop it, so he says no more.

"Lily, do you need any help setting up the guest room?"

"No. It's been his room all weekend," Lily answers. Savannah snaps out of her gloom for a moment to be surprised, but then she remembers that she was the one who forcibly encouraged his presence.

"Night, you two." She starts down the hall and just before she opens her door, she turns back to them.

"Thank you, Dari. For reminding me that hope can take many forms."

Dari lies on the bed in the guest room staring up at the ceiling. Worrying about small things like what time should he get his shower in the morning? What chores should he do to help around the house? What about all his stuff locked away in the old apartment? Ignoring the bigger things that are knocking at the door at the back of his mind, like what will he do after tomorrow? Will he end up in a shelter? Or worse? No. He can't handle those questions just yet. Instead, he thinks of the family who's welcomed him in as if he were one of them. He can't believe there are still people this kind in the world.

When he's tired, his mind will wander off into forbidden territory. Tonight, it wanders right over to a vivid image of his mother, standing before him in leopard-print leggings, knee-high boots, and an oversize cashmere sweater. He wants the image to evaporate, but it won't. She stands there as real as the bed he's dozing on, and she looks so sad. So sorry. She should be. If she were here right now, none of this shit would be happening. None of the bad shit.

There is a tiny knock at the door, and before he can say anything, Lily eases the door open. "You still awake?"

Dari looks to where his mother just stood. Gone. Ghosting. As per usual. "Yeah." He turns on the desk light. He lies back down on the bed and she sits next to him.

"What happened with your dad?"

He shakes his head. "Things went too far, I guess. And by that, I mean that I fought back."

Lily's eyes widen. "Good for you," she tells him.

"Hope I wasn't overstepping earlier with your mom."

"Oh. Yeah. Don't worry about it. I think you were more help tonight than I was anyway."

"You gonna tell her about that photo?"

Lily closes her eyes and blows some air out through her lips, making kind of an unintentional mouth fart. "No. She's dealt with enough of my drama. I can take care of it myself," she says.

"You know I got your back, right?" he says. She beams. "I don't think I can ever thank you enough for this." He's about to say more when Lily cuts him off with a kiss. A gentle kiss. She stops and looks at him. Dari traces her hairline with his fingertip, staring into the dark pools of her eyes.

"I can't thank *you* enough." She moves back to his lips, then his neck. He massages her hair and lets the tiniest moan escape from his throat. Damn. He didn't mean for that to slip out. Then, ever so delicately, he pulls away.

"We should go to sleep." He can barely look at her as he says it.

"Why?"

He envelops her for a moment—a really intense moment wherein he manages to kiss her face and neck and firmly caress her left breast simultaneously. Then he lets go.

"Because your mother is sleeping twenty feet away."

He then gently kisses her cheek, stands, and opens the door.

"See ya in the morning," he says.

Lily raises her eyebrows, but doesn't argue and heads back to her room. Dari closes the door and lies back down. He is awake. Certain parts of him are more awake than others. He thinks about Dick Cheney, Donald Trump, and Rush Limbaugh rolling around naked in a tub of baked beans. Effective. As he drifts off to sleep, he thinks about celibacy and how deliciously depriving it sounds. Then he thinks of his father. He's certain that that man hasn't held a woman in at least four years.

11

BOUNDARIES

Monday morning. Shit. This weekend almost made me forget that Monday would eventually come. Yet here it is. Like always. One thing is different: I had the privilege of walking to school next to Dari. He has this amazing way of giving me happy amnesia. When I'm around him, I forget everything terrible in my life. I'm not so sure that's a good thing, because it all comes back to me in dizzying, vivid detail as I walk into Mrs. Waters's office.

"Good morning, Lily. How are you?" Her attempts to sound casual have the opposite effect. She's usually anxious—not an ideal state for a guidance counselor.

"I have to, um, report an issue."

"Oh, no. What's happened?" she asks, trepidation in her voice.

I never actually thought the school would allow this to be published. But if I don't say anything, if I just roll with it, I'll feel like the biggest victim that ever lived. With shaking hands, I show her the photo.

Mrs. Waters sighs and shakes her head. "Where did you get this?"

"The literary office."

She nods. "Don't worry. I'll take care of it. Before lunch," she promises.

"Thank you," I say, feeling a bit relieved. I stand to leave, but she stops me.

"Lily? It isn't any of my business, but are you talking to anyone?"

I'm talking to you, right now, aren't I? I think it, but I don't say it. I know what she's asking.

"Yes. I just started seeing a therapist."

"Oh, good. Which one?"

Which one? We live in New York City. The number of practicing psychologists here could very well be in the seven-digit range.

"Dr. Maalouf," I reply.

Her face lights up. "Ariel Maalouf?"

Wow! How did she do that?

"Yeah. That is her name."

"She's young, but smart. Please give her my best."

I leave her office dazed. No matter how much I think I know, I am always surprised.

Ariel Maalouf is pretty cool. My first session with her was last week. I wasn't sure about her at first, but I think she might get me. Still too early to tell.

But I was impressed with her questions.

"What's your favorite band?"

"That's the first question you're gonna ask me?"

"I heard you were into music."

"I like a lot of bands," I said.

"What if you had to pick one today? Which would it be?" she pushed.

Since I wasn't prepared for this topic, I had to give it some thought. I like lots of bands, and I LOVE fewer, but the list is still lengthy. I rarely pick a "favorite" because I think that's for laypeople who don't understand the infinite possibilities of music. One day you might desperately need to hear power chords and indulgent drum solos. Another might be a day for orchestral sounds. Picking one band above all else is just wrong. But, then again, it's not like what I say has to be etched in blood.

Changing my mind later doesn't necessarily mean I'm a total waffler.

"I've been really into Sleater-Kinney lately."

"Cool. What is it about them?"

"Have you heard of them?"

"Nope. My music tastes tend to be a bit poppy. But my favorite stuff is classic rock and Motown."

She has no problem talking about herself freely.

"I like some pop stuff," I offered.

"Tell me about Sleater-Kinney."

"They're an indie rock band from the Pacific Northwest. I love that they don't seem to care. If they want to sound like riot girls, they do. If they want to sound like cute, twee girls, they do. If they want to sound goofy or obnoxious, they do. They just do whatever they feel like."

"They sound awesome. I'm gonna Spotify them as soon as I get home," she promised. I dug her usage of "Spotify" as a verb.

We talked more about music and the fact that I love to listen to it and sometimes I try to write it. Talking so much about it made me especially miss playing it. I taught myself to play bass and I took drum lessons for years. Why do these things fall away as we get older? Playing made me happy. If I know that I can do something that makes me happy, why do I allow myself to get so depressed? Seems like a no-brainer.

My next session is tomorrow. Dr. Maalouf assigned me to think of a question that's important to me and that I haven't found the answer to yet and share it with her. I strangely like the idea of approaching therapy as if it were just another class. Makes it less pathetic somehow.

Chemistry sucks. We now have to do some end-of-the-semester project with our lab partners, which means I'm going to have to spend some precious nonclass time with Tara. Nothing like being forced to work with someone who hates you. As if I had any illusions that I was the only person unhappy about this situation, as soon as the bell rings, Tara grabs her books and storms out. Yes, that could be about any number of things, but I don't think so.

Come to think of it, all of my classes suck. Maybe Tara was right weeks ago. Maybe I should just drop out. Who'd care? Other than my mom, and I'm sure she'd get over it. There are worse things I could do. Maybe I could work on my music. If I could get myself to start playing again. The best rock musicians never went to college anyway.

"What would you do?" I ask Dari at lunch.

"Are you asking my permission to quit school?" He sometimes has this annoying way of answering a question with a question.

"I'm not asking for your permission. I'm asking for your opinion," I correct.

He munches on his fajita thing.

"I don't think you're the high-school-dropout type," he finally says.

"I just don't think I can do it anymore. Graduation is more than a year and a half away. That's forever," I whine.

"No, it's not," he argues. Why does he always have to act all wise? Why can't he whine like a normal person?

"Every day in this school feels like a year. I guess what I'm really asking is, would you lose respect for me if I quit?"

"What makes you think I respect you now?" he asks, then quickly winks. I throw a grape at him. He throws some lettuce my way. We laugh and throw food at each other like a couple of summer camp geeks until I feel someone watching. I look up. Tracy stands by our table, a pained look on her face.

"Uh, hi," I say, settling down. Dari quiets himself too. He casually removes a straw wrapper from my hair.

"Can I talk to you for a second?" she asks. This can't be good.

"Okay." She's already moving toward the hall, so I follow her, shrugging in Dari's direction.

"I'm sorry. I am. But I didn't do it," Tracy whispers urgently.

"What?"

"The picture! I had nothing to do with it, Lily. I swear to God."

"I believe you." I don't know what else I can say.

Her eyes dart all over my face, searching for something.

"Mrs. Waters wants me suspended. It'll go on my permanent record. I want to apply to Yale next year." Her voice breaks into a cry. "I don't know what to do," she sobs. I don't know what to do either. Part of me—a big part of me—aches to see her like this and wants to hug her and assure her that everything is going to be all right. But she's treated me like a leper since school began. I hate that we're not friends anymore, but we're not.

"I didn't even mention your name, Tracy," I tell her honestly. "But I had to report it. What else was I supposed to do?"

Tracy wipes the tears away with the back of her hand. She hiccups like a little kid who just lost her balloon.

"You believe me?"

"Yes. I believe you."

She stares down at the floor. "Will you help me?" *Wait, what? Help you? Why should I? I was in the hospital, former BFF! You never came to see me. You didn't care! You treat me like crap.*

"Help you with what?" I try to make my voice as gruff as possible.

"Can you just tell Mrs. Waters that it wasn't me that did it? I wasn't ever gonna let that get published, you know? I wouldn't have even let it get to the faculty approval level. I swear." She's practically on her knees in front of me, begging. It is unbecoming and embarrassing. For her. I think about it. Will it kill my pride to speak on her behalf to Mrs. Waters? Not really.

"Get up, Tracy," I tell her. She does, clearly feeling like a fool. "I'll tell her," I say. She looks amazed for a second, then she embraces me in one of the tightest hugs I've ever had.

"I'm so sorry," she says into my ear. "I miss you."

Despite everything, I feel tears springing to my eyes, but I resist them. I'm not ready for a full-scale forgiveness reunion with Tracy.

"That's enough," I quietly tell her, and she lets me go. "I have to go get my things. On my way to class, I'll stop in Mrs. Waters's office," I say.

Mrs. Waters isn't exactly inclined to believe me. She says she's very observant and knows way more about what's happening in the halls of this school than most people would think. I ask what that means and then she clarifies. She brings up Mr. Motherfucker and the sad events of last spring and apparently she knows how close I once was to Tracy. The more she talks, the more I realize that she thinks Tracy was behind the whole thing. This tells me she doesn't know nearly as much as she thinks. I have no great love for Tracy these days, but this is not something she would conceive of let alone carry out.

"Tracy's too prissy, Mrs. Waters. She's never been in trouble for anything before. She's too afraid to do anything interesting enough to get in trouble," I explain. My lack of enthusiasm might actually help Tracy's case.

"All right, Lily. I'll take it under consideration." Then she gives me a tight smile and turns her attention to her computer screen, which tells me our meeting is over.

I wait in the main hall. I texted Dari I'd be here if he wanted to walk home with me. He hasn't replied. I don't know if I should stay or what. I'm assuming he's coming home with me again, but does he need space? Should we set boundaries? Boundaries. Ugh. I hate that word. I hate myself for thinking that word.

"Hey." He says it right behind me and I don't know if he intends it or not, but it has a potent sensual effect on my entire being. So much so that I hop about a foot away from him.

"You all right?"

"Oh, yeah. Great. No worries," I say. And then we stand there looking around, neither one of us wanting to take the first step toward the door for some reason.

"Do you . . . do you want to walk home with me? It's cool if you need some space or whatever. I totally get it." I try to sound as nonchalant as possible.

"No. Yeah," he says, weirdly distracted. "I mean, of course I wanna walk home with you. I just need to make a phone call first. Do you mind waiting?"

"Sure," I say, relieved.

We walk outside, so he can smoke, and I sit on the steps while he dials. He barely says, "Hey," before I hear the muffled sounds of someone flipping out on the other end. He says he's sorry, he didn't mean it, whatever "it" is. He sits, head in hands, blowing gray smoke from his nose and mouth. I think about his mouth. I don't think I've ever kissed a smoker before. I thought he would have gnarly breath, but somehow he even makes that work for him. He tastes like charcoal-laced cinnamon. Oh, no. I'm starting to swoon. *Stop it. You never want to swoon when the object of your adoration is sitting less than two feet away. Get a grip, Rothstein.*

"I know, Izzy. I can't really . . ." He glances at me briefly, then lowers his voice. "I'll tell you about it later. I can't go into it right now."

I feel an irrational pang of jealousy. I know he's talking to his sister and he's known her way longer than he's known me, but I now have confirmation that there are still things he's not comfortable with me knowing.

"Yeah. Thanks. I just . . . I don't know yet," he stammers. More yelling on the other end. I thought she'd calmed down, but I guess that didn't last.

She says something and then she waits. Dari says nothing. He stares straight ahead. I now clearly hear her say: "Dari? Dari are you there?"

"I'm here," he says. "Yeah, I heard you. But I . . . I can't do that." He puffs on his cigarette, it's burning down fairly close to his fingers. A little too close for my liking.

"Can you go over there and get some of my stuff? Please?" he asks.

They talk for another few minutes, and I don't hear much more from Izzy. They seem to have gotten past the yelling stage. He tells her he loves her and hangs up. His *I love you* sounds robotic, devoid of all meaning. If he ever says that sentence to me, I really hope it sounds better than that.

"She wants me to stay with her," he says.

Oh. Yeah. Of course she would. "Are you going to?"

"I don't know. I don't want to. Her girlfriend Trisha's a psycho. One time they broke up and Trisha called her sixty-three times in one day. I went to the movies with them once and it was horrible. Trisha made me get a separate popcorn because she didn't want to risk accidentally touching me. Later, she pulled Izzy aside and made her promise to never bring me out with them again. Know why? Because she's jealous of me. Her girlfriend's brother. She's a nutbag. You can't reason with her. You can't tell her things like not only do I share blood with Izzy, I have a dick! I'm not her type."

I can't help but laugh even though I know Dari's being totally sincere right now.

"I don't know. She's gonna bring me some stuff and some money. I'll figure something out."

"Well, our home is your home. As long as you want it to be," I tell him, feeling my cheeks go pink. So embarrassing. But he smiles. A grateful smile. And kisses me. It's short, but strong and just as electric as all the others that have come before it.

"Thank you, Lily," he says, his lips grazing the ridges of my ear. This time, he knows what he's doing.

I sit in the plush red chair in Maalouf's office. I chose it as mine the first day I came, and it feels right to go back to it.

"How are things?" she asks like we're just two friends having tea.

"They're not bad. I think they're good, actually."

"Tell me more." Dr. Maalouf sits forward on her seat. Perhaps she's unaccustomed to good news.

"Well, it's weird and it all happened kind of fast, but, uh . . . Dari kissed me."

"Sounds like things are very good," she says, smiling.

"Yeah. There's another thing, though. It's good in a way, but bad in a way too. He doesn't get along with his dad and, well, his dad kicked him out, so he's kinda staying with us right now." I don't know why I phrase all this as if I'm making a confession. There's nothing wrong with our situation, and if there were, Dr. Maalouf is not some all-powerful goddess from whom I should be asking absolution.

"Wow. That's intense," she says.

"I don't know. It's just unexpected."

"How long has he been staying with you?"

"The funny thing is, he kind of stayed with me all weekend while my mom was out of town before the shit went down with his dad, so it feels like almost a week."

"What was the 'shit' that went down?"

I draw a blank. All I know is what Dari tells me, which isn't much.

"He said he fought back. He didn't tell me how."

She nods. I can tell she's thinking. I can't imagine what, though.

"Do you know how long he's going to stay?"

I shake my head. In a flash, I remember why I don't care for therapists and why I didn't want to do this in the first place. They judge. Even if they don't mean to, they do. They think they know best and, worse yet, they can convince you that it's true.

"What are you thinking about?" she asks.

"I don't know. It's hard to trust people." Why did I say that out loud? She's gonna jump all over that.

"You having a hard time trusting Dari?"

Where did that come from?

"No! Not at all. I just meant . . . people in general. I totally trust Dari," I say a little too fast.

"That's good, but it would be understandable to have your doubts. There is something mysterious about him, isn't there? He has a way of keeping you at arm's length. That's what I'm sensing, but you can always tell me if I'm wrong," she says. I don't say anything. I have a feeling she's leading to something. Why can't we just talk about what a fantastic weekend I had?

"Does he remind you of other people in your life?"

"Like who?"

"Friends? Family members?" Her face is still gentle, warm, but I can so see the little wheels turning in her head. She's trying to make some weird connection so she can have an *Aha!* moment. Therapists love that crap.

"Not really."

"It's interesting that you're so drawn to him."

No, it's not.

"But there's something alluring about those who don't feel familiar to us, huh?"

"Do you want to talk about my assignment?"

She smiles. "Sure. Did you give it some thought?"

Huh. I thought for sure she'd forgotten all about it and I was gonna catch her. Unless I did and she's just a master poker player. Very possible.

"Yes. This is the question that I cannot answer. Why isn't there another option for me right now besides school?" There. I thought about it and I think that's quite a good question.

"What would be your ideal option?"

"No. I need you to answer my question first," I inform her. I'm not gonna play her head games.

"That's not quite how this works. I wanted you to bring in the question so we could talk about it and work on it together. Sorry if I misled you." She doesn't look sorry.

"That's disappointing," I say.

"What's the worst thing about school?"

"Going there."

"How long have you been thinking about this?"

"A while. Off and on. I'm just tired of it," I complain. I know she's not going to help me. I know when I leave here today I'm not going to have some magical school escape plan. I shouldn't have bothered bringing it up.

"Other than Dari, do you get along with other students?"

"Not anymore."

"Imagine for a second that tomorrow is going to be your perfect, ideal day. You get to spend the day doing exactly what you want and nothing else. What would you do?"

"Like what? I can do anything?"

"Okay, you don't suddenly have supernatural powers or billions of dollars, but being who you are today, if tomorrow you didn't have to go to school and didn't have to for the foreseeable future, how would you spend your day?"

Of all the therapist types I've encountered over the years, I'd have to say that Ariel Maalouf asks the most creative questions. These kinds of questions don't feel nosy for some reason. I don't mind them, even if they don't end up helping me.

"Well. I'd get up and eat breakfast—"

"What would you eat?"

"Specific. Um? Probably cereal and bacon. No! Blueberry pancakes and bacon. We never have bacon in the house because my mother is a vegetarian except on Thanksgiving. Then I'd—I'd play some music. Start on bass and move into some drums. Try to write a song if I still can. Early afternoon, I'd go all the way out to Queens to have Indian food in Jackson Heights, but the whole ride there, I'd be working on my song in my head. After lunch, I'd walk around the neighborhood, maybe go to some shops. Sometimes they have really nice handmade purses. They're beautiful. Then I'd head home and have some dinner with Mom, and Dari, and maybe I'd play some music for them. The stuff I'd been working on earlier in the day. Then maybe we'd watch a movie on Netflix."

"What movie?" she jumps in.

"*This is Spinal Tap*. Or if we're in the mood for drama, *Mona Lisa Smile*. Then I'd go to bed—in an ideal world, with Dari—and I'd go to sleep and I'd have the most peaceful dreams. Like dreams of being on a sailboat in the ocean at night and the moon is blood orange and the waves rock me to sleep. To sleep in my dream." I stop myself and it feels like I've been talking for an hour. It feels like I've lived this day because I am a bit fatigued, but in a good way.

"That sounds like an amazing day," she says.

"But it's not reality."

"Can you have a day like this anyway? Maybe not everything on your wish list, but I bet you could achieve at least 90 percent. On a Saturday? Or a holiday? There's nothing to stop you from having a day like this whenever you can. You just can't every day." She looks a little proud of herself, like she learned this exercise in a junior psych class and had no idea she'd ever use it in the real world. Proud. But not smug. I wouldn't be able to handle smug.

"It's not the same thing," I say.

"Why not?"

"Because it's like taking a vacation from real life, and real life is mostly terrible."

"It doesn't have to be. It just takes work," she says softly.

"I don't know where to begin."

She stares at me intently for a moment. Her lips purse just slightly, and I can tell she's taking a deep breath, but doesn't want me to notice.

"I think we need to talk about what happened last spring."

I stop breathing. Nirvana's "In Bloom" blasts inside my head. Why Nirvana? Mom is way more of a Nirvana fan than I am. There are at least ten other groups that should go off in my mind before Nirvana. Then I think, *Do I have some kind of a dark connection to Kurt Cobain? Am I going to be a heroin addict? Be betrayed by the love of my life? Put a gun in my mouth when I hit twenty-seven and pull the trigger?*

"Lily!" Dr. Maalouf has just raised her voice for the first time with me, and she looks more frightened than I feel.

"Where did you go?" she asks, lowering her voice to almost a whisper so I strain to hear.

"Nowhere." My voice cracks like a tiny kid hidden in a cave.

She looks concerned, afraid she screwed up. She did. She pushed me too hard, too fast.

"Do you keep a journal?" she asks, with a hint of desperation.

"No," I answer and before I'm aware of it, I'm easing into my jacket.

"We still have fifteen minutes."

"That's okay. I feel fine," I say, standing and grabbing my backpack.

"Lily, please just listen to me for one minute. Please."

She sounds so worried. I feel bad for her, so I sit back down, but teeter on the edge of the red chair, prepared to escape.

"I want you to write your story. All of it. As you see it. Everything that went down. Everything that hurt. Everyone that pissed you off. If this means you write a bunch of songs, that's great. If it means you write a two-hundred-page memoir with illustrations, that's great too. I just want you to try it."

"Why? I know what happened." I tremble.

"To get it outside of yourself. So it doesn't become an ulcer or, God forbid, a tumor in there. I might be wrong, but I truly believe it will make things better."

I have no interest in looking at all of that shit written down. I would rather have a root canal. In 1705.

"I'm just asking you to consider it."

"Okay," I say, and I bolt. I can hear her saying something behind me, but I don't need to know what it is. I remember the deal I made with my mother. Four weeks is all I committed to. Two weeks down. Two to go.

12

SAVANNAH THE CELEB

Dari waits outside for Izzy. He hopes Savannah doesn't know about his sad nicotine habit, though she can probably smell it on him. He considers quitting. Again. Maybe he can try the patch. Nicorette? Of course, that's the least of his concerns at the moment.

His phone vibrates. He checks it. A photo from Kendra. It's a selfie with her new beau. They look happy. Dari texts *congrats* and hits send. If she's hoping he'll get jealous, she doesn't know him that well.

A few minutes later, a yellow cab pulls up and Izzy steps out carrying a large box. Dari runs over to grab the box from her as the cabbie speeds off.

"There's a bunch of clothes, some art supplies, toiletries, and I tossed in a few books. I don't know," she tells him.

"Thank you," he says. "Did he give you a hard time?"

"No more than usual. He asked where you were. I think he misses you. But you know how he is." Izzy shakes her head. "I don't like this, Dari. I'd feel a whole lot better if you'd reconsider."

"I just don't feel comfortable staying with you and Crazypants."

"Call her by her name, Dari," Izzy says through a tightened jaw. Proof for Dari that their potential *Three's Company* arrangement would be a disaster.

"Lily and her mom like me. I won't go where I'm not welcome." He searches Izzy's face for signs that he's in any way wrong about how her partner feels about him. He finds none. She rubs her forehead, opens her wallet, and pulls out a wad of cash.

"You don't have to do that," Dari says.

"Just take it, Dari." He does, recognizing the impatience in his sister's voice. "Are you ever gonna tell me what went down?"

"When?"

"You know when."

"Didn't he tell you?"

Izzy shakes her head again. She takes the cigarette from Dari's fingers and inhales big before handing it back to him.

"I tried to hurt him. Bad. I just lost it. He was whaling on me and I lost it."

Izzy closes her eyes but doesn't look surprised. She probably suspected as much. "I know you don't want to, but it wouldn't be a bad idea to apologize. He's old. I don't think he knows how to be anything else."

"No."

"Maybe I should move back home," she says, and her spine seems to crumble right before Dari's eyes.

"That wouldn't help anything."

"I might be the buffer that keeps you two from killing each other," she reasons.

"I'm not going back," Dari announces.

"You won't stay with me. You won't go home. Dari, what are you gonna do? Just freeload off your girlfriend and her mom forever?"

"I'll get a job. I'll find a place," Dari decides.

"I don't think you have any idea how hard that's gonna be. I'm an adult and it took me months and months."

Dari understands that Izzy is worried about him. Nonetheless, he does not appreciate her doomsday attitude. Yeah, it'll be hard. Any harder than living alone with his father? He doubts it. He believes he can do it. And even if he fails, at least he tried. Can't be worse than giving up before he's even done anything.

"Thanks again, Izzy. I should go inside."

"Aren't you going to invite me in?"

He honestly hadn't considered that. Dari has a tendency to keep the different parts of his life separate, and that is how he likes it. But she did go out of her way for him. It couldn't have been fun going over to the apartment to pick up his things.

"Come on," he says and carries the bulky box into the lobby as Izzy trails behind.

"This is a nice building," Izzy observes as they wait for the elevator. "What does her mom do again?"

"She wrote some huge bestseller."

Izzy nods. "Gotcha. You know the title?"

"Think it was called *Heal Your Beautiful Self, Grow Your Beautiful World*."

The elevator arrives and Dari's inside it before he notices Izzy still standing in the hallway, mouth agape.

"Izzy, get in."

But she just stands there, so he plunks the box down and pulls her inside before the doors close.

"Savannah Price? Her mom is Savannah Price?"

"Yeah," Dari answers, unfazed.

"Why didn't you tell me before?"

"I didn't know you'd heard of her."

"Dari! I've read her book like fifty times. I've quoted it to you! I can't meet her. I'll sound like a crazy fan."

"Apparently, you are."

"Goddammit, Dari!"

"Shh. Don't be dumb. She's just a regular person."

Izzy bounces around nervously.

"I can't believe you're living with Savannah Price. The best things happen to you."

When they get to the door, Dari drops the box again and rings the doorbell.

Izzy whispers, "Do you have to do that every single time you come in?"

He shrugs.

Lily opens the door and smiles in surprise when she sees Izzy standing there.

"Oh, hi, I'm Lily. You must be Izzy."

"It's nice to meet you, Lily," Izzy greets.

Lily runs to get Savannah. They sit down and Izzy stares at Dari with an inquisitive expression. He tries to ignore her, but she's not the type that can be easily ignored.

"What?" he finally snaps.

"Nothing," Izzy says. "I was just caught off guard. Why, I don't know, since I know who her mother is now and—"

"Stop it," Dari whispers through clenched teeth.

Savannah enters the room in her yoga clothes: a lavender leotard with a pair of baggy purple yoga pants. She looks like she's just stepped out of an ad for a very cheerful/girly yoga studio.

"Hi, I'm Lily's mother, Savannah," she says to Izzy.

"Hi," Izzy squeaks. "Thanks. I mean, thank you for being so generous to my brother."

"Oh, he's a pleasure." Savannah smiles.

"I'm . . . I just wanted to . . . it's so great that—"

"She's read your book," Dari says, helping Izzy out.

"It's amazing," she says quietly. "Thank you for writing it."

Savannah's face brightens. "That is so kind of you."

"It's the truth. There were some tough times a few years back, and I don't know if I would've gotten through them without your book."

Dari eyes his sister, wondering if this is true. Sounds far-fetched to him.

Izzy and Savannah exchange smiles, but neither of them seems to know what to say to the other. Dari gets why Izzy is clamped up, but finds Savannah's silence puzzling. She brushes a strand of hair away from her eyes and stares at the hardwood floor. Sometimes she looks absurdly young to him. Way too young to have a daughter his age.

Lily breaks the silence.

"I love your hair," she compliments Izzy.

Izzy frowns, but then gently pats her head as if to remind herself that she does indeed have hair.

"Thank you," she says. "And"—to Savannah—"I don't ever want Dari to become an imposition. He's welcome to stay with me until we . . . Well. My dad can be difficult . . . ," she trails off, avoiding Savannah's eyes.

Savannah nods, concerned.

"I had a difficult dad too. I understand."

Izzy smiles apologetically. Dari's face flushes; he hates the idea of evoking the old man here in his safe haven. More than that, he hates seeing his sister feel this kind of embarrassment. No. Not embarrassment. Shame. She doesn't deserve to feel that.

"Would you like some tea or coffee?" Savannah asks, relaxing into her parental role.

"That's nice of you, but I have some work to do this evening. I just wanted to check on Dari and meet you. He speaks so highly of you both, but he didn't tell me he was staying with *the* Savannah Price," Izzy says. She seems like a teenager in this moment.

Savannah beams. She goes over to the bookshelf and reaches for a small ceramic pig wearing a red monk robe and mediating. She snickers to herself.

"This was a gift. I swear I don't shop at Hippies 'R' Us."

Izzy laughs, still awestruck.

"Would it be tacky if I asked you to autograph my copy someday?"

"Of course not." From the Zen pig's belly, Savannah pulls a simple card and gives it to Izzy.

"Here's my number. Call me anytime. If you want to talk about Dari or . . . anything else," she offers. Izzy takes a deep breath. His big sister is tough and wicked smart. She had to be to stand up to her old corporate crook bosses. But right now, she seems so tired and vulnerable. Unsure. Dari hopes that she will call Savannah.

"Thank you."

Dari follows Izzy to the door after she says good-bye. All the way to the elevator, they are both quiet.

Dari presses the button for the first floor.

"Are you gonna be okay?" he asks.

"Shouldn't I be asking you that question?"

"No. I'm gonna be fine," he asserts.

Izzy shakes her head with a smile. "I don't know where you get this confidence from. Can't be genetic," she jokes.

Dari walks her to the subway station.

"Why didn't you tell me you were dating a white girl?"

Dari shrugs. "I don't think about it that much."

"Be careful," she warns.

"Why?"

"You know why. This is New York City."

"It ain't the Jim Crow South," Dari argues. To this, Izzy gives him a serious stare. A stare that says *you know damn well how fucked up this city can be.* He gets it. He doesn't want to, but he does.

"I will," he promises.

They hug. Izzy can be emotional sometimes, so it's not such a shock for her to get a little misty, but the strange thing is, Dari fights tears too.

"What's happening to us?" Izzy asks, her face smushed into his upper arm.

"I don't know," he answers into her hair.

But, he thinks, *I know we're gonna be better because of this. Whatever it is. We'll never be the same. It's a good thing.* He doesn't feel brave enough to say this to Izzy. He'd be hurt if she laughed at him. He believes it, though, with 100 percent certainty.

What he does say is, "Don't worry. I love you."

* * *

He can't think of the "guest room" as his room. Too presumptuous. He doesn't want to get too comfortable here.

Lily's calico, Sheila E., hops up on the bed and makes herself at home on his legs. He checks out Craigslist, hoping for some leads job-wise. Nothing looks good. He doesn't want to be a tattoo artist's apprentice or an interior design assistant or a photography intern, and he's not qualified to be anybody's art director. Perusing the administrative jobs just depresses him, and he'd sooner tap-dance in the park for coins than wait tables. There are a lot of requests for male models, but 1) he's not fond of narcissists, so he'd rather not become one, 2) they might be fronts for pornography, and 3) the pay will most likely be shit. Unless 4) they *are* pornography fronts, in which case the pay might be decent, but the cost to his soul too high. For now.

He shuts his laptop and gets out his sketch pad. He draws. When in doubt, he draws. When certain, he draws. Drawing and (if he's lucky enough to have the room and supplies) painting are really the only constants in his life. Except maybe Izzy.

Dari does his best to think practically. For him, this means finding money—or a means of making money—and then finding an apartment. He has always dreamed of living on his own. Even when he was quite young, which probably isn't normal. What Dari is not thinking about is the fact that he is only sixteen. What landlord in his right mind is going to sign over an apartment to a minor? He hasn't gotten that far yet. He's stuck on step one. So he draws.

"Hey," Lily calls. It's her way of simultaneously alerting him of her presence and asking for permission to enter.

"Hey, yourself," Dari says. Permission granted.

Lily sits on the floor. "Your sister's nice," she says.

"Mostly."

"Is she freaking out?" Lily asks. Dari stops drawing for a second and looks down at her.

"Kind of. I think she just feels bad . . . ," Dari replies, trailing off in much the same way Izzy did when she brought up their dad. "I'd rather not talk about it."

"Cool," Lily mumbles.

Dari returns to his sketch. Lily remains seated on the floor, her back to him. He's obsessing on the feet today. He's usually more into drawing shoes, but he felt like he should give her the gift of bare feet, so he works on finding the definition of the phalanges, the metatarsals, the taut skin covering it all, and when he gets this obsessed with details of this nature, he tends to lose track of time. Which is why, when he lifts his head to give his eyes and wrist a rest, he's startled to see Lily still sitting there, completely silent. It's a little spooky.

"You all right down there?"

"Huh? Oh, yeah. I'm doing homework," she answers. That makes sense. And isn't spooky.

Dari inches toward the edge of the bed, and then not-so-gracefully slides his butt down to the floor so he's next to Lily. She pulls a bent box from her jeans pocket and holds it out to him.

"Junior Mint?"

"No, thanks. Besides, you don't want me raiding your stash, junkie."

"Shut up." She giggles.

Dari takes the textbook she's working from and inspects it. "French, huh? *Français est terrible*. Why you bothering with homework anyway? Aren't you planning to be a high school dropout?" Lily pokes him in the chest. Then she pokes his ribs, his armpits, and abdomen. He just stares at her.

"What the hell are you doing?"

"Aren't you ticklish? Anywhere?"

"No."

"I don't believe you." Lily tries his neck, his back, his thighs, his calves. He finally laughs, but not because she's found his tickle spot.

"You are wasting your time," he tells her.

"I think you're withholding valuable information."

"Oh, yeah? What about you?" Dari goes right for the rib cage, and Lily starts laughing like a damn hyena.

"What about here? Or here? Here?" Dari tickles her in pretty much every body part he can get to, and Lily gasps for air, tears rolling down her face.

"Stop! I can't breathe," she hollers.

"Really? Have we conquered them all?" Dari teases. In defense, Lily tries to tickle him again, to no avail.

"Dammit," she squeals. They collapse in joyous exhaustion. Somehow Dari ends up on his back, Lily straddling his midsection. She leans down and plants her lips on his. And his face and his neck. Dari's hands slide under her top and in seconds, the bra is unsnapped. He can tell she's impressed, but it's not that hard to do. They move quickly and easily, like they've always done this. Lily tears at his belt, but he grabs her hands before she can unbuckle it.

"Wait," he exhales sharply.

"*What,*" Lily wails.

"We can't. Your mom—"

"Oh, come on!"

"Lily, she's letting me stay here out of the goodness of her heart. I can't"—he hesitates, looking for the right word—"defile her daughter in her own house. That is beyond disrespectful," he whispers rapidly.

"She's not here. She went out to get Boca Burgers," Lily says.

Dari shakes his head. "Doesn't matter. I'm sorry. I just don't feel good about it."

Lily adjusts her top and puts her bra back on. Dari zips his fly.

"Lily, I like you. It has nothing to do with . . . It's not you. Seriously."

She nods, but something has shifted.

Lily opens the door to leave. She hesitates in the doorway and turns back to Dari.

"You wouldn't be defiling me, Dari. That happened ages ago."

Before he can respond, she shuts the door. Dari falls back on the floor. Still feeling the weight of her hips against his pelvis. Still seeing the coldness that settled in her eyes.

Fuck.

13

PERFECT SONG

I am copying down French conjugations from the board, which feels beyond pointless to me right now. I've taken three solid years of French, and I can barely speak a word. But I copy them down like a good little robot, and later I'll study like it actually matters. Because I'm stuck here and I don't see the way out. School sucks. Home is a den of frustration. I do love Dari, but he can be so stubborn. It's been days now of us barely touching each other and it is making me insane. God. I thought guys were supposed to be the desperately horny ones. This isn't fair!

"Ah, ah, ah. *En Français*," Madame Eichmann flirtatiously upbraids stupid Jason Chung, who just wants to go to the bathroom. Every day is retarded. Shit. I said I'd stop using that word. Even in my mind's voice. It's evil. It's insulting to the people who actually are retarded (mentally delayed? There must be a better word by now . . .) because it's not them I want to insult when I use it. Whatever.

I look down at my new notebook. I bought it for the express purpose of writing new songs, because I thought if I had a nice new notebook, somehow that would inspire me to write nice new songs. That has not happened, but I think about using it anyway. Maybe Dr. Maalouf's journal idea isn't completely idiotic and terrible. I don't know if I really need to write "my story." That feels overly dramatic. I might just write whatever the hell I want. She can deal.

The bell rings, mercifully, and I leave. In study hall, I open up my notebook and write a long collection of words about a beautiful black artist boy who is a cock tease. Is that right? Is someone a cock tease if they're teasing somebody's cock or teasing you with their cock? I scribble it all out. I start to write about last weekend. I start to write about my ideal day-to-day existence. I write for a while about my secret fantasy of living in Rome for a year, like Mom did when she was young. Well . . . it *was* a secret until I yelled it over Tenth Avenue. This stuff could be song-worthy someday. Maybe. Regardless, it doesn't feel bad to write it down. Doesn't feel magical or anything, but it passes the time. And I unclench my jaw.

Someone's staring at me, and I look up to see Tara in the doorway. She's not supposed to be here. She rolls her eyes and walks over to my desk.

"What?" I greet her.

"We can start working on the project. If you want. Crenshaw said our study hall teachers wouldn't care if we went to the library to do it."

"How do you know?"

"Seriously?" She sighs. "He said it this morning during class. Do you listen to anything anyone says?"

Not really.

"Fine." And I get up to follow her. I expect Mr. Lawson to say something to me, but he's too busy tweeting to notice my exit.

I slump into a chair as Tara takes out her notes and—you've got to be kidding me—index cards. She's actually put some real thought into this dumb thing.

"I have a few topics to propose. Once we decide, we can split up the tasks. I'll tell you right now that I don't plan to do all the work myself. I'm willing to let us both fail if it comes to that," Tara threatens.

"Fine."

"So we could look at Kelvin's work and the second law of thermo-dynamics—"

"Fine."

"History of the periodic table and Seaborg's revisions—"

"Fine."

"Or we could try to prove or disprove Walter White's television version of chemistry. But not by making anything dangerous. I don't know if Crenshaw would go for that one."

"Sure."

Tara chews on the insides of her cheeks. "Would you like to propose any topics?" she asks.

"Nope."

"Do you have a strong opinion one way or the other about which one we choose?"

"Nope."

Tara's lips tighten.

"Why did you ask me to be your lab partner?"

Her question takes me by surprise. Why does that even matter now? I try to take a breath without her seeing.

"I needed a partner and so did you."

"You rushed over to me, breathless. Why? Why not wait for Crenshaw to stick you with someone?"

I can't believe Tara remembers that day and my behavior so clearly. She seemed to be on another planet, as I recall.

"I don't know. What difference does it make?"

"You thought I'd leap at the chance to be your partner, didn't you? 'Poor, pitiful Tara McKenzie. There's no way anyone would want to work with her. She's perfect!' That's what you thought," she declares.

She's correct. I feel my pulse quicken. Shame sometimes does that to me.

"You didn't have a partner and you weren't looking for one. I thought I was making it easier for both of us," I mutter. This is sort of true, but pretending my motivation was purely altruistic would be a lie.

"You have never been nice to me. You never bothered."

Maybe not, but I always thought I'd been decent enough to Tara. I have no memory of ever insulting her or participating in any of the torment she received.

"You could've been. But you weren't," she says.

"I'm sorry," I tell her. "But I know you're not exactly wild about me either."

"You don't get it. You'll never get it," she growls. I have the sensation that I've just been slapped. Tara's more than a little scary right now. She should've unleashed this version of herself on her bullies. "Screw it. Let's just pick a topic."

"We could do the periodic table thing," I suggest.

"Fine. I'll work on the outline, you start researching. Tomorrow we can start putting stuff together."

I nod, oddly impressed with her focus, and try to forget the mini-assault I just suffered at her hands. She looks at me as if she's waiting for something. I don't know what she wants. Then she sort of waves me off with her hand.

"The computers are over there, the books over there. Why are you still sitting here?"

"Sorry. God!" I leave her and plop down in front of a computer. I don't know what she was expecting to happen just now. Was I supposed to fall down blubbering? Apologize for not going out of my way to be kind? Was she trying to pick a fight? I have trouble believing I am, or have ever been, anything special in Tara's life. The one person who could've protected her and didn't. That's not me.

Why did I stay here? I should've left. Dari skipped out before lunch. He asked if I wanted to join, but I declined in an effort to punish him. But he's totally oblivious. So, as usual, I'm just punishing myself.

I type up some notes. Mostly URLs that I'll look at later. Not like it matters. With me involved in this project, we will certainly earn a well-deserved F. Why don't I care? I used to. I used to worry about these things. My grades from the first marking period this year were inadequate to say the least. I'd never seen so many Cs all in one column. Mom wasn't too pleased, but she hardly said anything about it. Guess she's lowered her expectations for me.

I casually look behind me. Tara has her head bent over our chem textbook and a few other books, rapidly taking notes. How is she writing that fast? She's such a nerd, she's probably able to take notes and analyze the theories in the books while simultaneously coming up with her own theories. I've never thought about it before, but she is super smart. Probably why she's always been a target for bullying. But then again, she's also kind of poor, which might've been a bigger issue than her above-average intelligence. She used to wear this blouse in the ninth grade that had ruffled sleeves. It was made from a silky material that was not real silk (even I could see that) and covered in a floral pattern. It looked like something a seventy-year-old woman might wear to synagogue. People laughed every time she wore it. I didn't, but I understood why they did. Jackie snapped at a few girls who were making jokes about it once. She said they were lucky they didn't have to depend on donations in order to have clothes. That actually shut them up. Too bad Tara was on the other side of the room. She probably has no idea that Jackie defended her. True, the tone of her defense was sanctimonious and condescending as Jackie is prone to be, but I never heard anyone fight on Tara's behalf before or since, which says something for Jackie, I guess.

The bell rings, and I realize that I've been watching "Mango loves Milkshake" on YouTube for about the ninetieth time instead of doing work. Tara packs up her things and leaves without saying a word to me. I so hope we finish this project soon.

Out the window, the gray clouds hide the sun. November already. In some ways, this fall has felt interminable. In others, it's flown. Cold weather is hard for me. Been that way long as I can remember. That might be proof that I have always been plagued with the big D. This discovery brings no comfort.

I don't feel like going outside just yet. It's definitely too chilly for a ferry ride. Not that I'm in the mood for one anyway. Since my trip with Dari, I haven't felt the pull. It would be nice to let go of that. Of Bobby. Forever.

Instead of heading for the main exit, I walk back upstairs to the third floor. Just out of curiosity. Haven't been in this wing in a long time. The doors to the big music room are closed. I open it a crack and peek inside. Empty. So I go in. My fingers gently brush the keys on the upright. I adjust a music stand for the heck of it and move toward the back corner. There are other music spaces in this wing, but this is the big one. When the full band or orchestra needs to play together, this is the room they fill. I'm amazed that no one is here. Don't musicians practice anymore? Before I can think twice about it, I slide onto the stool behind the five-piece drum kit. The only sticks I see are the cheap hickory kind. They'll have to do. I start by lightly tapping the high hat. Then an easy snare roll. I get my foot involved, pedaling out a downbeat on the bass drum. And I go. I drum like never before. I haven't played in so long. I don't have a drum kit at home anymore. Too loud. Too many 311 complaints. This. This feels like freedom. This feels like me! This feels *fucking awesome*!

I beat those drums like I'm mad at 'em. I can't stop. My hands are burning and sore, but I do. Not. Stop. My face hurts. Aches. An unfamiliar pain. Now I do stop. Out of breath. Letting the clash of my echo and the sudden, deep silence hang in the air. I touch my face to find the source of the ache. I find it. I think. I'm smiling. I'm smiling so hard, it hurts. This cracks me up. I'm probably the only person in the world that feels physical pain as a reaction to joy.

I make some crazy expressions, stretching the muscles, then I rub out some of the tension in my face and I start again. This time I close my eyes and hear all the other instruments around me. The bass guitar comes in, then the keyboard, and then lead guitar. What are we playing? It's something new. Being created for me—by me—right as I sit here. I can hear the chords, the strings, the bridge. I start to hear lyrics. I want to stop and write this down, but I don't want to stop playing.

What if this is the only way I'll truly feel happiness? I have to play it out. I'll keep going. I'll keep going until the song tells me to stop. Yeah. It's coming. This is what I've been waiting for. This. This is that light feeling. The free feeling. This—

A wolf whistle. I drop the sticks, shaking and sweating. I scramble to pick them up, holding on to the seat to keep from falling over completely. He laughs.

"Very nice."

Oh. Him.

"Didn't know you gave private concerts."

"Why are you here? You don't play an instrument."

Derek Miller smiles deviously. I have never liked this guy.

"I heard someone rockin' out so I thought I'd see who it was. Never would've guessed it was you. You're full of secrets, huh?"

I grab my things to go. He's ruined my time here.

"Keep playing. Don't mind me."

"Don't you have anything better to do?" I yell.

He suddenly takes out his phone and a flash momentarily blinds me. He looks down at it.

"Nice. Now I have a set."

Blood rushes in around my ears. I can't think. I can't breathe.

"I have to know. Did Mr. Wright pay you? Or do you do porn for free? Either way. Maybe we can work out some kind of arrangement."

I push him out of my way and he falls backward into chairs and music stands, but he isn't hurt. I race out of the room and I can hear him laughing so hard he can hardly catch his breath. I bust through the doors, fly down the stairs, and run out of the building at full speed. I'm three blocks down the street before I stop, unable to run anymore. My heart tears through my rib cage, beating way too fast. I hold onto a chain-link fence, gasping for air. I'm not crying. I'm too tired to cry. Too angry to cry. I try my hardest to think back to my face hurting with happiness. It was only a few minutes ago, wasn't it?

He took my perfect song.

* * *

Dari chops vegetables. Mom drinks coffee and watches. What is happening in my kitchen?

"Hey, honey," Mom calls as I enter the room. "How was your day?"

"Superb. What's going on?"

"Dari offered to make dinner. Can you believe it?" my mother practically screams. You'd think she'd just won the goddamned Pulitzer.

"That's nice. What're you making?" I ask Dari, who hasn't bothered to look at me or greet me yet. So focused on the asparagus.

"Veggie stir-fry with teriyaki tempeh over brown rice," he replies with an astonishing air of normalcy. Like him cooking dinner in my kitchen just happens all the time.

"Cool. Thanks," I say.

Mom's delighted expression wilts once she really sees me. "What's wrong?" she asks. I shake my head, shrugging it off. But it's no use. I'm awful at hiding it when I'm miserable. Sometimes I think if I were better at it maybe I'd be able to fool myself. Trick the misery right out of me. She carries her coffee into the living room and gestures for me to join her. Dari still hasn't looked up.

"Is everything copacetic between you two?" she asks in an urgent whisper.

"I don't know. It's not that."

"What is it?"

Oh, God. If Dari weren't here, I'd break down crying and fall into my mother's arms, but I can't let him see that.

"I don't think I can keep going to school, Mom."

She sighs. "What happened?"

"They're never gonna forget what happened is what happened! And they're never gonna let ME forget."

"Should I talk to that counselor? What are we dealing with?" she asks, going straight into parent-on-the-case mode. But she can't help me out of this.

"No. Forget it." I turn to go to my room.

"Lily, I can only help if you talk to me. I want to understand, but I can't say it's okay for you to never go back to school. That's not an option."

I go into my room and close the door behind me. I wish Dari would come, but he probably wouldn't be any help either. I collapse on my bed and wait. I honestly do think someone will come at some point, but no one does.

Invisible girl. In my own home.

Late that night, after I mope through Dari's delish dinner, there is a knock at my door.

"Come in," I say, but I don't mean it. Dari gently pushes the door open.

"What's up?" It isn't meant to be small talk. He doesn't do small talk.

"Nothing," I mutter.

He sits on the edge of my bed. "You mad at me?"

"No." I say it automatically. But I am kind of mad at him. Why can't I tell the truth?

Dari sighs and stares straight ahead.

"I'm gonna leave soon. I'm gonna focus on finding a job. That's top priority. And then I'll go stay with Izzy and crazy Trisha."

"You don't have to go, Dari."

"Yeah, I do," he says sadly. "I'd rather be homeless than lose our friendship," he says so softly, I barely hear him. I rise up a little and hug him around the waist. My head rests on his thigh and he gently caresses my hair. Right now, I want him to stay here forever. And be with me forever. Wait. Did he just say . . . ?

"Friendship," I repeat. "Is that all we are?"

For a split second, Dari's hand stops moving. But in an instant, he resumes.

"No," he says, but with a question mark instead of a period. "Relationships are complicated. I prefer friendships. They last longer," he reasons.

I don't know what to say. As much as I try, I don't think I'll ever understand him.

"I want you to be my boyfriend."

I hear the slightest intake of air above me. He continues caressing my hair silently for several seconds. I decide in this moment that if he can't respond to me at my most vulnerable, then we will no longer be friends. Period.

"I'm not an ideal boyfriend."

"So?"

"I like you, Lily. Let me focus on finding a place to live and then we can revisit this question."

I sit up on my elbows and look him in his eyes.

"It's not that deep. Either you want to be with me or not."

Dari kisses me firmly on the mouth, but it's my turn to pull away. I want an explanation.

"If I didn't give a shit about you it wouldn't be that deep. But I do, so it is." He stands up then to leave.

"You're weird," I tell him.

"Can't help that," he says, and I'm alone again.

I turn my iPod on and find some Radiohead. I'm attracted to difficulty, I think. I'm attracted to guys who have truckloads of baggage. With them, it will never, ever be simple. And then they do or say one little magical thing and they own me. I remember something that Bobby said to me once. I wish I could forget it. He said, "There's nobody else like you on this earth. You're worth the risk."

Me. I was worth the risk.

14

WHITE FLAG

The class is engaged in what constitutes still-life drawing in ninth grade: a bowl of apples posed on a multicolored blanket. Dari stands several feet away from his painting-in-progress. So much more to do. But he doesn't know where to go next. He feels stuck. This is unusual because Dari never feels stuck.

"Obsessing on the white spaces?" Ms. Spangler asks him.

They're not white; they're eggshell. The miracle can of paint that bounced off the back of the Ace Hardware truck and rolled right up to Dari's feet was eggshell. Perfect for merging your collection of junk into a solid canvas.

"Probably," he answers.

"Then you might want to look at what you've already done and see what needs more of your attention," she advises.

Dari sighs.

"Everything all right?" She treads lightly, knowing how cagey he is about his personal life.

"I need a job."

"Don't we all?" Ms. Spangler snorts. "What kind of job?"

"I don't know. I just need income. It's serious," he adds, noticing her smirk.

"I'll keep my ears open. Anything you'd be opposed to doing?"

"Yes." Then he gets an idea and begins to add some blue to one of the corners he's already painted. Ms. Spangler studies him and his work.

"You must've really liked the Rauschenberg book."

Dari stops cold, a mild panic setting in. "Do you think it's derivative?"

She shakes her head. "No, I just see the influence. Don't be paranoid: It's a good thing."

He returns to his work as Ms. Spangler moves on to one of her student tables. He lets his grip go slack, softening some lines. *I'm not Rauschenberg. I'm Gray*, he thinks to himself, determined to be an original.

He can see his name at the Whitney. Galerie Richard—here or in Paris. König Galerie in Berlin. Dariomauritius Raphael Gray. He will only use his full name in print. If someone addresses him as Dariomauritius, he'll say, "Call me Dari or Mr. Gray or nothing." He'll distinguish himself as a painter by eschewing the color gray. When a buyer purchases a "Gray," he'll be hard-pressed to find a speck of gray anywhere in the painting.

"Nice," she says, passing him again. Dari startles for a second, remembering that he's still just an art student in high school and not the cultural phenomenon he is in his daydreams.

"Welcome. Come in." The balding man appears to be in a great hurry, but this doesn't affect Dari's normal pace. He takes his time entering the studio assessing the space and the artist's work.

"Here, have a seat," Baldy instructs, offering him a clear plastic chair, which faces the artist's white desk. Dari imagines that this furniture might be considered "space-age" if it were currently 1969 and they were set pieces from *2001: A Space Odyssey*. Since neither of those things is the case, the chair and desk look more like relics from the distant past. Or some kind of hipster commentary.

"So? Have you ever assisted a working artist before?" Baldy asks.

"No, I haven't," Dari replies. *Isn't every artist a working artist?*

"That's fine. And you're still in school, correct?"

"Yeah, for now."

The artist chuckles and types something into his tablet.

"Well, let me tell you what I'm looking for. I need someone who can give me at least twenty hours a week, and some of those can definitely be on the weekends. Most of what I need in the short term is help prepping for a series of upcoming shows. Are you good with silk-screening?"

Dari nods. *Silk screening? Who are you, Andy Warhol?*

"That's terrific. That would be the lion's share of the work for the next few months. I also need standard assistant-type help. Grabbing coffee, food as needed. I may need you to take calls for me when I'm working, and you'll probably have to make some as well. Hope you don't mind talking to people. You'd also need to arrange my appointments and travel plans, which will be plentiful this winter. It's pretty straightforward. Does this sound doable to you?" This guy talks a mile a minute. Does he have a plane to catch or is he on amphetamines?

"Who's your favorite painter?" Dari asks.

"Uh? Sorry?"

"Just curious."

The artist again chuckles. "Well. We can get into all that later. Are you interested in the job?"

"Maybe. But seriously: Who's your favorite?"

He sighs. Was that an eye roll?

"Rothko. He's the reason I paint."

Dari swallows. He tries to nod politely, but he knows this isn't going to work out.

"So? You interested?"

"What's the pay?"

At this question, Baldy's smile fades. "Well, it's negotiable. Depends on your experience, and it seems that you don't have . . . much."

Dari stands and walks over to some of the mounted paintings, apparently leaving the interview and entering a gallery.

"But," the man continues, "we can discuss it. I try to be fair."

"That's okay. I mean, that's cool of you and everything, but . . ." Dari shakes his head. "*Rothko*? No, I can't. I just can't." Dari stares intently at one painting. It's the simplest on display. A midnight background and a hairless, genderless figure at its center painted to look like television static so it moves even though it's still. Eyes shut, mouth open, and what's inside is even darker than the background. Screaming from nothingness into more nothingness. Dari imagines the figure without vocal cords, screaming with no way to make a sound. Perhaps this is a response to Munch?

"This is the one," Dari tells him. "This is your true voice."

Baldy titters—a nasty, dry sound. "They get younger everyday."

"Huh?"

"You can leave my studio now," the artist sneers. Dari nods a good-bye or a thank-you or something and gladly exits.

He gets a cup of coffee from a truck and walks through Washington Square Park. He sits. Despite wanting to, he does not begin a secret drawing of any chess players. He gazes at all the new buildings that have gone up in recent years. Monstrosities. They just tear down and build. Tear down and build. For what? Why is nothing ever satisfactory? Who was it that decided that new always trumps old? Dari suspects it is somehow connected to fear of death, but he's not sure. He should ask somebody old.

A job. Dammit. Damn damn dammit. Maybe he should've just sucked it up and said yes to the Warhol wannabe–slash–Rothko fanboy. But Dari sucks at sucking things up. School is a problem too. Wasting precious hours sitting in mind-numbing classrooms when he could be out searching for work. But doing what? He worries that he might be un-hireable.

His phone rings. Unknown number. Dari grins. Unlike just about everyone else on the planet, Dari loves unknown numbers. In his experience these are either telemarketers or scam artists who deserve what they get. The last time he got an unknown number, he convinced the sales rep on the other end of the call that he—Dari—was in the midst of a Molly comedown and having a serious freak-out. The telemarketer ended up near tears. "Dude, I don't know anything about Molly. I'm just supposed to sell subscriptions to *Vibe* magazine! I didn't sign up for this!" Dari laughs, remembering. Good times.

"*Hola, amigo! Esto es* Juan Pepe's! Would you like to try our South of the Border special?" Dari sings into the phone. He's good at staying in character once he gets going, but with a rush of alarm he wonders if maybe the Spanish was going too far. He took it last year. Three Bs. One C.

He can hear someone on the other end, but no one says anything.

"*Hola?* Señor Juan speaking. May I . . . *ayudas?*"

"Son?"

Dari drops the phone and gets down on his knees to pick it up. Scratched but intact. His hand shakes.

"Are you there?" he hears.

He wants to hang up. He really does. But he doesn't.

"Dad?"

"Where are you?" his father asks him.

Dari takes in a breath. "Washington Square Park."

Then they're both silent for a moment. Long enough for Dari to consider how difficult making this call must have been for his proud father.

"And you're safe?" he asks slowly.

"Uh-huh."

"Maybe you'd like to come home tonight? Or we can meet at a restaurant. Maybe the Afghan place you like so much?" This is a major concession for this man. Dari has never experienced this side of his father, so it's hard for him to believe. It's sort of like his father grabbed the biggest white flag he could find and decided to tackle Dari with it.

"I don't know."

"Where are you staying? I know it's not with your sister."

"I know more people besides you two."

"Dariomauritius, I'm trying." He sounds desperate.

"By changing the locks?"

He hesitates. "Perhaps that was going too far."

"Why did you call from an unknown number?" Dari asks.

His father takes a deep breath. "Because I knew if you saw it was me, you wouldn't pick up.

"I know we've had our differences, but you're still my son. I am willing to forgive you and let you come home," he tells him.

He's *willing to forgive* ME?

"I don't think so," Dari says flatly.

"You're sixteen. Do you honestly think you can live on your own as a grown man now?"

Dari's eyes search the park. The old and the new. The classic and the garish. It would be easy to just give up. Go home. Certain worries would disappear. But the others would come right back. He used to feel a heaviness in his stomach every day. Especially right before six o'clock. He doesn't want to feel it again.

"I don't know. But I'd have to figure it out eventually, right?"

His father says nothing.

"How old were you when you left your parents?" Dari asks.

"Things were different. It was a different time."

"Well. We'll just have to see."

"Dariomauritius! I know you're smarter than this."

"Thank you, by the way. For ruining unknown numbers for me forever." Dari ends the call. He's still a little shaky, but it's a good shaky. Mostly. If there's a part of him that is willing to choose potential homelessness over going back to his dad, then he can probably handle whatever's coming.

15

GRAVITY

I rifle through the mess of my locker, searching. I know I have some. I know I do. Not behind the books, not under my scarf or gym clothes. Aha! Under a pile of old Wendy's napkins, I find my precious generic Duane Reade ibuprofen. I pop open the bottle and swallow three without water. The cramps today are no joke. I reach in my jacket pocket and find some loose M&M's to help the medicine go down. Sweet relief. It's coming. Soon. It'll be here soon.

I shut the locker door and Derek Miller stands there, two inches from my face.

"Bitch."

"What?" What's happening?

He *spits* on me! I scream and jump backward. I scramble to find the contaminated spot on my clothing. Left boob. Ugh, so gross! I wipe at it with Wendy's cheery face and when I look up, Derek's gone. *What the hell?*

In the bathroom, I frantically scrub at the spot. I'm sure Derek's spit is long gone, but I'm so skeeved out, I just keep scrubbing. Who does he think he is? I've never done anything to him. I'm still looking in the mirror when Jackie appears behind me, putting her hands on my shoulders, looking at my reflection with sorrow. What is she doing here? I know the bell already rang. She's not your typical class cutter.

"Are you all right?" she asks.

"Why?"

"I saw what happened."

"Yeah? What is going on? I hardly know that asshole!"

Jackie's eyes go big. I've seen this look on her face before. She's going out of her way to act surprised. It's fake. "You mean you didn't hear?"

"What?"

"Mrs. Waters was gonna take Tracy down for that photo? Of you? You know, the one where you're—"

"Yes, I'm familiar."

"Well, she begged and begged, and the only way she could save herself was by ratting out Derek. He's the one who sent it to the journal staff."

My legs get shaky. Feeling a little woozy. Why won't last year die already?

"They put him on disciplinary probation and won't let him play for the rest of the soccer season, and he has to wait for a hearing to find out if he'll be expelled." Jackie must have some idea of how much pain this situation has caused me, yet she's telling this story as if it's any other piece of juicy gossip.

"Do you know how he got the photo?" I manage to ask.

Jackie's face goes flat. Before transforming into the Jackie face that I loathe most. This is Judgmental Jackie's face.

"Well, I assumed it was Photoshopped. You wouldn't be dumb enough or crazy enough to pose for something like that. Would you?" Is she seriously challenging me?

"Yes. I would," I inform her and I leave the bathroom. I drink some water from the fountain and consider going to class, but then again, who am I kidding? I asked her the question, but the answer is so obvious. I know how Derek got the photo. Bobby liked to hang out with the jocks. They were all "bros." If I think about it, I would guess that Bobby sent it around to his "bros" as a joke. But I don't want to think about it.

"This doesn't make any sense," Tara complains, looking over my notes.

"Can you be more specific?"

"Uh, I don't see how this connects to our thesis, like, at all. It's almost like you just Googled the words 'Seaborg' and 'periodic table' and this is what you came up with."

Well, that is exactly what I did. It doesn't mean my findings are any worse than they would've been otherwise. I did actually put some effort into this. Compared to most of my academic ventures of late, what I've done here is stellar work.

"What would you prefer I do?" I try to sound casual. I don't want to lose my temper with Tara because God knows she's right about me, but I am on my period and a shithead spit on me today.

"I'd prefer you care more, but I'm sure that's asking for too much." She sighs and puts her head down on the desk the way little kids do when they're in trouble. It kind of makes me feel bad for her.

"I'm just not good at this stuff. Chemistry is way more your subject than mine. The only reason I'm in this class is because Ms. Keegan wouldn't let me register for Behavioral Science. She said that class was for the slower kids. I tried to convince her I was slow, but she said that was offensive."

Tara actually laughs a little with her head still down. The library's practically empty. Only a few other losers working on sucky projects and a kid getting tutored. Nobody wants to be here.

"I can do most of it. It's not that big of a deal," Tara groans.

That's not right. I can't let her do that.

"That's bullshit. I can do it." I sigh and look at the pages. She's right. It's sloppy work. I know I can do better, though I never guessed my motivation to try harder would be because of sympathy for Tara.

I close Google and log in to some sites that are actually science-based.

Tara keeps her head down on the table. She stays like that for so long, I wonder if she's asleep. Her breathing doesn't sound like that of a sleeper, but you never know. If she's totally passed out, will I have to wake her up when it's time to leave? That would be weird. Today's the first day in our recent history when we haven't actively hated each other. I don't know if I can deal with tapping her on the shoulder. Touching should be reserved for people we love. Beyond that, I'm not that into it.

But I don't need to worry because she's not asleep. She lifts her head and turns to the side, still resting it on her crossed arms.

"When we were in sixth-grade gym, the girls hid my clothes and I had to go out into the hall naked to get help from the principal."

Jesus. I completely forgot that happened. That was awful.

"You were the basketball team captain, and you didn't pick me last. You picked me fourth. You treated everyone on the team the same. You weren't mean. You weren't nice, but you weren't mean. Do you know where they hid my clothes?"

She's really asking about this? Some mean girl nonsense that happened five years ago?

"No. I don't know, Tara. I didn't see what they did," I tell her truthfully.

"You pretended you didn't hear me. You were at the other end of the locker room, and I called out to you because I thought you would help me. I thought you'd tell someone so I wouldn't have to leave and be humiliated. But you were laughing and talking to someone else. You heard me. But you pretended you didn't." Tara continues staring off into space. She remembers every detail as if it had just happened. I guess she would.

"I'm sorry, Tara."

"You wouldn't have had to do much. Just tell a teacher or something." She doesn't necessarily seem sad talking about it. It's more like she's just trying to understand.

"You're right. I should've done something. I don't know why I didn't. I'm sorry."

Tara shrugs. She's goes quiet again, and I continue working. I can't say it to her, but I thought about that day a lot right after it happened. I did hear her, but I couldn't bear to look at her. I was afraid. Afraid whatever she had that made everyone hate her would rub off on me. I was a coward. And I was horribly ashamed for a long time. Then I forgot about it. Completely. In fact, had I remembered that day when school began this year, I might have been more charitable. But that's no good either. That would've come out of pity, which might have been worse. It's hard to know what to do.

"Can I ask you a question?" She cuts her eyes at me. Now she seems suddenly awake and alert.

I brace myself. Nobody ever asks for permission to ask you a question you want to hear. Nobody ever says, *Can I ask you a question? Would you mind if I gave you a massage and warm brownies every day for a month?*

"What?" I reply.

"Why did you do it?"

I gaze at her over my laptop.

"Do what?"

"You were totally normal. Accepted by everyone. Why did you give that all up?"

I want to be patient and not freak out, but I am already seeing red. Not a good thing.

"It wasn't my choice," I say through a freshly tightened jaw.

"Well, maybe not the aftermath, but everything that led you there was your choice. Mr. Wright, and how that all ended. At some point in there, you probably could've made a different choice that might have saved you. I just wonder if you ever thought about everything you could lose," Tara finally finishes.

Sure I thought about it. I just figured it'd be fun to be a social pariah!

"It's my personal business, okay?" I'm giving her a chance. She does not want to open up this door.

"You were set. You could've graduated unscathed. It blows my mind."

"You don't know what you're talking about," I warn.

"No. You never thought about it. Because you never had to. You thought you were immune."

"Can we just get this over with, please?" I whisper.

She continues staring at me. I don't get this girl at all. One minute, she's a bitchy headache. The next a sad victim of middle school cruelty. And now? Why is she tormenting me just when I was starting to like her?

"It's just interesting to me. I've never been accepted, and I didn't do anything wrong. You've probably been doing wrong all along, but you finally got caught and exposed. So your behavior led people not to like you, which actually makes sense. It makes no sense in my case."

"What do you want, an award? Congratulations. You're way more virtuous than me," I say, and I try to go back to work, ending this discussion.

"Yes. I do want an award." She is now sitting upright, arms crossed. Challenging me.

I shut my laptop. "What do you want from me?"

"I want you to stop treating me like I'm pathetic. *You're* pathetic!"

"Tara. Don't mess with me."

"What was that? Sorry, I didn't hear you. I was too busy laughing and being popular and ignoring your pain."

"Not cool! I said I was sorry and I meant it!" I don't want this with her. This is too much anger even for me. I look over at the librarian's desk. No one's there. The other students left in the room are all focused on us now.

She leans in close. "I heard a rumor that you saved the bloody sheet from when he popped your cherry, and you wrapped yourself in it like a cape all the times you kept showing up at his house. Is that true?" Tara's eyes twinkle with malice. The rumor was false, but I am beyond rationale.

"At least I never fucked my brother!"

I'm on the floor. Tara is on top of me, pulling my hair. She's got a clump in her hand. I push her off and stand and she takes a few steps back and then runs into me with all her strength, headfirst like a bull. She knocks me against a bookshelf, where an African violet was perched until we send it crashing to the floor. None of it hurts. I feel nothing but rage. I let her get in a few puny punches, and even a scratch that tears open the skin above my eyebrow, and then I go berserk. I hit her as hard as I can in her stomach, get her on the floor, and then I hit her again and again until someone grabs me and pulls me backward. I try to kick my way loose, but can't.

"ENOUGH!" Vice Principal Monaroy's voice splits my eardrums. Mrs. Waters helps Tara to her feet and glances at me with terror. My head suddenly returns to the present moment and out of the buzzing, angry place it was just in. Tara looks bad. Really bad. One of her eyes is red and puffy, her shirt's ripped, and blood drips from her lips. She's barely moving. I know she hurt me too, but I can't feel the pain yet.

In the vice principal's office, Mrs. Waters pulls up a chair to sit between Tara and me. I'm guessing this is to prevent us from throwing any last-minute swings. Monaroy stares at both of us a long time. First me, then Tara, then back to me. He shakes his head in disgust. His face is so red it looks sunburned.

"I'm shocked. In all my time as an administrator at this school, I have never seen two ladies behave in such a disgraceful way," he begins. He refers to both of us, but he mainly looks at me. I try to glance at Tara, but can't thanks to the wall of Mrs. Waters.

"What do you have to say for yourselves? Miss McKenzie?"

"I'm sorry. I lost my temper," Tara mutters in a tiny, pained voice. "I'm very sorry, Mr. Monaroy."

"What about you? Miss Rothstein?"

He knows all about what happened last year. I'm sure his opinion of me, if he bothers to formulate opinions about students, wasn't so high before this afternoon. And this can't be the first time he's seen a girl fight. He's full of it.

"I was angry," I answer.

"And," he continues impatiently.

"And . . . what?"

"Don't you think you owe everyone in this room an apology?"

I am about to repeat Tara's words verbatim. He liked that. But in an inexplicable flash, I think to myself, *What would Dariomauritius do?* WWDD.

"Not really," I say.

"Excuse me?" He is outraged.

"I'm sorry for wasting your time, Mrs. Waters. I'm sorry if I hurt you, Tara, but I'm not sorry I hit you, because you had it coming. And Mr. Monaroy?" I try to think of why I would possibly apologize to him. "I'm sorry you had to stay late. I know typically you like to leave as soon as the bell rings, sometimes sooner, so I'm sorry that my conduct kept you from the loft in Tribeca that your lawyer girlfriend pays for." That. Is what. DWD.

I do not want to look at his face, because it is a real-live horror film: blood, veins, thumping temple, bulging eyes. But I can't look away. Will his head explode any second like the only part I've seen from that movie *Scanners*? It might. If it does, I don't wanna miss it.

Spoiler alert: His head does not explode. Unfortunately. Because Tara squeezes out a few tears, she gets a slap on the wrist and one day of detention. One day! Because I chose not to take the high road, he hits me with five days' suspension and a big, black mark on my permanent record. Technically, there's supposed to be a hearing before you get a suspension of that size, but evidently he felt that that wasn't necessary in my case. And in the event there was a slight chance I could keep this misfortune from my mother, I had the pleasure of remaining in his office while he called her, and listening to the whole horrendous conversation. Happiness be damned. Lily is here to ensure her own misery.

"Is that really what you think?" Dr. Maalouf asks. She's been patiently listening to my bitchfest for—I glance at my watch—the first full fifteen minutes of our session. I suppose it's fair that she get a chance to speak too.

"About what? I mean, which part?" I ask.

"I know you're being facetious and there's nothing wrong with that, but do you think you are the one ensuring your own misery?" Dr. Maalouf likes to do that. She likes to take the last few words I say and throw them back at me as a deep question. It's annoying.

"I don't know. Maybe?"

"What makes you uncertain?"

Oh, God. Who knows? Some people might think that it was some kind of luck or serendipity or something that I just happened to get into a brutal fight and get suspended on a therapy day. I, however, do not. The last thing I feel like doing right now is analyzing my actions.

"Well, I'm involved somehow. Aren't I?"

"Yes," she agrees. "You're also involved when things go right. Aren't you?" She did it again. *Stop parroting me.*

"Dr. Maalouf? Can I go? I don't feel like being here today."

"You're not a hostage. But we can switch gears. We don't have to focus on the fight if you don't want to."

I say nothing. I don't want to focus on the fight, but I'm not sure I would want to focus on anything she might bring up. I didn't even tell her about the spitting incident. It's been a full day.

"Are you worried about being punished when you get home?" she asks. Is it just me, or is this still fight-related?

"Not really. She doesn't punish me."

"No?"

"Not anymore."

Dr. Maalouf shifts in her seat, keeping her eyes on me as she does. This makes me want to shift in my red plush chair, so I do. But I end up shifting into an uncomfortable position, so I awkwardly revert.

"What's the harshest punishment she's ever given you?"

"Once she got rid of the Internet for a month. I thought she was bluffing, but she did it."

"What had you done to prompt the punishment?"

December 30. Nothing happening on New Year's Eve eve. I asked if

I could stay out late with the girls. Whenever I said "the girls," I meant Jackie and Tracy. She said sure, just be careful. Instead of girl time, Bobby took me to see *The Nutcracker* at Lincoln Center. I liked some of the music, but it was mostly boring. To make up for it, I made him teach me how to drive. So we took his car and he taught me and I practiced and we rode into the night laughing and eating snickerdoodles and I almost drove into a ditch. When I started to get a little sleepy, I finally checked the time. 4:23 a.m. We'd driven all the way out to Amagansett. By then, I knew I was in deep trouble, so rushing back would've been pointless. We stayed and watched the sunrise on the beach and when we got too cold, we had hot cider and bagels at Mary's Marvelous. I got home around eight that morning. Mom had talked to Jackie and Tracy and their parents. They hadn't covered for me. I could tell she'd been crying and hadn't slept. Bobby, of course, couldn't come to my aid. I was on my own.

"Lily? What was it you did?" Dr. Maalouf asks again.

"Oh. Yeah. I got an F in Geometry."

She nods.

"Do you consider yourself to be spoiled?"

"Yes," I reply.

"How do you feel about that?"

"I don't care." Here come the judgments. Always waiting right around the corner. Here they come. . . .

"Why not?" she pushes.

I slump in the chair. I may not be a hostage, but I feel like one and I don't have to automatically answer her just because I'm sitting here. Just to be polite. She stares at me and I stare right back. She's trying to wait me out. She wants me to answer the question, and she's not going to say anything else until I do. I've seen so many therapists use this technique. I'm no amateur. She has no idea how stubborn I can be.

I hear the clock ticking behind my head. Very strategic placing. If it were behind her head, I'd be checking it every ten seconds. She folds and unfolds and refolds her hands in her lap. Ticks. She's got a lot of them. How long has she been doing this? Staring contests are normal, and we haven't been at it that long at all.

"What are you thinking, Lily?" she finally asks. *Ha! I win!*

"I'm thinking I promised my mother I'd see you for four weeks. This is week three. So I'm almost done," I say.

She presses her lips together and looks down at the floor.

"Have you starting writing in your journal?" she asks gently.

I nod.

"How has that been?"

"Fine. I guess."

"Good. It's up to you, of course. Forcing you to see a psychotherapist would be counterproductive. The hard work falls on your shoulders. Not mine. If you're unwilling to do that work, it would be a waste of time and money," she tells me.

I'm processing her words when I start to cry. No warning. The waterworks just start like a floodgate has been opened and I can't shut them off. She runs to a shelf and grabs a box of tissues. She hands it to me and then she sits across from me on her coffee table so she's much closer. I sniffle and hiccup, attempting to curtail the tidal wave coming out of me.

"Don't, Lily. If you need to cry, just cry. It's not gonna hurt anyone," she assures me with the smallest smile. I don't get the smile, but it doesn't feel unkind, so I just keep going. I don't have any thoughts. It all feels physical and overwhelming. Like a bucket of paint that's been tipped over. It can never be untipped. Gravity. This is like messy, painful gravity. A force of the universe. Far beyond my control.

I'm not sure how long this lasts. I look over at the window and it's dark outside now. Was it dark before I got started? I can't remember.

"What are you feeling now?"

"Angry. I'm so. Angry." I say it and it feels like cement blocks have just fallen off my back. I can sit up without effort. I can breathe.

"I would be too," she assents. I do my best to loosen the grip of my jaw. It's giving me a blinding headache. But then again, that might be due to Tara punching me in the face.

I want to ask her something. I just got through crying and I'm afraid if I say it out loud I'll be swept back down into that sea. But I need to know. She's the only person I can ask.

"Do you think there's hope for me?" I say all the words clearly. No mumbling. I thought it would hurt much more to say those words.

"Yes."

Before heading home, I slip into the bathroom, thinking I should splash some cold water on my face like women do in the movies. It always looks like it helps them. I cup the water in my hands and throw it on my face and cry out in pain. The skin and muscle is tender and I just reassaulted myself. I catch my eyes in the mirror. This is the first time I've bothered to look at myself since the fight. My bottom lip is gigantic, my left jaw bruised purple, and my left eyebrow is all scratched. Tara messed me up, but she looked far worse.

Just like the first day of school, when I turn my key in the lock, Mom is standing there waiting for me. The mood is quite different today.

"Oh, dear God," she yells when she sees my face.

Dari runs into the living room.

"Shit, Lily! Um, sorry, Savannah."

"No. *Shit, Lily* is pretty accurate. Come on." She drags me into the bathroom and starts to fix up my injuries, but she's never done this before and doesn't know how, so she starts by applying rubbing alcohol to the open sore on my mouth. My screaming and cursing brings Dari running into the room.

"You don't need that," he says, referring to the alcohol. He wets a washcloth and gently dabs at my face to clean the remaining dirt. With his free hand, he searches the medicine cabinet and mysteriously finds a tube of white cream. He administers it lightly where he can.

"Lily, I don't know what to say. What were you thinking?"

I wince as Dari presses a cotton swab to my eyebrow. I can totally smell him right now and, despite the pain, I hope he never finishes dressing my wounds.

191

"Are you listening to me?" Mom bellows.

"Yes."

"What is going on?"

Again, I don't answer. There IS no answer.

"Lily," Dari breathes into my ear. It's so subtle, Mom misses it. He barely moved his mouth. I know he wants me to cooperate. He's worried.

"If it matters, she attacked me first." It's true. I think.

"Dari? Thanks, honey. Could you excuse us for a minute?" Mom sweetly asks him. He nods and leaves and she watches him fondly. Perhaps he's the child she wishes she could claim as hers right now.

"Fighting, Lily? You know this is beneath you. Why?"

"I don't know. It happened. There's nothing I can do about it now."

Mom rubs her face in exasperation. "Are you even a little bit sorry?" she asks me.

"Yeah. It's not like I wanted to do it. I'm sorry I upset you. It's not gonna happen again," I say.

"All right," she says out of resignation. "Can you go to your room for a while? I need to think."

"About what?"

"Can you just do what I ask?" she snaps. I jump. She's not a snapper. She must really be angry.

I slump off to my room and get out my notebook. The journal. I try to write. I think about being angry. I don't like it. It sucks. It makes me feel like a great big jerk. Why did Tara get me so mad? Am I mad at her? Not really. But the person I'd really like to punch is nowhere near.

Illogically, I feel like finishing the stupid chem project, so I do more work on it. The kind of thinking required to do this actually calms me. There is no connection to anything germane to my life, so I can concentrate on it and get my focus off of myself. Or my mother's fury.

In the almost sixteen years I've known her, my mother has rarely shown her wrathful side. But there was one time I remember. I was really little and we were living at our old place in Hoboken.

We'd gone to the park to ride the carousel and feed the geese bread crumbs. On our way back, I was making goose noises, which usually cracked her up, but she didn't notice. She was tense and kept walking faster and faster. "Mommy, why are we going so fast?" I asked, but she said nothing and continued at the speedy pace. As we walked up the steps to our door, my mother whipped around and shouted, "What do you want?" It scared the daylights out of me. This was the first time I noticed the man. He was heavy, had reddish hair and a beard, and wore glasses. He was right behind us. I didn't understand why he was standing just below us on the steps. We only had one neighbor, Miss Katherine, who was old and lived alone. Why was this man trying to come inside?

"Nothing," he said in a funny, fuzzy voice.

My mother's face was red with rage. Looking back, it was probably fear, too.

She turned her back on him and raised her key to the door, like always. He was still standing there. She twisted the key in the knob, and he took one more step toward us. At that moment, my mother elbowed him in his shoulder before turning around and kicking him in the jewels. As he stumbled backward, Mom picked me up, opened the door, got us inside, and locked it behind us. She peered through the window in the foyer to see him staggering around outside. When this went on too long for Mom's liking, she opened the window and yelled out at him.

"Don't make me come back out there. Get the fuck off my street!" And he did.

"Who was that?" I asked my mother.

"A bad man. Don't worry. Mommy will never let anybody hurt you." For a long time I had nightmares about the redheaded "bad man." If he lived in our neighborhood, I never saw him again after that day. I also had daymares about the bad man if I was at the park. Why did he want to hurt me? Now that I think about it, he probably wasn't interested in me at all. He wanted to hurt Mom.

I finish up my portion of the project, which is probably all that was left anyway. I'm sure Tara's all done. I consider e-mailing it to her. Just acting like nothing happened. I don't, though.

I've been in here a while now. I'm starting to get hungry. Would that be my punishment? They'd just eat dinner without me? No. I am not cool with that. I quietly open my door and start walking down the hall. I freeze when I see Mom and Dari deep in some kind of hushed conversation. I get closer and when Mom notices me, they both suddenly shut up. What. The hell. Was that?

"Are you guys talking about me?"

Dari shakes his head, but he couldn't look any guiltier if I'd just caught him reading my journal.

"No, honey. We were just . . ." Mom shrugs. The aroma of ganja hangs heavy in the air. Great. Well, at least she's no longer furious. "You hungry?"

I nod. Something feels off, and I'm not sure what it is. In the kitchen, dinner is ready. The table is set. This is not how we do things in my home.

"You cooked?" I ask (more like accuse) her.

"No. Thank our houseguest." She points to Dari, who smiles shyly.

"Again?"

"I don't mind," Dari says.

Chipotle vegetarian chili. Seriously?

We eat in silence. The chili is awesome. Probably the best I've ever had, but I don't feel like telling him that. I don't feel like shining a light on how much more wonderful he is than I'll ever be.

"Well? Should I punish you?" Mom asks me.

"I don't know. That's up to you."

"Let me rephrase the question: Do I need to punish you?"

I shake my head. "But I understand if you do."

Dari stares at his bowl, smiling to himself. I wonder what he finds so amusing.

"Maybe tomorrow you and I can go and see an exhibit or something," she suggests.

"For what?"

"Well, I don't want you sitting around watching TV. Suspended or not, you might as well learn something."

"There's a Cy Twombly retrospective at the Guggenheim," Dari says.

"Really? Too bad you can't join us, since you're the expert. Though I remember a little about abstract expressionism from college," Mom brags.

"I don't know if I want to do that," I interrupt.

Mom eats. She doesn't respond. Can't I just hide all day long in my room? I don't want to learn anything.

"You should go, Lily. Twombly's fun," Dari says.

"I don't know where you got your cooking skills, but this is delicious, Dari. Thank you," Mom says.

"I don't mind."

"Of course you don't." I think it to myself, but I make the mistake of mumbling it out loud.

"What?" he asks.

"Nothing."

"Lily, are you getting sarcastic?" Mom asks.

I keep eating. "I'm sorry, Dari. Your food is amazing. You are amazing and I'm sure my mother wishes you were her kid."

They both stare at me in shock.

"What is wrong with you?" My mother's patience with me is coming to an end . . . fast. And the thing is, I don't know what's wrong with me. I don't know why I said it.

I'm not finished eating, but I'm finished sitting here. I throw my bowl in the sink and head out the door.

As I wait for the elevator, Mom opens the door.

"Where are you going?"

"For a walk," I say calmly.

Mom stands there looking at me. I look elsewhere, but from my periphery I can tell she's hurt. What am I supposed to do? Just nod and be silent and pretend I feel fine when I feel horrible? What would all her followers say if they knew she just wanted a well-behaved beagle for a daughter?

The slow elevator finally comes, and I step in. I take a deep breath. Blissfully alone. Until Dari sticks his arm in the door seconds before it closes.

"Why are you so mad? I can stop cooking if that bothers you. I just don't wanna be a freeloader."

I stare at the numbers lighting up, wanting to be on the ground floor so I can run.

"You don't trust me," he whispers.

We hit ground level and as if he'd been reading my mind, Dari grabs my hand firmly. If I try to flee, he'll be right there with me.

"Sometimes I feel like every day is the worst day of my life," I say.

"If you only feel that way sometimes, how can every day be the worst day of your life?"

Despite everything, this makes me laugh.

"Your mom's freaked."

"Can we go somewhere and not talk about her or anything else related to today?"

Dari shrugs. "I'm all yours."

16

SEA SPELLS

The wind is merciless. Slicing through their clothes like an ice pick. But the air smells intoxicating and the sea waves crash against the sand with such force that they could easily be in Brighton Beach, England, instead of Brighton Beach, Brooklyn.

Lily might be literally crazy. Certifiably so. She's ripped off her shoes and is running into the water. It is freezing out here! Dari smiles weakly, but he's not the least bit comfortable with wading into the Atlantic on a blustery November night.

"Are you insane?" he shouts, but his words disappear in the wind. After tearing down the beach like a wild woman, Lily just stands at the water's edge, watching the tide. Her feet leave perfectly formed prints in the damp sand. Dari catches up to her.

"Aren't you cold?"

"No moon tonight," she says.

"I know. Too cloudy."

They go quiet, but the world around them is loud and alive: waves, wind, the train in the distance.

"Think we should head back soon?" Dari asks.

Lily turns and stares into Dariomauritius's eyes. Is she studying him? Sizing him up? His irritatingly long, curly eyelashes, the slight dimple on his left cheek that's always there even when he's not smiling. Even when he's frowning. Like now.

"No," she answers.

Dari nods. He knew that would be the answer. He studies her sharp cheekbones under the bruises from the fight earlier, the sparse freckles on her nose, the slight twitch in her lower lip. Even when she's trying to smile. Like now.

They need to go back, but he can't just drag her to the Q train like some Neanderthal.

"What do you want to do?" he asks softly.

"Make music. Be free. That's all. It should be easy." She smiles at him and it isn't a crazy smile. It's a weary smile, but one he understands. He thinks about being free every second of every day.

He grabs and squeezes her hand. Lily raises herself up on her tip-toes so she's at eye level with him. She plants a simple and sweet kiss on his face. Then they're back to staring at each other. But differently now. His arms firmly around her lower torso. The faint aroma of her cocoa butter body lotion teasing him. The cold melts away, the waves calm themselves until they are no more than a gentle caress. The water tickles the shore. He kisses her differently now, a little harder, a little more insistent. She does the same. They find themselves moving back and forth, but to where? There's nowhere to go. What are they gonna do? Whatever it is, they need to do it immediately.

"Come on," Lily whispers.

"Come on where?"

Lily looks all around. With no direction, they walk briskly, hand in hand away from the ocean, desperate for a way to be alone. Now. At the same time they notice a tiny abandoned building. A storage space for playground equipment perhaps? They race over. Shit. Door's locked. Dari heaves a giant sigh-grunt, but Lily notices something both alarming and delightful: A window next to a side door has been busted.

She bravely sticks her arm inside and fumbles around until she finds the door's lock and pops it open. They are inside. He touches her gingerly, afraid of bumping wounds he can't see, but she guides his hands to move faster, hold tighter. They're kissing with greater intensity now. With freedom. They are making music. Dari somehow reaches around to his back pocket to get his wallet and from that, a condom. Lily waits breathlessly for him to open the plastic and slip it on. She reaches down to help him, but it's dark. It's too dark in here, and that is regrettable. They'd both like to see each other now more than ever, but they have to make do with what they've been given. Dari slides his mouth over Lily's neck and the smallest squawking sound escapes from her throat, which startles him. And prompts their first exchange of dialogue since the beach.

"Are you sure?" he whispers into her ear.

"Yes."

An ancient man glares at them—specifically him—on the Q train. He looks like he's about ninety and he does not like what he sees. Dari holds Lily's hand in his lap and he's not about to let go of it. So this old piece of shit can glare until he drops dead. *It's the 21st century, asshole!* Dari briefly considers making some obscene tongue gestures at the old man, but he's not feeling especially prankish at the moment. He feels peaceful. Lily smiles though her eyes are somewhere far away. He decides not to disturb her in her quiet place. He leans back, closing his eyes to the parade of freaks, bigots, and hipsters that is the Q train after midnight. He can still taste her Burt's Bees lip balm on his lips. He's never been with a girl his age before. They've always been older. He liked it. He likes her. It's not like being with Kendra. Being with Kendra was like being with a distant star, and when she lost the distance, he lost interest. Lily has no pretensions. She is who she is and nothing more or less than that. She's what he needs right now.

"Hey, Lily," Dari whispers.

"Hmm?" She returns from her mental quiet place, and her eyes sparkle.

Dari removes his jacket and lifts his shirt. On the right side of his torso, near his rib cage, is a large *D* that looks like it's been shaded with a black crayon. Inside the *D*'s empty space is a crude, smirking cow with black spots. The tattoo isn't so big, but detailed. Must have taken some time.

"That's my tag," he says shyly. Lily runs her finger over it. And then she cracks up. The old man across from them mumbles something and finds another seat.

"Is it bad if I think it's funny?" Lily's genuinely concerned.

"I hope you think it's hilarious."

She laughs for a few seconds and then stops. The echo of her laughter hangs in the car.

"I love it," she says.

They walk to the door. Dari lights a cigarette. Feels like he's been holding Lily's hand for hours. Dari's phone buzzes, and he gently pulls away to check it. He reads the words *Thank you* and smiles.

"Who's that?" Lily asks.

Dari shakes his head, brushing it off, and blows bluish smoke though his nostrils. So what if he sent a few texts to Savannah over the course of the evening? He's a guest in her home. He couldn't have her worried about her only child. So he set her mind at ease. No big deal.

"I don't know what to say to you," Lily tells him in a dreamy way. Like maybe this is a good problem to have.

"Then don't say anything," he replies. He gradually finishes his cigarette, stomps it out, and they turn to go inside. The night is eerily quiet. He playfully nibbles her fingers before checking his watch: 2:24 a.m. *Wow. Getting up in four and a half hours is going to be a freakin' blast.*

"Dari?"

"What's up?"

"Do you remember when you told me you were an asshole?"

Dari presses the button for the elevator, unable to stifle an epic yawn. "Uh-huh."

"What did you mean by that?"

"That's what you're thinking about right now?"

Lily nods. If she's worried, it doesn't show. She seems to be framed in a soft glow.

"Because I am," Dari says and they get into the elevator.

"I don't think so. I think you just maybe want people to think you are," Lily surmises. The doors close. Dari turns to Lily and wraps a few of her curls around his fingers.

"You think too much."

Lily giggles and reaches up to kiss him just as the doors open. She barely gets a peck in before he jerks away, moving toward the apartment door.

"Really? You're still weirded out because of my mom?"

"Shh!" Dari takes out his newly acquired set of keys, but Lily stops him.

"Tomorrow. We're telling Mom about us."

"Telling her *what?*" Dari asks, alarmed. The idea of sitting Savannah down and telling her that he just had sex with her daughter in an abandoned public building in Brighton Beach fills him with terror.

"That we're intimate. We can't pretend we're not." Lily is firm. If she weren't smiling so sweetly, Dari would be convinced that this was a threat.

"I just don't . . . I want to respect her daughter in her home. Does that make sense?" Dari is desperate. He's worried Lily's idea of declaring their intimacy might include sloppy PDAs at the breakfast table.

Lily grabs his face and kisses him assertively. Not assertively—aggressively. She releases him.

"We'll talk about it tomorrow." Having closed the subject, she allows him to open the door.

The living room is dark, which seems to surprise Lily. She was probably expecting a lecture of some kind. Dari smiles to himself. She has no idea how lucky she is that the worst punishment she'll ever get is a lecture. Maybe a grounding, though he doubts it.

Lily flips on the light in her room and sees a sheet of a paper on her bed.

I am asleep. But I am aware that you're coming home at an unreasonably late hour. You will be punished. It's only fair. —Mom

She doesn't seem upset or anything. Dari then gives her hand a quick squeeze and vanishes down the hall to the guest room without so much as a sound.

Moments later, Dari falls into a deep slumber and dreams that the ocean pulls him down to the seafloor, where he can see lost shoes, bracelets, eyeglasses, jump ropes, and a painting. Naturally, the painting intrigues him, and he tries to get close to it, but it stays beyond reach. He just wants to see it, but he can't. He keeps chasing it. Junk from everywhere begins to pour into the sea on top of him. Bottles, DVDs, loose change, dirty laundry, books. He tries to swim up to the surface, but the junk hides the light, creating a blanket of darkness. A darkness of crap. The things are heavy and they cover him and weigh him down and the wet sea darkness drags him back to the bottom. But then a light appears! And a sound. A loud, high-pitched, grating sound. It is an ambulance with its lights flashing and sirens blaring, crashing down amidst the junk into the sea and heading straight for Dariomauritius. He wakes up to learn that the blaring sound is his alarm clock because—holy shit—it's already seven a.m. He hits the snooze button and turns over and thinks of Lily's soft mouth. And the ocean. And being buried alive.

He has to get out of here.

17

SLIPPERY

I wake up around seven out of habit, and then I remember I'm suspended. I'm glad. I'm happy to be suspended. I know I could use a shower, but I want to hold off as long as I can. Keep last night on my skin as long as I can. I think of him and his fingers slipping up between my—

"Lily, get up," Mom interrupts. She's wearing the stone face. She wears this face when she has to be stern with me, and there's no penetrating it, so I don't argue. I sit up, and once she's sure I won't sneak back under the covers, she leaves me alone.

It's a challenge to have the guy that you want to look your absolute best for in your house in the morning when you look your worst. Usually, I try to wait him out. I can hear him coming past my room and then, when his shower starts, I get all my stuff together so the minute he reenters the guest room, I can zip into the bathroom and lock the door. The only problem is sometimes I barely get any breakfast because by the time I'm ready, he's finished eating, and if I stayed behind to eat, I wouldn't get to go to school with him. But then again, maybe he wants that sometimes? I have to be careful. Don't wanna scare him. . . .

I hear him leaving the bathroom, but I'm still not dying to get a shower.

I rake a comb through my hair, throw on my slippers, and briefly consider making a surprise visit to his room. Is he dressed yet? (Hope not.) Will he be happy to see me? (Hope so.) But I do look like shit. I wish I could get over my vanity. I just wish I didn't care. Or more specifically, I wish I didn't *have* to care. I just wish nature would take care of all that beauty nonsense so I could concentrate on other things, like how I'm going to convince my mother to let us sleep in the same room together despite the fact that I'm currently in some degree of trouble.

I open my drawer to find an old sweatshirt to throw on, and I reach for my heather-gray standby without thinking. I shake it out and I look at it. It's old and about three sizes too big for me. DARTMOUTH 1769. It was his. HIS. Bobby's. I take a small breath. I inspect my face in the mirror. I look normal. Not good, but not pale or unhealthy. I feel fine too. I feel . . . good. Like if I step outside of myself and really look at how I am compared to how I was just a couple of months ago, I'm different. I smile at myself in the mirror because I have a strange thought: What if the person staring back at me right this very second is the person I'm really meant to be? A person who can easily smile at seven a.m. even though she hates mornings. A person who feels okay just to . . . be. I have an idea. I look down at his stupid shirt. I am not wearing this thing ever again. I know what I have to do.

She opens the door. "What are you doing?"

I shrug, caught off guard. "Dari was in the shower and I didn't want to—"

"Just get out here."

"But, Mom, I'm not—"

"Now, Lily." She is not playing around. I quickly arrange my hair so that it sort of hides my face. She leads the way and, as I walk behind her, I check out my morning breath. It's bad, but I come into the living room and it's all for naught. He's gone already.

"Dari already left?"

"Obviously."

"He didn't say bye or anything."

Mom stares at me, really trying to make her stone face do the work she isn't prepared to do.

"I'm thinking I should ground you, except I'm afraid you'd like that too much," she begins. "Clearly I'm out of my element. But I have to do something, Lily."

"Why?"

"Because nothing's working! Therapy, finally making a new friend? I feel like you're just getting angrier." And then come the tears. I was dreading those.

"Come on, Mom. Don't cry."

"Dari might have to go back home."

"*Why?*"

"Because I don't know how else to punish you." She wipes at her eyes and stares at the floor. She has to know how unfair this suggestion is.

"I'm sorry. I'll do whatever you want. Just don't do that," I plead. "I won't get into any more trouble, Mom. And I won't stay out late or be sad anymore. Just please let him stay." My own voice starts breaking. I am so tired of crying. It never ends.

"For now. I know it isn't fair to Dari. I just don't know what to do."

I feel a slight shiver. I've never known Mom to use somebody like a bargaining chip.

"You could shut down the wireless again."

She shakes her head, resigned. "You should eat something. Do you want to do the Guggenheim today?" she asks, trying, and failing, to shift gears.

"I promise I won't get into any trouble, but I was wondering if maybe I could, uh, be alone today?"

She looks doubtful and still vulnerable enough to roll up into a ball of tears if I'm not careful.

"Dr. Maalouf asked me to write a journal. To write my story. Like the bad things that happened, I guess. I haven't had much time to write in it, and I don't always want to even when I do have time. Can I go to the library and write in it today? Please?"

She sniffs, brushes her hair out of her eyes.

"How do I know you're telling me the truth?"

I run back to my room to get my book bag. I pull out the notebook and bring it to her.

"It's real." I even show her a few pages. "It might not seem like it, but I think it might . . . be helping. I don't know why. But when I write in it, I feel calm. Less angry."

"Why can't you write in it here?"

Good question.

"I can, I guess. The library just puts me in a good mood. Reminds me of going there for story hour when I was little. When I felt happy. That's probably dumb."

And there are those pesky tears again. How did I upset her this time?

"I'm sorry," I say, confused.

"No, no, no." She weeps and then she hugs me. "I'm just proud of you. You know? I've been wanting you to do this for years, it seems. But maybe you just weren't ready yet. This is good, Lily. This is a step." She smiles through her tears and grants me permission. The trade-off being that I have to come home by dinnertime, and then I'm grounded for the rest of the week. By "grounded" she means no Dari. How I'll be able to avoid him while we're living under the same roof will be interesting, but I don't argue with her.

On the train, I open my notebook. I have an important question and I don't know the answer. Perhaps if I write it down, an answer will come.

I feel freer and stronger than I have in months. I don't feel his hold over me anymore. Is this because of Dari or is it something else entirely? Dari seems like the easy answer. Passage of time, easier still. Something's going on inside of me and it's way different from what was going on inside of me when school began and I can't help but think that, in my case, different is definitely better.

I get off the train and make my way through the crowd. Before moving any farther I stop, right in the middle of everything. A few idiots bump into me and curse me, but I ignore them. I don't want to live my life today on autopilot. If I'm going to do this, I want to make sure it is exactly what I want to do. I close my eyes, and I breathe in, and I breathe out, and I smile. Opening my eyes to the cold sun, I know what I have to do. So I follow the throngs like I have so many times before and I don't have to wait more than a minute before the next ferry hits the dock.

Staring out the window on the S48, I briefly think about how well I lied to my mother and feel guilty. Today, I know what's best for me, though. As much as she'd like to, she can't possibly have this knowledge. It's better that she isn't involved in this anyway. For her sake.

It's cold out here, closer to the water. I'm wishing I wore my heavy jacket now, especially since it's a hike from Forest Avenue. It's been a long time, which is why I took the wrong bus at first, but there it is. Red brick. White siding. Purple swing set. Toyota Corolla in the driveway. I had an idea. I had an idea that I'd come out here and say, *You hurt me, but you don't hurt me anymore* or *You've disappointed me. You've disappointed everyone in your life.* Something devastating like that. But now I'm looking at his house and his sad little yard and it doesn't matter. It doesn't fucking matter.

Before I can bail, before I can think, he comes out onto the porch. My heart pounds. He could call the police right now and I'd be toast, but he doesn't seem to be reaching for his phone. He just stands there. I don't move closer. At least I'm not in the yard. I'm on the sidewalk, outside looking in.

"What are you doing here?" he finally calls.

I just stare at him. I know why I came here, but nothing about this scenario is the way I imagined it.

"Speak or I call the authorities," he threatens.

I'm looking for something familiar. Something to remind me of why I thought my life was over not so long ago. Why he mattered so much to me. I can't find anything. Not only does he seem shorter, he's gained weight in all the wrong places and . . . is his Mets cap hiding a rapidly receding hairline? I see nothing in his face or his diminutive form to suggest that I should've thought about him twice.

"I remembered you differently," I tell him.

"So?"

"I think you want to believe that you ruined me. You didn't. You may have damaged me, but I'm not ruined at all. *You're* ruined." I feel electricity vibrating through my pores. I had no idea it felt this good to tell someone off. I don't even feel angry. I feel righteous. I feel superior to him.

"Get out of here." He then tries to open his door. It's locked. He struggles with the knob then searches his pockets for keys. He's locked himself out! His struggle quickly morphs into panic as he pounds on the door.

I can't help but laugh. Just a little. He turns slowly and glances over his shoulder to see if I'm still watching and drops his head in humiliation once our eyes meet. He curses and bangs and kicks the door. I leave before anyone opens it for him. I almost feel sorry for Mr. Wright. Without the adoration of students, he's just some unemployed man-child with a paunch who's locked himself out of his own house in broad daylight.

Unconsciously, I start to skip. I stop because how dumb must I look? But for some crazy reason, I do it again. I skip for a good seven minutes, maybe longer. I feel so light, I bet I could jump high enough to dunk a basketball right now. I whistle and come close to singing "It's Such a Good Feeling" from *Mister Rogers' Neighborhood*, but as a damn-near adult, I decide there are limits. But I'm smiling. Yep. Smiling again. Because it *is* a good feeling.

"I feel happy today," I say to no one. A lady walking her dog stares at me. I'm sure she thinks I'm crazy, but I don't mind at all.

There's a pretty park out here called Snug Harbor. I sit near an elaborate fountain, open my notebook, and examine the question I wrote on the way here. Dari is part of what is different about me, but he's not all of it. If I wasn't evolving, I would have never had the courage to talk to Dari in the first place. No. It's me. I jot some of my observations down (so I wasn't totally lying to Mom). As I write, I sense that I'm being watched. I try to ignore the feeling; this is New York and somebody's always staring. But I feel a chill that has nothing to do with the weather. I look up and lock eyes with a woman. A woman I've seen before.

"Hello," she says.

"Uh, hi," I say, but I really don't want to have a chat. I just want to write in my notebook and be alone with my thoughts.

"I remember you," she says. At that moment, I know exactly who she is, and seeing her here is super weird.

"Yeah. You're the lady from the window," I say, making her sound more like a Dutch prostitute than a psychic. "Do you live around here?"

She shakes her head. "I like this park. I like it on cold weekdays because typically I have it to myself." She studies me closely.

"I'm never here and I won't be returning," I tell her, as if to assure her that she won't have to share her park with me again.

"You're getting closer, but you're still holding on. Get rid of the things you don't need," she instructs, and then she pops one of those freaky e-cigarettes into her mouth. She sits near me, not too close, but close enough for me to hear her without straining.

"I don't have any money." I don't know if she's trying to corner me into paying for her services again or what.

"Don't worry about it. I'm not staying long." She stares at the water fountain, or rather she stares *through* it.

"I don't usually do this, but I could feel you calling out to me long before you acknowledged me. If you're interested, you're in a good place right now. Everything takes time, but you're going in the right direction. Just don't depend on others for your happiness. People are slippery."

"Slippery? Like con artists?"

"They slip between your fingers if you hold on too tight." Her olive face turns a ghostly white for a moment and then goes back to normal.

"Be careful. Your rage is a powerful thing. Keep it in check." She then stands up and heads down toward the road. No "good-bye" or anything.

"Wait a second," I yell. "What do you mean rage is a powerful thing? Am I in danger? That's so vague!"

She turns to face me and her eyes narrow on mine.

"I said *your* rage is a powerful thing. That is specific."

Tara's freshly pummeled face appears to me in a flash, and I blink it away.

"So are you haunted or something? Did you go to sorcery school or have a supervillain-type accident in a science lab?" Why I need to be a smart-ass about her trade is beyond me.

"Runs in my family. Like cancer," she replies.

"How do you know?"

She glances out at the water toward the dock and all at once, seems terribly exhausted. Maybe I'm annoying.

"My grandmother and my mother predicted their own deaths. Date, time, and location. If that's not proof, I can't give you any."

"So? Do you know when you're going to die?" I ask.

She smiles sadly. "My dear? I know when *you're* going to die."

I can't speak. I just stare as she continues down the hill to the road and is soon obstructed by the trees. I am curious to know when I'm going to die, obviously, but she didn't seem willing to share any more, so I let it go. It's also possible that learning any concrete details about my death might terrify me. I sit back down and tell myself that I don't believe in clairvoyance. That it isn't at all strange that I just ran into the random psychic reader we found on "yes night" and that she's probably just a sad lady that likes to go around scaring people. I reach into my bag and I pull out the gray sweatshirt. She just said I should get rid of things I don't need. Did she know what I was planning to do? No matter. I'm not really taking her advice if I thought of it first.

I follow her path down to the road and inch closer to the water. Last night I could've done this in the ocean. Would've been way more dramatic and fitting, and Dari would've been with me. But this is good enough.

I unroll the shirt and try to forget about how happy it made me when he first gave it to me. How I couldn't wait to wear it, and got a strange thrill knowing I could never wear it to school. Then I think of Bobby from today. Not the Bobby of last year or the Bobby in my memory. This Bobby is a gross little man who I suspect is completely useless now that the schools won't have him. His life is depressing. This helps. With no more nostalgia, I drop it into the water, watch it darken with moisture and then sink below the murky surface. I feel nothing. I feel fine.

I do feel like he's gone. From me. He doesn't exist anymore. I never thought I'd be able to feel that. The happy rush from earlier has settled. I don't feel overjoyed or especially sad. Maybe sad for all the time I wasted, but mostly I feel nothing. On the ferry, I try to focus my thoughts on last night. I loved last night, but even that won't take hold of me. I open my notebook and write: *I think I love too much.* Then I cross it out and I write: *I think I love too hard.* Then I sigh and cross out the words *I think.* I don't want to replace Bobby with Dari. Dari is special and deserves better. I glance outward as we pass Lady Liberty and imagine she's me for a second. She'd be smarter. She would use her head, and I bet her head is filled with logic. She would probably slow things down with Dari. Even though she doesn't want to, she knows that things that get too hot, too fast have a tendency to blow up in her face. She's been through a lot, Lady Liberty.

After we dock and I make my way out into the station with all the other passengers, my legs begin to carry me in the wrong direction, wanting to get back on line to ride the next one again before I can stop them. Probably out of habit. My old dance teacher would call that "muscle memory." It's been programmed. That's all over now. I have no reason to ride this ferry ever again if I don't want to. And I don't.

It's lunchtime and I feel like walking, so I start going north, grab a Papaya Dog along the way, then a milk shake. I just keep going. Before I'm fully aware of my surroundings, I realize how close I am to the big, beautiful old library on Fifth Avenue. Maybe I'll make a stop there after all.

* * *

4:10. Feels like a good enough time to head home. My phone rings just before I go underground to catch the train. I look at it and read the name that flashes across the screen in disbelief.

"Hello?"

"Hi. Lily, I just want you to know that I am sorry if I came off as . . . uncaring yesterday. I am deeply concerned about you and only want the best." Jackie says all this slowly and deliberately as if she's reading from a teleprompter.

"What?"

"I am going to make an effort from now on to be more sensitive and"—she pauses for a moment—"less judgmental. Your life is your business. I don't have any right to interfere."

"Thank you."

"You're welcome."

A pigeon poops on the wrought iron gate separating Bryant Park from Forty-Second Street while Jackie and I say nothing.

"Why did you call?" I ask.

"I was worried. I didn't want you to fall into a bad place or do anything rash cuz of me."

"You were afraid I'd tried to end it all because you were being snotty?"

"I don't know! I don't know how fragile you are! I don't want to be a negative contributor in your life."

"Oh my God. Jackie, I'm still a person. You treat me like I'm nothing more than a psych ward patient."

"That's not true," she protests, but she does not sound convinced.

"It is! You didn't call me because you actually want to talk to me. You called me because you feel guilty."

Jackie is completely silent, quite possibly for the first time in her life. I feel a crazy boldness right now. Something about today just makes me want to be totally honest, and I do not care about the consequences.

"Jackie? I am breaking up with you."

She gasps, then laughs. "Wait. What? What?!"

"You know how in life people sort of grow apart? We've already done the growing bit, now we need to just stay . . . apart. Please."

"Seriously? You're doing the friend equivalent of dumping me right now?"

"Yeah. It's time. I wish you the best," I tell her.

"Whatever, Lily. I hope you're being heavily medicated!" And she hangs up on me.

The train is crowded, so I have to stand. Otherwise, I might pull out my notebook and write something about this occasion, which feels significant. I might write something like, *I am officially no longer friends with Jackie and I don't feel bad about it at all.* It's so much more satisfying to unfriend someone in real life instead of on social media.

I enter the apartment and the living room's empty. I grab a celebratory handful of gummy worms from the kitchen and shove them into my mouth. As I chew, I walk back toward my room and notice the light bleeding out from under Mom's office door.

I open the door and stop.

I open the door and everything stops.

They stop. They, they, they.

My senses dull and fail me. I think I'm having a stroke because I can't feel my hands or my feet and I can't have just seen what I've seen. I can't have heard what I just heard. They. Them. Someone says "no" three times, four times, a hundred times, and that someone is me. Water mysteriously gushes into my ears from somewhere. All I see and hear blends into an underwater blur. With no actual water. There is movement, but I can't interpret it. None of this can be real. My mother's mouth is flapping up and down and all I hear is water. I saw it. They. Them. Her hand on—Her Star of David tattoo on her lower back.

"Lily!" She screams my name. I hear her clearly now. Everything comes into sharp focus. I can't be here. I run.

I saw her lips. And his lips . . .

I don't wait for the elevator. I run down the stairs and he's right on my heels. I can't breathe. I can't find the air. Where is the air?

"Lily! Please listen," he cries.

There is no listening. There is no explanation. There is no nothing. My mother has always been very beautiful. Dari will always be beautiful. Why didn't I see it before?

I run out into the street. I just keep running. I want to run until I die. Run until my lungs explode. Run until the world comes to an end. My mother. My Dari. Who are they? Why?

The sick thing is . . .

They look like they belong together.

[A BRIEF DETOUR: THE BALLAD OF LILY & BOBBY]

Spoken, NOT sung! Like Lou Reed:

I was alone
Sometimes it got so bad
You grabbed me by the hand
Cuz I didn't have
A dad.

But you messed it up, man!
Like a psycho in a van
You're just like Peter Pan
Wanted me to be your fan.

That sucks. Hard. Trying again.

Sung, NOT spoken! Like Anne Wilson:

You dreamed you were my drum
Kept me under your thumb,
This is so fuckin' dumb!

There. I tried to write it out in song, but I can't. Lyrics are hard enough without trying to come up with some about the worst year of my life.

Soooooooooooooooo. This is kind of awful, terrible, stupid, but I guess I'll give this telling-my-story thing a try.

Robert Wright used to teach at my school. He taught English to sophomores and seniors and was the faculty adviser for The Folio, the poetry and arts magazine. He was also my friend. (This is not easy to write down.) It was his idea for me to be The Folio's editor. First time a sophomore had ever been given the job and I really liked it.

Sometimes I'd stay late after school to work on The Folio and Mr. Wright would be there. This is how I found out that he was a huge Radiohead fan like me. I didn't know that teachers could have good taste in music. This is also how I found out that he was a guitarist for a Brooklyn band called the Radical Faulkners. He said I could come and see them sometime if I wanted, but he understood if I never did. Their gigs were usually way out in Brooklyn somewhere and he figured I had better things to do than watch my teacher's band in my spare time. He was wrong about that, but I didn't let him know. I told him to bring his guitar to school so we could jam. He was very impressed that I played bass and drums, but especially drums, because it's long been a male-dominated instrument, he said. To this, I said, "Duh."

A few times we snuck into the music wing when no one was around and we played all kinds of shit. Random old shit I never told anyone that I liked out of embarrassment. Van Halen, Def Leppard—he even knew "Cannonball" by the Breeders. He had eclectic tastes just like I do. He asked me for drum lessons, so I gave him some. He asked me to guide his hands, so I did. He asked me how resonant the average human body was. I said, "It depends." He said, "I bet I'd make a good drum. You should smack me sometime and see," and he winked and I blushed harder than I ever have before. I said, "I'd never, ever smack you, Mr. Wright." (Gag me.) Then he said, "Whenever we're alone, just call me Bobby." He said it like it was no big deal, but it was a huge deal for me. It's so embarrassing now.

When we finished putting together the fall portion of the magazine, he said he'd never met anyone like me before. He wished we had met under different circumstances and at a different time in our lives. I agreed, and I only meant to hug him. Then I only meant to kiss his cheek. He lingered there and when he didn't show any signs of moving, I kissed him for real.

I have thought about that kiss way too much. Sometimes I wish I could go back to that one kiss and just freeze time right there. Right when everything was wonderful. Sometimes I wish I could go back in time and not hug Bobby at all. I wish I could just nod and say something wise like, <u>Good thing you have a beautiful wife at home that loves you</u>. But I didn't. I rarely thought about her at all.

I was too busy thinking about the lies I had to keep coming up with to explain to Jackie and Tracy why their third musketeer was suddenly MIA. I told them it was a guy and it was complicated. That much was true. If they'd been satisfied with that answer, I wouldn't have needed to lie at all. But they asked me questions all the time. "Does he go here?" "Is he in college?" "Where did you meet him?" Because of shit like that, I had to invent a boyfriend they could accept. "He's a senior." "He goes to school uptown." "We met at Starbucks." "You can't meet him because he's really shy and he has this big scar on his face from a car accident when he was little, so he's super self-conscious about meeting strangers." The scar bit helped a lot. It made Jackie feel instantly sorry for him and freaked Tracy out. They stopped asking questions. My mom wasn't as concerned at first. She thought I was entitled to my privacy.

Once I stayed late though there was no reason to. The Folio had already gone to the printer's. I just wanted to see him and not in class because that didn't count at all. The journalism room was completely empty, so I just sat there and did my homework. It was cold that day, and someone had left one of the windows open, so I got up to shut it and about had a massive heart attack when I found Bobby there standing by the window, hidden between the wall and the bookcase. He'd been standing there the whole time, not making a sound.

"You scared the crap outta me!"

He just kept staring straight ahead, like I wasn't there. The air blowing in made the room freezing, but he didn't seem to notice.

"What's wrong?" I asked. Everything about him was freaking me out that day.

He didn't say anything for a few minutes, so I just stood there like an idiot, doing nothing. When he did, though? Okay. This is a paraphrase or whatever, because I can't remember exactly what he said, but it was something like, "There's no one I can cry out to. No one would want to hear me if I did." And then he said something about rats chewing the wires in the walls. Nothing he said made any sense. It was frightening. When he finally moved, he turned his head to look at me and told me to go home and said I shouldn't stay after school anymore. I said sometimes I was going to have to so we could get our work done, but if he ever wasn't feeling well or needed to be alone, all he had to do was tell me. He just smiled this supersad smile and said he'd be fine and that I should get home. He came away from the window and let me shut it. While my back was turned locking the window, he left without making a sound.

I didn't see him outside of class for a few days, but when I did, he seemed normal again and apologized.

"What was wrong with you?" I asked him.

"I don't always take care of myself the way I should," he said and shrugged. Okay, this is more paraphrasing, but it's pretty much what he said: "It's hard to be happy. As you grow, your life is like a collection of newspaper stories and some headlines are great ones that you're proud of. But there are so many that you wish you could just erase. And you can't. The things we do stay with us till we die." This was easily the most serious conversation I'd ever had with him.

"Well. The parts of you I've gotten to know

so far feel like really good headlines. If it's any consolation."

"It is." He smiled the special smile that he saved only for me. "Wanna go to the Strand? I need the latest Jennifer Egan."

I never saw him act like that again. A smarter person would most likely have stayed clear of their teacher/boyfriend for a while if they'd witnessed him bugging out. Not me. It made me like him more.

Last birthday, December 12th. Bobby wanted to do something special for me. I got permission to spend the night at Tracy's and she agreed to cover for me just in case. A cold wind was blowing us all over the place that night when we stepped out of the car. He blindfolded me and led me to a spot in the woods. I could see nothing. I could hear the wind knocking the trees back and forth, which made the wooden trunks sound like screechy rocking chairs. I heard water and other nature sounds. Oh my God. He could've been a SERIAL KILLER! He could've been plotting to kill me and eat me and I would've just followed him right to my pitiful death with this big, goofy smile on my face. Such an idiot!

"Stop here," he said and he removed the blindfold and I couldn't believe what I saw. This gorgeous, big, wild waterfall with snow and ice all around us. It was the most beautiful thing I'd ever seen. For some reason it made me want to cry, but I stopped myself because I was scared my tears would freeze to my face. I didn't know where we were at the time since I'd stopped paying attention to our surroundings once we were on the interstate. Later, I found out we were in Ithaca. A magical place I'll probably never go back to.

He bought me a steak for dinner and we had profiteroles for dessert. I told him he could order wine if he wanted to. I didn't mind. He said that was thoughtful of me, but he didn't drink alcohol.

I don't remember too many details about the hotel. It was nice but generic. Just a regular, clean hotel. I don't like admitting it, but thinking back to that night it was more like it was _his_ birthday.

He was relatively gentle. I'll give him that. I didn't know we were going to go all the way that night. I can't believe I didn't guess that he had that planned, but I didn't. When he entered me, I screamed then covered my mouth. He tried to be more careful after that, but it hardly made a difference. I was glad when he finished. I just wanted to hide in the bathroom.

"Are you all right?" he asked from the other side of the door.

"Yeah, I'm fine," I lied. "I just need a minute."

I felt weird. Sore, yeah, but it wasn't just physical. I wanted to go home right that second and spend what was left of my birthday just with Mom, watching cheesy movies. I'm not sure when I changed my mind, but when I opened the door, I saw him sitting on the bed with this sad I-just-lost-my-puppy face and then all I wanted to do was make him smile again. So I gave him a kiss and suggested we order room service sundaes. His lips curled into a smile though his eyes remained sad.

"Do you have any idea how much I love you?" Yeah. He seriously said that to me! Those exact words. I had no idea how to respond. I was shocked, flattered, and a little scared. He didn't need an answer from me, I guess. He picked up the phone to order our sundaes. While he held the phone up to his ear and had his back to me, he said, "I hope you don't end up hating me one day." For a second, I thought he was talking to room service. I figured it out and then I glanced down at the bed and thought I might faint. There was a lot more blood than I'd expected. ~~███████████~~

Here comes the bad stuff.

We tried to make plans for the future. This was like early February. I still had three long years to go until turning eighteen, which felt like decades. We decided that when I did turn eighteen, I would of course go to college, but should stay in state and far enough away to make sure I could live in a dorm. This way, when he came to visit me, we could have our privacy. I think his definition of "privacy" was the fact that my mother would be miles away. He was also waiting for his youngest child to reach middle school age. His marriage was over as far as he was concerned, but he wanted to wait until he thought the baby could psychologically handle the concept of divorce. I told him that all my friends were children of divorce and every one of them wished that their parents had done it a lot sooner. He was impressed by this. It wasn't actually true, though. I never knew my father and having been raised just by Mom, the whole idea of divorce is baffling to me. Two people can't live together anymore, so they stop doing it. That's it.

Yeah, I'm sure it's sad for a while, but then you move on. It's especially confusing to me where kids are concerned. There are kids in the world who are sex slaves and child soldiers, for Chrissakes, and we worry that a kid can't handle seeing one parent less frequently than the other?

I got off track. Divorce. His. Whatever.

I fed him my fake divorce statistic and he couldn't get over how mature I was for my age. He understood why I didn't have a boyfriend before we started seeing each other. He was sure that no boy my age would be able to stimulate my mind. I was sure he was right. The more I got to know him, the more I loved him and the harder things became. By this time, my mother did want to meet my boyfriend, mainly because she felt disconnected from a huge part of my life. Lying to her was much more challenging than it was with the girls, so I just started avoiding her altogether.

If "The Ballad of Lily + Bobby" were a real song, it would be in hopeless D Minor.

On Valentine's Day I was blue. I pretended to have big weekend plans with my fictional Bobby when I knew where the real Bobby was. He played hooky and took his wife on an overnight romantic getaway. To Ithaca. I couldn't stop myself from imagining him making love to her on the same bed that I bled on, and I vomited in the hallway and got sent home for the day.

"You're making yourself sick. And for what? Some guy too afraid to meet your mother?" She said something like that to me. I had no fever or any other flu symptoms. She knew my illness was coming from a mental place.

"Are you hiding something?" She wasn't making an accusation exactly. I think she was just worried. I told her it wasn't that serious. That mostly I was sick with PMS. This ended the conversation, though I have no idea why, since she clearly didn't believe me.

On President's Day we did something reckless. His wife took the kids to see her parents for the weekend, and I went out to his house on Staten Island and stayed with him. How stupid was that? Did we want to get caught? I honestly don't think I did. I can't speak for Bobby, though.

Nobody had ever told me I was beautiful before. Not like him. Mom said it, but she told me that when I was a twelve-year-old mutant, so it didn't count. When Bobby said it, he meant it. It felt like he meant it. He thought I was so beautiful that he took a few photos of me. We'd just done it on the dining room floor, which I did not enjoy. Floors are hard. I was raising my leg to see if a sore spot was becoming a bruise when I heard the unmistakable clicking sound of a phone camera. We both laughed. Then I did a goofy pose and he took another. That one was just plain ridiculous! But then he did it again and I quit laughing. He apologized and promised to delete every single photo on his camera that day. ALL of them. With and without clothes. Which is the opposite of what he did.

I always felt sad when our time together ended. I knew I'd have to go back to school and pretend he was just my English teacher and Folio adviser and nothing more. Seeing him at the front of the classroom talking about J. D. Salinger or the concept of allegory or whatever nonsense he was supposed to be teaching us was soooooooo depressing. Nobody knew him like I did. Nobody knew that he'd accidentally gotten his wife pregnant and done the right thing by marrying her, though it crushed his dreams. He'd dreamed of traveling around Europe and writing short stories. He'd especially longed to visit Prague and Vienna. The kids in my class dozing through his lectures had no idea how miserable he was inside. They probably wouldn't have cared anyway.

When it was time to go, I slowly put on my boots and concentrated really hard on NOT crying. He gazed at me from across the room with sad eyes of his own. Then the phone rang.

"Hi, honey," he said with a little sigh. He smiled, but rolled his eyes at me, so I knew he had to take the call. He went into the kitchen to talk to her. I didn't understand how she could be so blind to his unhappiness. I thought maybe she didn't love him any more than he loved her, but had the dumb idea of staying together for their kids. It didn't make sense that she'd want to be with someone who was tired of her.

I had to know what he was saying to her. I crept close to the kitchen door and listened. I couldn't hear too well, so I pushed it open, just a crack so I could see. Something she said made him laugh so hard, he had to grab the tabletop to keep from falling over. Then he whispered something that I couldn't make out and he smiled. The smile I thought was only for me. He said a few things so softly I couldn't hear them at all, and then he turned away, making it much harder to catch words. I'd started to get bored when I heard something that I hoped I heard wrong. "I miss you." He then turned enough for me to see a corner of his face and I knew he'd said it then because his face missed her too.

I backed away from the kitchen door and ran upstairs. I had to make a quick stop. Real quick. Then I went into the bathroom and flushed the toilet. Then I flushed it again and again and again. I think I flushed it six times before he came upstairs.

"Lily? What the hell? Are you sick?"

"No," I said and I made him drive me to the ferry at that moment. When he leaned over to kiss me, I jumped out of the car. He might've gotten some hair, but he made no contact with any part of my face. I wanted proof that I was the one he truly loved. His words weren't enough anymore.

The next day in class, I was terrified and excited waiting for him to get there. Tracy and Jackie were so on my nerves that day! They wanted me to do a "girls' Saturday" with them. Something Jackie read about in <u>O</u> magazine probably. They wanted all three of us to go get massages and mani-pedis and cupcakes and crap. I politely said no (a bunch of times!) and glanced at the clock. He was late. Then they got these concerned, serious faces like they were all worried about me or something, because apparently cake and strangers painting your toenails can fix all your problems!

Finally, he showed up. He seemed totally normal, not a care in his mind. He started writing some notes on the board and asking discussion questions about <u>Native Son</u>. It was like I wasn't in the room. Then, to make matters worse, he gave us a pop quiz! Yeah, like I had plenty of time to read that damn book out at his house all weekend! He passed my desk after everyone was focused on the quiz and with almost no movement at all, he dropped a piece of paper on it, which said "See me in room 306. <u>Now.</u>" I looked up and he was already gone. As soon as I entered 306, he calmly closed the door and started whisper-shouting.

"What is the matter with you?!" he snapped. I just stood there stunned. He'd never spoken to me like this before.

"Answer me," he ordered.

I shrugged, thinking I might be able to play dumb for a while. Then in a flash, his face changed to the Bobby I loved.

"Was it an accident?" he asked in a gentle voice. "If it was an accident, that I can forgive. We have to be much more careful, but if it was an accident, then I'm sorry, baby. I'm sorry for yelling at you. Was it?"

It would've been so easy to say, <u>Yes, Bobby. I certainly didn't mean to leave my panties between your sheets on your wife's side of the bed. I didn't mean to leave the panties you bought for me special that say "Little Drummer Girl" with pink hearts dotting the i's.</u>

"Please answer me, Lil. Was this an accident?"

"No."

His face fell onto the floor. I'd betrayed him. I'd broken his heart.

"You want to destroy me?"

I shook my head, not knowing how to explain. I thought it was obvious. I was just trying to make it easier for him. His face. Oh my God, that sad, SAD face! He opened his mouth to say something, but it was like he couldn't remember how to form words anymore. Until he got his memory back.

"I'm . . . I'm sorry, Lily. But, um, I think we're through now." And he turned his back on me and left me alone in room 306. There was my proof. All he had to do was take the opportunity I'd dropped in his lap and choose me over his wife. He didn't.

~~I think~~ I love too hard

He wouldn't let me apologize. There was nothing I could do. He wouldn't return my phone calls or texts. It was like I didn't exist. Like nothing had ever happened between us. I began to feel crazy and very, very unhappy. I went to his house. No one would answer the door. I KNOW they were home, and I know they heard me! He wouldn't look at me or call on me in class, and he knew I was way too insecure to cause a scene in public. He stopped working late on the magazine, and when I politely-and calmly, calmly, calmly, dammit!-said we couldn't make the deadline without extra help from him, he told me he'd put me in charge for a reason and trusted that I would figure it out. So I blew it off completely. Tracy was on staff and a flash fiction piece she wrote was supposed to be published. Because of me, no one was sure if the last issue of The Folio would come out by the end of the year or not. She kept asking, "What's wrong? What's wrong?" but I couldn't tell her. So I disappointed her. We missed our hard deadline, then two subsequent deadlines, and I was fired.

One night I sat in my room and listened to Feist's "Let It Die" 57 times in a row. I know it was exactly 57 times because Steve Jobs was a demon and made sure that iTunes could keep track of such horrors. This was Sylvia Plath-level despair. Mom was terrified. During one of my crying jags, she joined in, begging me to tell her what was really going on. I was exhausted, so I told her everything. She took it well, considering. She hugged me a lot and cried a lot and cussed a lot and threw some shit. We went to school together the next day and talked to Vice Principal Monaroy. (Side bar: Who the hell is our regular principal? Is he dead? Is he a man? I have no idea.) He seemed totally stunned. He even asked me at one point if I was sure. I'm going to write that again. He asked me if I WAS SURE!!!!

Mr. Monaroy called Bobby/Mr. Wright down to his office. As soon as he came through the door and saw me and Mom, I saw his eyes go a shade darker, but then he just walked in and acted like he had no clue why he'd just been summoned. Vice Principal Monaroy suggested I leave while he spoke to Mr. Wright, but I refused to go. I wanted him to have to look at my face. To acknowledge my existence. He spoke very softly to Mr. Wright, explaining each accusation. My mother sat there bristling. I know she wanted to rip his stupid face off his stupid head. When Monaroy was all done, Mr. Wright cleared his throat and launched a counterattack against me. He said we'd spent some time together after school working on The Folio and that I'd developed an unhealthy attachment to him. He cited my recent behavior on the magazine staff and the dozens of phone calls and texts I'd sent that had gone unanswered, and he claimed he was in the process of filing an order of protection against me because I'd been coming to his house to harass his family. Then this man who took my virginity away long before I was ready to give it to anyone looked me in the face and said, "Lily, you're a very special person. I'm sorry you feel the way you do, but I'm your teacher. There have to be boundaries."

I might've laughed for a second before I lunged at him. Thank God my mother was there to grab me so he couldn't add assault to my list of crimes. I would have killed him. I would not have left him alive.

There was a full-scale investigation. It took some time and it was awful and everyone knew about it. Most people believed Mr. Wright, because he was well liked and nobody knew or cared who I was. It wasn't much better when people believed me. Jackie did and she couldn't stop lecturing me. Told me he raped me and no matter what I thought or did, it was still rape. She kept saying that word over and over again. She said it to me on the phone at night, during study hall, during English (we had a substitute by this point and she was a mean old lady and everyone blamed me for that), and she said it again one time during lunch, which caused me to throw my yogurt against the wall.

I still don't know if Tracy believed me. Like most of his students, she loved Mr. Wright, and at the time she didn't love me so much. She was mostly nice to me when she wasn't avoiding me, but she did admit once that she just couldn't picture me and Mr. Wright together and she wondered if there was a slight chance that I might've misinterpreted his actions. "I don't know how many ways penetration can be interpreted," I responded. She never spoke of it to me again.

The scariest times were when my memory got hazy and I felt confused and sad and I sometimes had trouble believing it happened myself. Robert Wright testifying that I was an obsessed, disturbed young woman couldn't possibly be the same Bobby who couldn't believe how much he loved me. It got so bad that Mom said I could switch schools or we could move. I don't why, but her willingness to completely uproot our lives sent me the message that my problems weren't fixable. That I wasn't fixable. Mom's never been the type to just throw up her hands in defeat. I think this was the closest she ever came to doing such a thing. I got tired of crying and tired of myself, and felt sure that I was not worthy of love. I tried to kill myself by cutting my wrists, which is harder to do than it looks in the movies. I failed. Duh. Mom begged me to have faith that this would all end someday like a nightmare. I decided to trust her, as much as it hurt. Mainly so I wouldn't leave her all alone. That didn't seem fair.

Somebody told Mom about this "homeopathic psychologist" that she made me see. He turned out to be a big fake. He burned candles and played Indian music in his office, but other than that, he was just a bad psychiatrist. He barely spoke to me and sent me home with a prescription for Cymbalta after meeting me once. I didn't want to take it. I thought taking medicine was not going to magically make my life better. I fought with Mom about it because she thought I should at least give it a try. So I took half the bottle in one sitting. This stunt led to my first extended hospital stay. Things were not going well.

Robert Wright was fired and charged with five counts of unlawful sex with a minor, sex assault, and one misdemeanor count of acting in a manner injurious to a child. He served fifty days in prison and was released on five years' probation. He was crafty about making most of the evidence somehow work in his favor. He might've gotten more time otherwise. I don't understand. Something about IP addresses and burner phones. I don't know. But the thing that he couldn't explain away was our room service sundaes on his credit card bill. He could explain being there because he went there often with his wife or alone to work on his lame-ass short stories that he'll never finish, but he couldn't explain two jumbo hot-fudge sundaes with a wife and two sons dangerously allergic to chocolate.

That's my sad story in a nutshell, Dr. Maalouf. It was my nightmare and now it's over. I'm not sure what the moral of this exercise is. Perhaps it's so I know that things can't possibly get worse. But then again, maybe that's just wishful thinking.

PART 3

18

THE WOLF

He runs and runs and runs, but she turns a corner, and before he can follow, a cop stops him.

"What's the hurry?"

"Just, uh, my friend." He's out of breath. Can't he just be trusted for once in his life?

The cop scowls and then barks at him to slow down.

So it's illegal to run while being black. Got it. Thanks.

Dari sits on a park bench, looking around to assess where he is. Sheridan Square. He dials Lily and gets her voice mail.

"Lil? Can you call me, please? You didn't see . . . what you think you saw. I'm sorry anyway." He hangs up, wondering just how stupid he could possibly be.

Hours earlier, before the sun has set, Dariomauritius stands outside the apartment building finishing his cigarette and contemplating a sensible exit strategy. He's made no earth-shattering discoveries when she joins him.

"Mind if I bum one?"

"Oh. Uh," he stammers.

She rolls her eyes, "Dari, I'm not dumb. I know you smoke. May I have one, please?" Savannah asks evenly.

He slowly nods and gives her one.

"I'm trying to quit," he confesses.

"I get it." She sits down on the steps. Dari sits too, and offers her his lighter. She lights up, inhales deep, eyes closed, and she holds it for so long, Dari worries that she forgot the exhalation part. Just before he panics, she lets the smoke billow from her lips.

"I have not done that in about twelve years," she shares.

"Why now?" he asks.

She inhales again and watches the traffic speed by.

"Trying to access that part of myself that isn't so tired. I'm sure it won't work, but it's worth a try.

"My agent dropped me today. It was very considerate." She immediately shakes her head. "No. No, it wasn't. It was pitying. He feels sorry for me, but he had to let me go nonetheless."

Dari nods, not knowing what to say.

"It's hard to blame him. The publisher nixed the contract a few days ago. I feel sorry for me too."

"Why?"

"Because I'm getting old. It's a bad feeling to know that you've hit your peak and nothing you do will ever matter in the same way again. If it matters at all. Then there's Lily. Great example I've been for her. I feel like I just keep striking out."

She finishes her cigarette and heads inside. "I'm sorry, Dari. You shouldn't be listening to all this," she says as she opens the door.

"I don't mind," Dari says, hurrying after her.

"That's because you're sweet." They wait for the elevator.

"Not really," he argues. "I think it's cool that you talk to us like we're adults. My dad talks to me like I'm his subject."

They get inside and the door closes.

"When's the last time you talked to your dad?"

Dari shrugs.

"He's called. I can't deal with him anymore. Probably just go live with my sister."

"I'm not trying to rush you out or anything," she quickly says.

"I appreciate it, but I should make some kind of move soon."

Once inside, Savannah starts a pot of coffee.

"Where's Lily?"

"She went to the library to do some work," she says.

Well, that sounds like a lie.

Savannah joins him at the table and they listen to the coffee percolate.

"Your agent sounds like a moron," Dari says. "Maybe you should go the indie route. Self-publish. Or go through a smaller publisher. If you need to publish at all. This might be a good thing, even though it doesn't feel like it now." Dari believes all of these things. He's been working on how to put those beliefs into words since they were outside on the steps. But Savannah's sad eyes and lack of a response make his words sound hollow. Almost rehearsed.

She attempts a smile and rises to get their coffee, but Dari stops her and pours each of them a cup. He knows how she likes it: almond milk and two spoons of agave. He sets her cup in front of her and sits. He drinks a lot of coffee. It may be his favorite thing not involving another person. Better than weed. He's on his third steaming sip when he glances up and sees the first tear.

"Did I say the wrong thing?"

"Nope. Everything you've said is perfectly, perfectly right." She wipes her eyes with her lavender-painted fingertips.

"I can't write anymore, and I can't write anymore because I no longer believe my own PR. I can't find any meaning in my little aphorisms because there is none. I am a fraud."

Dari takes a long gulp of his coffee. He can't tell if she's beyond consolation yet.

"Sometimes I want to burn every piece I've ever made in my life just before I make something brilliant," he tells her.

"That's different."

"How?"

"You make art. I make a product."

Jesus. Time to switch things up.

"Wanna do something stupid?" he asks.

She laughs. "Of all the things I expected you to say, that was not one of them."

"Seriously, though. Do you?"

"What is it?"

Dari holds up a finger and runs to his room. He grabs a pad of cheap newsprint paper and brings it back to the kitchen.

"Ever play Exquisite Corpse?"

Savannah shakes her head. "Isn't that a song from *Hedwig and the Angry Inch*?"

Dari frowns in confusion. "Maybe. I don't know. It's fun and ridiculously easy. All you have to do is make some bad art."

"I'm sure I can manage that."

"Let's agree to make the ugliest monster anybody's ever seen."

"Why would we do that?"

"Because it's fun and funny."

Dari rips a sheet from the pad and draws something and then folds over what he's done.

"Okay. Let's say that I just drew some feet. Or something. Now you add to it."

"But I can't see what you did."

"That's the point. We're drawing in the dark. Just try it."

Savannah draws something then folds over her contribution and hands it back to Dari, who hesitates.

"You know? This is more fun with several people playing, so . . . I'm going to be a different person each time."

"What?"

"I will draw as a different person each time it's my turn. Now I'll be Ms. Spangler, my art teacher." He closes his eyes then makes a strange expression, wrinkling his nose as if cradling glasses. Savannah snickers. Dari draws while constantly crinkling his nose. When he's done, he drops the face, folds the page, and passes it across the table.

"I'm just gonna be myself."

"Of course. I just like a challenge," he explains. Savannah draws something, folds, hands it back. Dari thinks. He smiles.

"Now I'm gonna be Lily." Again he closes his eyes and when he opens them, he sighs and looks up toward the ceiling sideways. Savannah busts out laughing as Dari draws with one hand while twirling a dreadlock around his pointer on the other.

"How was that?"

"That was my daughter. I think I'm afraid of you," Savannah jokes.

This continues only a few more rounds and then Dari unfurls their monster. A creature that would easily scare Leatherface.

"Oh, this is dreadful," Savannah howls.

"Yeah, it's awesome," Dari replies.

Dari explains the power of creating something repugnant: It's just yours because no one else would want it. He can tell by the time he finishes his spiel that Savannah is thoroughly intrigued and no longer feeling so sorry for herself. Victory.

In her office, she shows him images that she's been using to inspire her. Images like a 1955 photograph of the Taj Mahal, a drawing of the Buddha as a teenager, a painting of Mother Teresa, and a framed letter of goodwill addressed to her from the honorable Desmond Tutu. She explains that lately her objects of inspiration haven't been helping her at all. Quite the opposite. As soon as she sits in her desk chair, she hears the doors of the Taj Mahal lock upon seeing her. Teen Buddha glares at her with disapproval. Mother Teresa detests her choice to live in comfort. And worst of all: Archbishop Tutu shakes his head in bitter disappointment, wishing he could tear that framed letter to bits. Dari tacks up their monster on the wall, next to Buddha. He suggests she use this as inspiration. No matter how bad her writing may be, it's not as bad as this thing, and even it deserves love.

"Where did you come from?" she asks him.

Dari swallows, taken aback. "I was born in Brooklyn."

"No. I mean . . . I don't know what I mean," Savannah says softly.

There is an extended moment that in literal time could not have been more than three or four seconds, but in life time it feels like hours. An extended moment that neither Dariomauritius nor Savannah fills with words or movements. An extended moment where maybe they each tap into something they can't explain, can't understand, and certainly can't express.

"My real name is Michelle Rothstein," Savannah says, breaking the silence. "I didn't relate to my family, so I changed it, but you can't ever change who you are."

Unconsciously, Dari moves slightly closer to Savannah. She stands.

"Well? Should we order dinner? Do leftovers?" she asks.

Dari doesn't answer, but he, too, stands. He leaves the office, goes back into the guest room, and retrieves the sketch pad he carries with him everywhere. He flips through it quickly. Dari finds the page he wants and returns to the office. Quietly, he hands her the sketch pad. She sits back down on the love seat, overwhelmed by what she sees. It is the drawing. The one Lily saw the night of "yes" and Bevvy Botswana and fire escape kisses. The drawing that Lily couldn't believe was her, it was so beautiful. The drawing that wasn't yet complete. Now it is complete. And it isn't Lily. Not exactly. It once was, but it evolved.

Time stops again. She still hasn't said a word, but her eyes say everything. She gives him a fast peck on the cheek.

"Thank you, Dari. You've made my day," she says. Dari stares back at her, not smiling. And quick, quick as a kitty on a mouse, she leans back into him and their lips touch. It's subtle, but it happens.

Dari pulls back. Savannah gasps. Both these things happen simultaneously.

Dari's heart pounds. What's he doing? What's *she* doing? How did he get so mixed up so easily? Dari sinks farther down in the love seat. Should he run away? Should he speak? Should he do anything?

"I'm sorry. I'm so sorry. This cannot happen," she whispers while quivering, though she hasn't moved. Dari nods, still unsure of what to do. Has he lost all sense of what it means to be drawn to a maternal figure? *Is that what's wrong with me?*

"You're a beautiful boy." Savannah says it so low that he isn't positive that those are her words, but he can't think of what else they could be.

"I'll leave tonight," he whispers.

"Yes."

Then, out of nowhere, she cracks up laughing. "I feel like we've invited you into our home and you've seen us both at our worst. I swear to you, I'm usually not this much of a basket case," she says. He laughs too and lightly taps her lavender fingers.

"I am," he says. They both giggle for a second and then they stop. Though they silently contemplate each other, though their close proximity has yet to change, a shared smile indicates that the tension has safely left the room, never to return. All wrongs have been righted. Until the door opens. Until Lily comes home.

He's stopped leaving messages. He knows she isn't going to call him back. So he searches. He goes to the Staten Island Ferry station, but she isn't there. He retraces their steps on the night of Yes. Coffee shop. No. Karaoke. No. Diner. No. Bevvy Botswana basement. No. Quite by accident, he finds himself standing in front of a garish neon sign. PSYCHIC READINGS BY AMELIA.

"I need an emergency reading." He comes in and sits down without waiting for Amelia to react.

"You again."

"I have money. Not much, but I can give you what I have." He digs a few crumpled-up bills from his pocket and tosses them onto the small table.

"What do you need?" she asks.

"She ran off and I can't find her and she hates me now and . . . I just want to know if she's safe."

Amelia nods. "Want a soda? I have some fancy root beer."

"What? No, I don't want any fancy root beer! Can you help me or not?"

She takes Dari's hand and inspects it. Then drops it.

"Why are you chasing her?"

"Excuse me?"

"No, I will not excuse you. Why are you chasing her? Worrying about her in this way?"

Dari is at a loss for words. *Isn't it obvious?*

"She is not your responsibility."

"Of course she is."

"Wrong. She needs to take care of herself and you need to take care of yourself. You two are like . . . you're like an iPod, let's say."

"Oh my God—"

"Just listen for a minute. You are like an iPod. To her. A fun toy with many capabilities and many secrets. To you, she is like a magnet. What happens when you stick a magnet on an iPod?"

She waits for an answer. Dari shrugs. "I don't know. It scratches it."

"It erases all its memory in an instant. It takes everything away and leaves nothing behind. To you? This girl is a parasite. She doesn't know how to give back what she's taken."

Dari thinks about what she's saying for a moment. He straightens out his crumpled bills with trembling hands.

"But I'm the jerk. I'm the one who screwed up," he explains.

"Yes. I know what you've been up to. You're like a wolf in a trap that chews his own foot off in order to escape. Stupid, but you're a kid. At the moment, anyway. What do you know?"

"Do you know where she is or not?

The woman sniffs then straightens out a crease on the tapestry covering her small table. She looks up at Dari and stares at him for several interminable moments.

"No," she says at last.

Dari leans back in his seat, assessing this Amelia person.

"You do. Don't you?"

"No, I do not." Amelia pops open a root beer and takes a long pull. "I'm tired. I'm not getting a read on you now."

"You're not gonna tell me anything I can use?"

"Stop looking for her. I can tell you that."

"This hasn't been helpful at all," Dari announces and tries to slam the door on his way out, but there's some device in the door frame that prevents this from happening. Amelia's prepared for an angry clientele. He's feeling far worse than he did before going in, and now he's out twenty bucks. Why did he give her so much? Racket!

It's getting late and he's getting hungry, but he doesn't feel like eating.

Any word? he texts Savannah.

Seconds later, she calls.

"Hi," he says gently.

"Dari, just come back. You need to eat and get some sleep." Her voice is so hoarse, it sounds like she's been crying for days.

"I have to find her."

"How? She could be anywhere."

Dari says nothing. He has no idea how he can possibly find her at random in this city of eight million people, but that doesn't make him any less determined.

"She's done this before. When she's been really upset. She wants to punish me. She'll come back. I know she will. And if I need to call the police, I will tomorrow. I know they're just gonna tell me she's a runaway, but what else can I do?" She laughs a little, or cries. Maybe she's doing both at the same time. Dari hears her swallow something. Probably wine. Or something stronger.

"Sometimes I wish I were twenty-one years old again and living in Rome," she says.

Twenty-one and living in Rome. These words are familiar. So familiar. And then Dari remembers he has heard this exact wish once before.

"Savannah, I have to go. I'll call you back," he tells her, and he runs to grab a crosstown bus heading west.

When he's close, he hops off and checks his watch. 9:47. Still time. If he's right . . .

Please be here.

He rushes up the steps, trying not to fall on his face. Because of the cold wind, no one is here. It's a wasteland tonight, reminiscent of what the High Line once was, minus the litter and crack whores.

And there is the glass wall overlooking Tenth Avenue, and there's Lily, leaning into it. Making another wish?

Her back is to him, but he knows it's her. No one else has hair like hers. He's dead still for a moment, afraid if he calls her name, she'll bolt. Afraid if he comes up behind her, she'll be terrified. No option is a good option, so he delicately walks closer toward her, and when he decides he's left a safe distance between them, he stops.

Still afraid to speak, he takes out a cigarette and lights it. Lily turns to him.

"I wish you would've talked to me," Dari begins.

Lily stares at him, stone-faced.

"It wasn't what you thought. Seriously. There's nothing going on between me and your mom. We're just sort of . . . friends. I promise you."

"I know what I saw." Ice in her voice. Ice in her eyes.

"How long have you been out here? You must be freezing." Dari moves toward her to give her his jacket, but she pushes him away.

"Don't touch me."

Dari looks deeply into Lily's eyes. She's no longer seeing him. She's seeing someone else.

"You're being really unreasonable," Dari scolds.

Lily slowly walks toward the stairs and heads down to the street level. Dari follows her easily this time.

"You might hate me right now, but I'm not the guy. I'm not the grown man who screwed you up. No matter what you may think of me, I'm not him!"

"YOU'RE WORSE!"

Dari is instantly silenced. He's never seen Lily so angry.

"You are worse because you knew I was broken and I trusted you!"

"You are not broken—"

"Oh, just shut up! I'm not somebody to play around with. I do not go around screwing guys in public! I have never done that in my life and it meant everything to me and it didn't mean SHIT to you!"

"That is not true!"

"Then why are we here right now? Why are we shouting at each other on a school night in Chelsea?!"

"You're kinda just shouting at me."

Lily starts to walk away in a huff, muttering more nonsense under her breath, when Dari grabs her.

"At least forgive Savannah. She didn't mean to hurt you."

Lily slaps Dari across the face, and it's a weak, messy slap. It's a slap that makes a thud sound because of her glove and how cold Dari's cheek is, but the intention is quite clear.

"What is wrong with you?" he sputters.

"All that time. All that time we spent together. All the fun we had. All the—all of it—you have never, NEVER, once looked at me the way you were looking at her in that one second. I KNOW WHAT I SAW!" Lily attacks Dari, hands flying all over the place. He tries to defend himself while containing her, which is a lot to handle, and in the midst of it—sirens.

Goddammit.

"Step away from her," the cop says on a bullhorn.

"Officer? I'm not—" Dari begins, confused.

"Step away from her now." The cop pushes Dari up against a wall harder than necessary, considering the fact that Dari is no criminal. He searches him.

"Is this man bothering you?" the cop asks Lily.

"Oh my God," she mumbles.

"Did you hear me?"

She heard him.

"Lily," Dari calls as Officer Dipshit pushes him back against the wall.

"Nobody's talking to you. What the hell is this?" The officer pulls something from Dari's back pocket.

Dari tries to turn to look at it, but the cop prevents him. Meanwhile, his partner has gotten out of the car.

"It's a palette scraper."

"A what?"

"Palette. Scraper. For paintings," he says slowly enough for a squirrel to understand.

"Oooh. Are you an artist?"

"Yes."

"You gettin' smart with me?"

"No, you asked a question, and I answered it."

"Shut up!" Tired of Dari and his direct answering of questions, the other cop turns back to Lily.

"Miss? Do you know this man?"

Lily looks at Dari.

See me, Lily. Please see me.

"No. I don't know him."

She turns away as he screams her name, and she doesn't turn back. She just keeps walking. She doesn't turn back when she hears the scuffle. Doesn't turn back when she hears more shouting. Doesn't turn back when he cries, "I didn't do anything." She just keeps walking and walking.

One of them kicks him, but he can still see Lily up ahead in the near distance. If only he could get her to forgive him! If only she would just acknowledge him! He reaches for her and for one glorious instant he tears himself free and breaks into a run.

Lily doesn't turn back. But she stops dead in her tracks when she hears the gunshot.

19

FROZEN

I want to turn around now. I have to turn around now. But I can't feel my feet. I hear commotion behind me. I bend my leg and do all I can to lift it from its planted position, and I pivot. I get myself turned back downtown again. I can't see what's happening.

"I know him," I cry, but it sounds like it's coming from someone else. Someone far, far away. "No! I didn't mean it! I know him! I do know him!" I'm moving as fast as I can, but my feet are bricks and my tongue is a swollen mass. What's happening to me?

An ambulance comes and I really make myself run now. I run like never before. My mind comes back, my body comes back, my heart comes back.

"Please," I scream.

They gently lift him onto a stretcher and get him inside.

"I know him! I do," I yell. The EMT workers don't notice me.

"Miss, you need to leave now," a younger cop warns me. He stops me before I can get any closer. Where are the other ones? They'd recognize me.

"The guy in the ambulance," I begin, and as I try to catch my breath, it pulls away, its lights flashing and sirens blaring. *"No!"*

"Do you have information about . . ." The cop's asking me something, but I can't hear him as I race after the ambulance. I can only run for a few blocks before my legs stop carrying me.

I mentally note the name on the rear doors. Beth Israel. Beth Israel. Beth Israel. Shaking, I reach for my phone and dial a number. A number Dari added to my phone. In case of an emergency. She picks up on the third ring.

"Hello?"

"Izzy, it's Lily. Get to Beth Israel hospital right now. Your brother's been shot."

Though it's long gone, I follow the path of the ambulance for a while not knowing what else to do. It makes more sense than doing nothing or sleeping on a park bench, which is still a real possibility. I'm cold in a way that makes the world seem large and slow. I want to stay cold. I don't want my mind to thaw out. I don't want to think about what I just did.

I hear a phone ringing. I know it's mine, but I cannot imagine why I should bother answering it now. What difference could it make? It stops ringing. It starts ringing again. Someone is relentless.

"Hello?" I manage to answer.

"Lily? Where are you, honey?"

"Who is this?"

"It's Uncle Ray. Your mom is really worried about you."

My brain is in no condition to decipher what's happening on the other end of this call.

"But you're in Uganda," I say, throaty and confused.

"No, I've been back for a week. I sent an e-blast about it. Don't you read—never mind. Where are you?"

I don't answer. I try with all my might to imagine the world of kindness that Uncle Raymond inhabits and I try to picture myself in that world. I can't.

"Lily, please tell me where you are. I can come and get you. Things are gonna be all right. I promise."

Promise. A promise. I promise too. I promise that if I ever find a time machine I will undo everything. As if tonight were just a horrible nightmare. I will go back and undo the events of last year and I'll still be BFFs with Tracy and Jackie and happy to be a curious virgin. I will go back and walk right by Dari's lunch table without disturbing him. I'll go back even further and make sure Dari's mom gets to live a long life and that he gets to visit museums with her in Paris. But if I am only allowed to make one short trip with my time machine, I will go back and I will not deny him.

"LILY!"

"Seventeenth Street and Sixth Avenue," I wail and hang up. Hoping that I just freeze to death.

A Time Before

L: You taste good.

D: Oh, man.

L: Seriously. Like Jolly Ranchers.

D: Thank you. That's weird.

L: This is the best night ever.

D: I think you're right.

L: You are the polar opposite of what I thought I wanted.

D: Thanks?

L: Yeah. You're so much better.

D: Happy Halloween.

L: What?

D: It's after midnight. So. Happy Halloween. Wanna go trick-or-treating?

L: Kinda.

D: What should we dress as?

I gave it a little thought. Precious little. I pinned my hair back on each side symmetrically, buttoned my sweater up to my larynx, and wrapped my scarf around my waist like a skirt. As a finishing touch, I pulled out my Maalouf notebook and held it innocently in front of my chest with a number two pencil.

L: Guess who I am.
D: Sylvia Plath?
L: No! I'm Anne Frank.
D: Ah. Yeah. I see it now.
L: Who are you gonna be?
All he did was pull his hoodie up over his head.
D: The boogeyman.

Uncle Ray pulls his car up to me slowly. Flurries blow in the wind. Mom's in the backseat.

He gets out and comes over to me.

"Are you hurt?" he asks.

"Hurt?"

"Did you . . . did you hurt yourself?"

"No."

I glance over and see that she's buried her head in her hands. If she has nothing to be ashamed of, why is she crying? If she has nothing to be ashamed of, why is she sitting in the backseat?

Snow blows into my hair and gets trapped there. I'm snotty and I need a tissue, but I'm not about to ask for one. The last thing I want to do right now is get into a car with my mother. But Dari. Oh my God. Dari. I follow Uncle Raymond and I get into the front seat without saying anything to her.

As soon as I slam the door, she tries, "Baby—"

"Stop. Take me to Beth Israel hospital."

"What's wrong?" they both ask at the same time.

"It's Dari. It's serious."

20

DARIOMAURITIUS RAPHAEL GRAY, AGE 16¼

The human body has 206 bones. I remember this from second-grade science. There is no way that number is exact and fixed. The human body is too mysterious.

Am I in my body anymore? Am I in a body anymore? Here and there. Gone and not gone.

Pain. My neck. My head. Bullets cause pain. Bullets cause death. Bullets cause paralysis. Bullets stop your conversation.

I do not want to keep remembering. Remembering. I am powerless to stop it from coming back. The sound, the cold, the hands, the shouting. I don't understand what I did wrong. I did something wrong. Something I did wrong. I talked. I got angry. I got angry. I got angry. I got angry. That was the crime. Remember: Don't get angry. It is illegal to be a black man and be angry. Right. Got it. I will remember this next time.

Next time.

Don't get angry.

The people who work in this hospital care. They think I matter. They want to save my body and everything it holds within. They rush around my body like little busy birds trying to put me back together. That means I'm broken. Lily says she's broken. She is not. She is going through a hard time. That is what the experts say on television. A hard time. A rough patch. A painful period. But it will pass. She is not broken; she's wounded. She will heal. She can be fixed. Savannah can be fixed. Not me. I will always be a broken toy. A walking scar. The scary one. To the blue men. To the people who cross the street. To the guards who stop me at the airport to check my hair for weapons of mass destruction.

Weapons. Mass. Destruction. Mass destruction is a positive thing if you have cancer. Mass destruction is not a positive thing if you are minding your business. Mass destruction is.

Safe things. See them. Neutral things. Don't look down at the table. Don't look down at the blood puddles on the floor. Look up at the fluorescent light flickering. Don't look at the monitor. Look up at the clock ticking the seconds away slowly. Don't look at the beads of sweat on the young resident's forehead.

I am angry. It is illegal for me to be angry. Remember: Don't get angry. It is illegal to be a black man and be angry. Right. Got it. I will remember this next time.

Next time.

I will be angry in this place I am in. I will stay angry to push out the sadness.

I can see my name at the Whitney. Galerie Richard. Here, or in Paris. König. Berlin. Dariomauritius Raphael Gray. I will only use my full name in print. If someone addresses me as Dariomauritius, I'll say, "Call me Dari or Mr. Gray or nothing." I'll distinguish myself as a painter by eschewing the color gray.

I wonder if my father will miss me.

21

MISTAKES

We've been waiting. No one at triage will tell us anything because we're not family. I don't want to call Izzy again. I don't want to drive her crazy. I don't know what to do.

Uncle Ray has gone to the cafeteria to get us all coffee. Mom sits on the ugly orange-cushioned bench. I stand several feet away from her. There's room next to her, but I'm not sitting there.

"I made a mistake," she says. I pretend I can't hear her. "A mistake," she repeats, raising her voice. "And I'm sorry."

I edge closer, but I don't sit.

"Lily? Can you answer me? Please?"

"That's not important right now," I tell her.

"I know. You don't have to forgive me. I just need you to know that I'm sorry."

I turn and look at my mother for the first time since opening the door to her office earlier today.

"What am I supposed to do with your 'sorry'?"

She visibly shrinks, but doesn't answer my question.

"Please don't shut me out, Lily. You're my whole life. If you shut me out . . ." She can't complete this sentence.

"You're no better than Mr. Wright." That. That may be the meanest thing I've ever said to my mother.

She crosses her arms, but in a strange way. Like she's trying to hold herself up. She locks her jaw, as if preparing for a fight, but her eyes remain glassy and she shivers. I feel awful. Like I just socked her in the face. That makes me hate her all over again, for making me feel bad for feeling how I feel.

"Mr. Wright was a teacher who . . . fucked his naïve fifteen-year-old student and then lied about it like a textbook psychopath. I don't think a small, stupid, closed-mouth kiss quite puts me in the same category." Now her glassy eyes sparkle because on top of being hurt, she's furious. I don't respond because I don't know how to and because I'm tired and because I'm scared and because I don't know who I am anymore. I don't think I used to be a cruel bitch.

"No. You're right. It's my fault. All this. You. Your misery. It's me. I fucked up." She sighs and collapses into herself.

But it isn't true.

"Not this," I say quietly. "Tonight . . . I fucked up. Just me." I say it and it lands at the pit of my gut like a tumor. My tumor. I earned it.

She slowly turns and gazes at me. "Lily? What exactly happened tonight?"

I stare into my mother's blue eyes. I tell myself: *We've been through worse.* But have we?

I get a text with a floor and a room number. Nothing else. No clue as to how he's doing. Nothing. I look up at Mom and she knows without me saying anything. We both head for the elevator bank.

Eighth floor. A room number. This has to be a good sign. He's been moved to a room. That's always a good sign, right? I look at the numbers on the doors, but quickly see that they're totally different from the one Izzy gave me.

"What's wrong?" Mom asks.

"Excuse me?" I ask the receptionist. "Can you tell me where I can find this room?"

She glances at my phone and then says we're in the wrong wing; we need eighth floor west. She directs us to go back downstairs and walk to the other side of triage and take those elevators. This is nuts. We're trying to decode crazy directions while God only knows what's happening with Dari.

As we race toward the west side of the building, we catch sight of Uncle Ray talking on the phone. He looks up and hands us our coffees—still hot—and mouths the word *sorry*, but Mom waves him off and silently says *thanks*.

We look out for our number on Eight West, and as we come toward it, I slow down and I stop. It's not a patient's room at all. It's a waiting room. As we get closer, we look through the glass window separating the room and the hallway. It's a smallish room, but there are a number of people here. Frightened-looking people. Close to the wall, I spot Izzy and a tiny, black woman in a red knit hat talking to a police officer. Izzy's hands move around wildly, hysterically. The police officer nods, but doesn't seem to say much in response.

When she sees us, she walks away from the cop and instinctively hugs my mother without saying a word, and Mom hugs back. Red hat joins her and scowls at me. She hates me. Does she know?

"I can't believe this is happening," Izzy says, still in Mom's embrace. She finally lets go and wipes her eyes.

The officer appears and touches Izzy's shoulder delicately.

"Oh. This is his friend," Izzy sniffs, referring to me.

My legs become Jell-O.

"Can you tell me what happened earlier?" he asks me.

"Is this really necessary now?" Mom interrupts.

"I'm sorry, but unfortunately it is." He wasn't one of the ones involved. He's a little older and seems tired and sad.

"Me and Dari were arguing and these cops came over to ask what the problem was, but there wasn't a problem. Not a serious one. And I was mad at him, so I walked away and I heard a struggle and then a gunshot," I'm crying again. They all just stare at me.

"Did you see how the struggle began?"

"No, I only heard it. I was walking away, so my back was turned."

"Did anything else happen?"

I shake my head. I'm lying. Lying and crying. It's not only for my sake, I think. The last thing I want to do is upset Izzy any more at this moment.

"Thank you. I may be in touch later with more questions." He awkwardly nods and disappears around the corner. Has he been waiting here to talk to me?

We all sit down in this dreadful waiting room. Izzy looks much older than her years tonight.

"Is he still in the OR?" Mom asks.

"Yes. Still working on him."

Still working. That has to be a good sign.

"They're doing an emergency craniotomy. The bullet only passed through one hemisphere, they said, but . . . there's swelling." Izzy breaks into sobs.

Hemisphere. Craniotomy. Bullet. His head. Oh my God. His. Head.

Mom grabs Izzy's hand. "We'll stay here as long as you need." Izzy thanks her, dabs at her eyes, and mumbles an introduction to her girlfriend, Trisha, who barely nods at us. I can't help noticing that so far, Izzy has yet to look in my direction.

"My father followed them upstairs, but they told him he couldn't go in. I don't know where he is now."

We sit quietly for a few minutes. His head. His brain? I can't think about it. I can't. In the background, there is an elderly couple speaking softly to each other. I think they might be praying in Spanish. A young family of Asian and white people that look like zombies. Their toddler is the only one among them that makes a sound. In the corner, the television plays *Hot Tub Time Machine*, and to keep from feeling nauseated with dread, I spend a decent amount of time trying to figure out who the hell would've put that movie on in this waiting room. A nurse? An orderly? A punk kid scared and waiting just like the rest of us?

"Lily," Izzy begins. I'm startled, but strangely comforted. At least she's addressing me.

"Why were you fighting?"

The whole hospital collapses on me for a tiny second.

"It was . . . I—I don't know." How can I answer her?

She stares deep into me with desperation.

"It was stupid," I say.

"But what did he do?" she asks me. *Nothing to deserve this.*

"Lily got into some trouble recently," Mom suddenly interrupts. "Dari wanted to give her some sensible advice and I imagine she was being stubborn." Mom turns to me with a stern look in her eye, but then lightly pats my hand. I am grateful for her adept lying skills, but I ease my hand away.

"I just can't believe this is happening," Izzy says again, dropping her head into her hands. Silent Trisha rubs her back gently.

This is an awful room. Death lives in this room. I hang my head low and close my eyes.

I don't really know much about praying, but I'm going to do my best. *Dear God, please take good care of Dari. I love him and he's a good person (even though he's always saying he's an asshole). He has a lot of life yet to live. I'm sorry. Please help me be a better person. Thank you. Amen.*

I open my eyes. All is quiet except for the sounds coming from the TV. I try to concentrate on the movie. George McFly from *Back to the Future* keeps almost losing his arm. John Cusack's high school girlfriend stabs him in the face with a fork. It is wildly inappropriate for this movie to be shown in a hospital. I walk over to the TV and the DVD player. Sure enough, some crazy person has intentionally played it. I hit the stop button, but nothing happens. I hit eject. Still nothing. Is it stuck in there? Does this film play on a loop here? I try to turn the TV off and still, nothing works. I feel a strange buzz in my pocket. I know it must be my phone, but it doesn't sound normal. Feels like it's buzzing the drum intro to "Hot for Teacher." I take it out and read:

Truth or dare?

What? OhmyGodohmyGodohmyGod . . .

Are you OK, I type, hands shaking so hard I almost drop the phone.

What did I tell you about keeping your rage in check?

I scream and someone grabs me from behind.

"Lily? Lily, look at me."

I turn to her and I scream again: no face. Dents where the eyes and mouth should be. A nose hole. Blankness.

"Lily?!"

Mom shakes me awake. Izzy and Trisha are no longer in sight. Uncle Ray hovers by the doorway anxiously. How long was I asleep?

"We have to leave," he begins. "I can take you back to your mom's or you can come with me to Brooklyn. Only thing is, I may not be able to bring you back for a couple of days. But it's up to you," he says. It's a fake choice. There's only one actual option.

"Fine," I mumble, knowing I'll have to go home to Mom's. Knowing I'll have to sleep in my bed. Knowing I'll feel a hole like none I've ever felt when I pass the empty guest room.

If you could take back one thing you've done in your life, do you know what it would be?

I do now.

22

WITHIN THE FRAME

I am in pieces.

I am a sack of meat in a bed. Red.

I am other places too.

I am at a picnic by the river and the sun beats down. Baby blue, dark yellow. Me, Izzy, Dad, Lily, Savannah, and my mother ghost. We are the auburns and cinnamons and burnt siennas. The day is too bright. Izzy grabs my legs and arms and moves them around to tease me. I can't stop her. We eat cold chicken, callaloo, and sweet potatoes, and we drink lemonade. Gold, green, orange, pale yellow. I can't taste. I can't chew.

We play a game. Dunk Dari into the water. The water is blue-green-brown. I can't protest. Dad dunks me down and I can't breathe and I choke and then Mother dunks me down and I can't breathe and I choke and then Lily dunks me down. She pulls me down with all her strength, but I can resist her. I go down and bob back up. She can't beat me. Victory = purple.

I am at the Louvre. I am with the Venus de Milo. She tells me her belief that someone has hidden her arms in the basement. Creamy white.

I am in the art room painting. Ms. Spangler whispers something in my ear about Rauschenberg and the Taj Mahal and her hot breath is too close. Eggshell, forest green, vermilion.

I am at home eating breakfast with the old man. I know he hates me. I know he lives to fight me. But, instead, he cries. He cries into his eggs with snot and whimpers and he almost touches me with his hand. But he doesn't touch me. Brown, dark brown, yellow, more eggshell, too many colors. This painting has too many colors.

I am far too many pieces. I am far too many nerves, bones, cells, and brushstrokes. I can't see the painting if I am the painting. All of me is tired. All of me is done. No more traveling. No more painting. No more breathing. No more looking for love and moms in all the wrong places. No more.

Tired. Brain tired. My mind keeps going. It needs to rest like my body needs to rest. Can it be switched off much like my body was switched off? Just to take a recess? I will find out.

Five, four, three, two . . .

One.

23

HUMAN

More than a month has passed. Winter break starts tomorrow. Dari is still in the hospital.

I visit him most afternoons. The first time I saw him, I covered my mouth so that his family wouldn't hear the cry coming from my throat. He doesn't look so good. There's a bald patch on his scalp where they operated, his skin is sallowish and he looks so small. Like I could pick him up and fold him into a bundle on my lap. I can't touch him. I can't go inside his room. I can only see him from behind a glass window. I can't bear the distance I've created.

But he's holding on. That's what his nurses say. "He's tough. He's holding on." To what, I don't know.

On my birthday, I requested we not have cake, but I blew out a candle. I keep coming in the afternoons to see if I'll get my wish.

Nothing is easy anymore.

I thought once that I'd hit my own personal all-time low, but I was so wrong. There are lows, ugly depths of the human soul that a normal person can't even fathom. I envy normal people.

Back when it happened, Dr. Maalouf suggested that I start

seeing her twice a week instead of just once. I agreed, and I do, but sometimes . . . sometimes her need to see a way out of this, out of me, just doesn't make any sense. I can never undo what I did to Dari.

I've been attending these meetings on Thursday nights at this old church in Harlem. I found out about them online. They're for family members of African-American kids—mostly guys—who've suffered violence at the hands of the police. Most of them were killed. I go to these meetings and say nothing. Sometimes I bring cookies (sugar-free because I overheard a man there say he was diabetic). The group members just stare at me, but I've never said anything. I don't have the right to.

Home. Things haven't changed radically. My mother and I communicate. I love her though I hate her, and she probably feels the same way about me. She used to apologize at least once a day, but that's petered out. Lately she keeps reminding me that she's human, that she's made horrendous choices and is bound to make more. I get it, though I wish I didn't. She's seeing a therapist now too. We both keep talking. When talking is possible. Talking once a week. Talking twice a week. Being human. We don't know what else to do.

School is school. Word got around about my Tara fight, and now some kids are scared of me. I eat lunch alone, not giving the slightest shit. You can be here one second and vanish the next. My isolation is actually a gift. I can't relate to anyone anymore. It's like I'm standing on this cliff of existence now, right at the edge. Below is a five-hundred-foot drop into a canyon of broken, stony memories and pain from a future awaiting me. In the distance, I can just make out another cliff, directly opposite. This is where everyone else stands.

"Hi," someone says to me during today's solitary lunch. I look up surprised, wondering how she possibly made it across that canyon.

"Hey," I reply.

Tracy sits. "I just want you to know, I never in a million years would've let that photo get published. I don't care what people say about me."

"I know," I say.

"Also . . . I'm sorry, Lily. I think I've been kind of a bitch to you," she says, staring down at the table.

I shrug. "Thanks."

"How is your friend?" she asks carefully.

"The same." I don't feel right discussing Dari with her.

"We don't have to or anything, but do you think we could be friends again?" she asks. Her voice cracking. I'm not up for an emotional lunch, but I'm happy she said it.

I nod.

"Good," she says.

"I missed you," I admit.

"Me too."

I don't know what prompted Tracy's visit today. I have noticed her watching me at lunch lately. She sometimes sits alone too. Jackie has drifted off to the jock girls' table, and who knows what's going on with Marie? I do know that a lot of people were mad that Tracy turned Derek in. I've heard them call her "rat" in the halls.

Before lunch period ends, I stop by the art room. Dari's unfinished painting hangs on the back wall. His sense of color is astonishing. I kind of prefer his simple sketches to this, but it isn't finished. Yet. *Yet.* I shiver, imagining it as a memorial encased in glass in the main hallway for everyone to see. I close my eyes and shake the image from my mind.

"Lily?"

I open my eyes, hoping I didn't look too stupid standing there with them closed, but not caring that much.

"How is he?" Ms. Spangler looks super worried.

"The same."

She nods sadly. "Can you—one minute." She walks briskly to her drawing table and pulls a card from her purse.

"It isn't much, but could you pass that on? To someone in his family?"

"Of course," I promise.

She makes an attempt at a smile and then returns to her desk to prepare for an incoming class. I head downstairs and as I start to put the card away, I realize it isn't sealed. Why wouldn't she seal it? I pretend for a few seconds that I have enough integrity not to read it, but I quickly give in to reality.

The cover has a shimmery, golden background and the design is nothing but a crude crown drawn in black. Looks like a child could've done it, but there's something magical about it. Inside her message is short: *Sending love and prayers. I'm very lucky to know this radiant child. When Dariomauritius pulls through this, please let him know that I could use an assistant with his level of talent. Barbara Spangler, Art Teacher/Artist*

I'm tired of myself. Not in an I-hate-myself-and-I-should-die kind of way. That gets old. More like an I've-been-through-hell-and-I've-put-others-through-hell-which-brings-me-to-a-new-level-of-hell kind of way. The only thing I've come up with so far to confront this self-fatigue is to try to make some lives slightly less hellish. I need to move my body. I need to be busy. I need to do things that are absolutely NOT about me. I thought I'd never ever board the Staten Island Ferry again, but I was mistaken. I've been helping to rebuild some homes in areas still badly messed up from last year's hurricane season. I like hammering nails into wood, picking splinters from my fingers, and getting pit stains in December.

The bell rings, signaling free period, and I head to the auditorium to wait for the other SI relief workers, but when I get there, I find out that the team is already on hiatus for the holidays. This seems like information I should've received beforehand and I'm momentarily angry that I didn't, but the anger passes when I remember just how little attention I tend to pay to teachers these days.

I pass the gym, where I see a group of girls huddled together. A gym teacher shouts, "Let's go," and they all file in and I lock eyes with Tara McKenzie. Dammit. Tara finally got her wish after the fight and Mr. Crenshaw let her join another lab team. He moved me to Jamie Paulsen's, and it's fine—she hates me so deeply that she won't even look at me. I don't do squat in that class anymore.

Tara glares at me.

"What is this?" I ask, referring to the clandestine PE class.

"It was announced this morning. It's women's self defense," she snaps.

"Oh, cool."

"*What?* No! You cannot take this class. I'm taking it BECAUSE of you," she shouts.

"McKenzie, you in or out?" Ms. Perry, one of the gym teachers, yells, and Tara runs inside. After a moment, I follow her.

I hide in the back because I'm not exactly dressed for gym, but I try to keep up. It's mostly easy since this is the first class.

"Go away," Tara whispers.

"No."

"Why do you have to ruin everything?" she hisses.

"I'm not ruining it."

Perry blows the whistle and everyone freezes. Crap.

"Problem, ladies?" she asks us.

I shake my head and Tara sucks her teeth.

"Maybe you two should be our first guinea pigs. Come on. Up to the front."

Why was I dumb enough to follow Tara?

"All right. Rothstein, you be the assailant. McKenzie, get ready."

I'm still in the process of getting ready when Tara screams, "BACK OFF!" and thunks me in the chest, sending me to the floor. Ow.

"Someone help her up," Ms. Perry orders. Some girl I don't recognize (freshman?) pulls me up by the hand.

"Switch off," she barks.

We do, and this time I get ready, prepared to pounce, but not ready enough because Tara anticipates my steps and sideswipes my leg before I can do anything. I'm back on the floor.

"Come on, Rothstein! You're not even trying! Switch again!"

I glance up at Tara. "Truce," I whisper.

I get up again and this time I only pretend to attack her. I let Tara try all the remaining moves we've learned, including a choke hold, with no real resistance. Perry blows the whistle to rescue me from probable death. Tara mercifully releases me and I do try to block myself, but Tara punches me in the stomach and I fall over. This time I don't rise. I can't. I gaze up at Tara. She's smiling.

"Truce," she finally says.

"Rothstein, I don't know where your head is at, but it clearly isn't here. Hit the showers," Perry tells me in disgust. I shrug and do as I'm told. Stumbling a bit, because she did hurt me.

"McKenzie! Nice work," Ms. Perry compliments. I glance back and see Tara following the moves with ease. Still smiling.

I walk into the locker room and long for a towel or a change of clothes.

My phone buzzes.

Call me ASAP. It's from Mom. I sigh. *Not another emergency,* I silently pray to myself as I dial. She picks up before it rings.

"Meet me at the hospital."

THE NATURE OF THINGS

Dari

I'm coughing. Get this damn thing . . .

Someone grabs me and restrains my hands. I'm just trying to get this damn thing out of my throat.

"Dario? D-Darius? I'm Nancy. Do you know where you are?"

Why is she holding me down?

"Can you understand what I'm saying to you, hon? Can you speak?"

I cough some more.

"Dari. My name's Dari." Feels like my mouth is full of dirt.

Her eyes light up like I said my name was Jesus Christ.

"Welcome back."

My father talks incessantly about everything that they had to do to me. Three major surgeries and that may not be the last of it. He also keeps mentioning a lawsuit against the NYPD. Now that I'm not dead or a vegetable, he feels comfortable getting a lawyer involved. I haven't said much, but I try to listen. If I weren't so tired and achy, I might be able to appreciate the strangeness of my father's behavior. He's not only acting like he loves me, he's acting like I'm his favorite child. Not the one who tried to kill him once. When I get out of here, I'll most likely go back to his place. He might take it easy on me now. Hard to say.

He continues talking as I doze off. If I have any dreams, I don't remember them.

I open my eyes, and it might be five minutes later or five hours later. The light outside seems the same, but that doesn't mean much. Nurse Nancy leads somebody into the room.

"Dariomauritius," a familiar voice says.

I don't believe it. My mother's here. And it's not my imagination.

"It's you," I say.

She looks me over like she's never seen me in her life.

"My baby. My beautiful baby," she cries and kisses me all over my face. It's too much. I feel suffocated.

"Stop it," I struggle to say. She does.

"My poor, sweet baby."

"You haven't called or e-mailed in ages." There is no way I'm going to make this easy for her.

"I'm so, so sorry. You have no idea how sorry I am, baby."

Yeah. I'm sure you're sorry NOW.

She pulls the chair closer to the bed so she can hold my hand and look me in the eye while being as close to my face as possible. She needs to back the fuck up.

"I guess we haven't talked since . . . August? Good Lord, where does the time go?" She genuinely seems confused and agonized by the passage of time and her role in it.

"This is—what it takes to get you to visit? I have to nearly die?"

She shuts her eyes and nuzzles her face against my hand. I want to pull it away from her, but I'm too tired.

"You know I love you more than anything."

"Do I?"

The tears fall. They dampen my palm, and it's a nice feeling. I like the feeling of her tears on my skin. Haven't felt that in so long.

"I hope you do. I'm gonna make things right between us, Dari. I'm much better than I once was."

So many words come to me that I want to say, to argue with her, to tell her she's a crappy mother who left me to be raised by a mean, sad man. But I can't catch up with them. I can't fit my mouth around all of them, so I just say what little I *can* say.

"How are you better?"

She lets go of my hand for a moment and opens her purse. She unzips a pocket and pulls out a tiny velvet box. Is she about to propose?

She opens the box and where a ring would normally be, sits a bronze-looking disk like a coin. She shows it to me. There's a symbol on it that reminds me of the illuminati triangle, but it's something else. This is a one-year pin.

"You haven't had a drink for a year? At all?"

She shakes her head. "No. A year, two months, one week, and a day. I'm working on myself, Dari. I will keep working on myself."

I try to nod, but that's a lot of effort. I'm skeptical, but this is a good thing. One little step in a humongous journey, but a step nonetheless.

"When you've healed, want to come stay with me?"

Despite all her efforts, I just can't believe that this is a real offer. Not after all this time. She's worried about me and she feels guilty. This is not real.

"For how long?" I will call her bluff.

"However long you want. I can work it out with Maynard." Her eyes shift a little nervously when she brings up Dad. "We can enroll you in school there."

"I don't speak–French. How am I supposed to go to high school in Paris?"

She chews her lower lip like she hadn't thought of this.

"Summer? Come for the summer. I can teach you the language or you can take lessons if you prefer and then if you want? Stay."

"You'd shit yourself–if I said–'yes.' Wouldn't ya?"

"No, I wouldn't. I'd be ecstatic if you said 'yes.'"

I shake my head. No. This cannot be real. Something I've fantasized about a hundred times cannot possibly be real. She's messing with me.

"I am the queen of making mistakes. I'd love the chance to do one or two things right."

It could truly be the morphine, but I think she may be serious this time.

"I can promise you: There is no better place to paint."

I hate how much I miss her. I hate knowing that there's probably nothing else in the world I want more than to live with her in Paris.

"I'll think about it," I finally say.

She smiles and caresses my arm. She tells me about her work and a show she has coming up in Lyon. I close my eyes and listen and enjoy it when she accidentally slips into French. She was born a black girl in bumblefuck Alabama and spent most of her young life being passed around to relatives that didn't want her and could barely take care of themselves. Things weren't easy for her. I don't know when she started drinking, but she was probably young. And it's funny to think about now, but I had no idea her drinking was such a big problem when I was little. I just thought that was her personality. I just thought she was a zillion times more fun than Dad.

Yes. I resent her. I can't help it. But some tiny, mysterious part of me that I can't help is a little bit glad that she found a way to be happy. I don't know how long her visit will last, but I'm also glad she's here.

Izzy's outside, her back to the window. The last time Mom called was before school began, I tried to give the phone to Izzy, but she wouldn't take it. I wonder if she's speaking to her now. She probably has to, given the nature of things. I hope she forgives Mom someday. Actually, I hope Mom earns her forgiveness someday.

Lily. I can see her peeking in from the hallway. She looks gaunt, pale. Like she's been ill. Maybe she has been.

"Dari? Baby? What's wrong?" My mother asks.

Nothing's wrong. Only that I've been shot in the head. Oh. She wants to know what I'm looking at. I don't say. I just keep looking until Lily realizes I'm staring at her and she jumps. If I had the energy, I might laugh.

"Who is that?"

"Lily." I don't have it in me to explain Lily to my mother right now. For that, she'll just have to wait.

"I want to see her now," I say.

She goes to get Lily. I do want her to come back. My mother. I do want to hear more about her life, but I need to see Lily.

Lily

I tear down the corridor like a tornado, but Mom catches up to me and holds on, forcing me to move at a normal human pace. I can't wait to see him, though I'm also terrified. He might not want to see me.

As we turn the corner, Izzy sees us immediately and smiles.

"Everything looks good so far. One of his doctors used the word 'miracle,'" Izzy says, and Dari's father rubs tears from his eyes and takes a deep breath.

Inside the room, Dari still looks pretty bad. He's talking to a striking, tall woman in designer boots.

"Do either of you need anything?" Mom asks.

"Thank you, no," his father says. "I am grateful to you. We haven't always gotten along, but I love my son very much." Mom nods empathetically. He slowly heads back to the waiting area. There's something shy about Dari's father. I hadn't noticed that before.

Mom pumps Izzy for specifics about Dari's prognosis and she gets out her phone, where she's been storing all her notes related to Dari. I peer through the window. He still looks incredibly frail. I've gotten so used to looking at Dari's lifeless body that I jump when I realize that he is now looking straight at me. The woman turns to follow his gaze and rises when she sees me.

"Hello, Lily," she says, popping her head through the doorway. She has a smooth voice, like she might be a singer.

"I didn't mean to—"

"That's all right. Go on in," she says and takes my place on the bench.

I walk up to the side of his bed. The machines beep. His jagged breathing accompanies the mechanized sounds.

"Are you in pain?" I ask, because I don't know where to begin.

Dari

"Not right now," I tell her, though that isn't exactly true. Too soon for another dose of morphine, though.

"I'm sorry," she says, and she says a few other things too. Things about her responsibility and her shame. And being a shitty friend. Things she should say. Things that make sense. None of which I feel like hearing.

"I don't remember a lot—from that night. I don't wanna talk about it. Let's just be quiet for a minute," I suggest. She nods, pressing her palms into her thighs nervously.

I don't like the smell of this room. Pine-Sol, starch, and metal. I try to catch a whiff of Lily's cocoa butter body lotion. I can't. Maybe she doesn't wear it anymore.

In a near whisper, she asks, "Will it hurt if I hug you?"

"It might." It *would*. I wanted to see her. As soon as I saw her face at the window, I needed her here. A burning, painful itch needing to be scratched. But now that she's here, nothing feels right.

"It's hard to get up and live my life. It's hard to, like, brush my teeth and comb my hair. To put on deodorant. To refill my MetroCard. Feels like all those stupid things I do, that I'm supposed to do, are insulting to you because you can't do them." She stops. I glance over at her and she's staring at the floor. I have a strong urge to tell her to stop brushing her teeth and combing her hair and putting on deodorant then.

Lily

Everything I say sounds stupid. Everything I do is stupid. Why am I here? Why can't I just leave him alone?

"What do you want me to say?" he asks.

"I don't know."

"Bullshit." He almost smiles after saying this.

"You don't need to say anything," I mumble. "I don't . . . I don't think I know the words to describe how I feel. I don't know if there are words that could do it. It's just ridiculous trying to pretend to be normal when nothing will ever really be normal again."

He starts to respond, but coughs for a second. Then he tries to turn his head and winces in pain. I figure out that he needs his cup of water from the night table and hand it to him, holding the straw to his lips until he gets enough.

"You have to feel how you feel, and so do I. That's how it is, " he finally says.

I nod. I'm grateful for the painful simplicity of that thought.

Dari
What do I want from Lily now? Do I even know? I think I might be too tired to want.

"Was she your aunt?"

"Huh?"

"The woman who was here. Your aunt?" Lily repeats.

"My mother."

The air falls from the room for a moment. Lily opens her mouth to say something, but doesn't. Of course she's shocked. I lied. It was a pretty serious lie. But honestly, there were times when it felt like the absolute truth.

"Your mother's alive?"

"Yeah." I say nothing more about it. My life, my choices. She wouldn't get it anyway. When your Mom leaves you to escape a bad marriage and to pursue her dreams and to have piña coladas for every meal (until recently), sometimes you wish she *had* died. At least in that case her desertion would've been beyond her control.

Lily
"Did you hear things?"

"What?"

"I mean," I try again, "when you were . . . unconscious. They say that people can hear things sometimes. Did you?"

He starts to raise his arm, but the IV hose gets caught on something and he can't. He sighs and leans back against his pillow. The tiniest movement takes all his strength.

"There's an awareness. I could see some things. Hear some things. I can't tell you what. It was like dreaming in 3-D or something."

He stops; he has to catch his breath. I want to touch him, but I'm terrified of hurting him. He's so fragile right now.

"I can just let you rest."

Dari

I know her. She doesn't want to leave, despite what she says. I don't want her to either. I still feel that burning itch that I don't know how to scratch.

"Say what's on your mind, Lily."

Lily

I shouldn't say it. I know I should let it go. I should leave him be. But I can't.

"Are you in love with my mother?"

He coughs a little, and I instantly feel ashamed for asking.

"No," he replies.

"I understand if you are."

Dari looks at me, really looks at me, and that night flashes through my mind once again. I don't have the right to ask anything of him.

"I said no. Who even cares?"

I shrug. Guilt-ridden.

"If you don't wanna believe me, then don't believe me." He sighs.

For the first time I can remember, he sounds completely unsure of himself. He sounds like a kid. He said no. I do believe him. I don't want to cause him any more suffering. None. I take his hand and gently squeeze, wanting to give him some comfort. He doesn't squeeze back.

Dari

I don't know. I'm tired. I don't know what I feel. I liked both of them. *Loved* both of them? Maybe. But differently. I don't know. I can't explain it, and she wouldn't understand. *I* don't understand.

"You were like a storm. She was the rain, you were the thunder."

"Destructive."

"Intense," I correct and lean into my pillow, closing my eyes, hoping this will be enough for her, though I may never put it in those exact words again. I melt into the vision of a downpour and a rumble of thunder embracing me and lulling me to sleep. The itch starting to ease.

Lily

All is quiet except for the machines and his breath. A storm. Sounds right. I remember that I should probably breathe, too and I exhale for the first time since entering the room.

Sensing that he's had enough of me for now, I tiptoe toward the door.

"Stay," he says, eyes still closed.

I do. I'd stay forever if he wanted me to.

"Dari," I begin, ignoring the knots in my stomach. "Do you think we'll still be friends?"

He takes a few breaths, those jagged breaths, before answering me.

Dari

"I think—I think if I ever get back to my old self, we'll always be friends." It's the first time I've considered the possibility that I might not fully recover. I might not. Valerie Solanas shot Warhol in 1968. He didn't die until '87, but he never felt right again.

In the midst of my Andy reverie, Lily starts to tremble, giving my arm a tremor sensation since she's still holding my hand. She still needs more from me. She needs more than I can give. If I'm going to get myself better, I have to focus on my needs for a while.

Lily

I study the IV hooked to his right middle finger. I suppose this is to prevent dehydration. It should be me in this bed.

"I love you," I say softly. "But that doesn't have to be your problem."

"I love you too, Lily. Like I love thunder. I need it. And sometimes I need distance from it."

Dari

That sounded much better in my head, but my head is Swiss cheese now, so it's the best I can do. All this is too heavy. Too thick with sadness. I miss laughing with Lily. Or arguing with her. I search my mind for the last time I can remember laughing so hard I almost pissed myself. It was at the Bevvy Botswana concert. I want to bring it up. I want to see if the memory tickles Lily as much as it tickles me. But I don't.

Lily

We sit in silence. Relative silence. I know I should leave so his secret mom can take my place. I'm afraid to leave, though. I'm afraid he'll cut me out of his life forever. And now that he's firmly and wisely pushing me away, I love him more than I knew was possible.

"Dari? You don't have to answer me now. Or ever. I don't even deserve an answer. But . . ." I briefly swallow the shame that will surely follow me for the rest of my life. "Do you think that you'll ever be able to forgive me?"

Dari gently opens his eyes and stares at me for a long time. Those stunning eyes. Even in this condition, his beauty remains intact.

Dari

I look at her. The best friend I have. Maybe *ever* had. I do love Lily and I do believe that we'll still be friends. She deserves the truth.

"No."

ACKNOWLEDGMENTS

There are many wonderful, generous people in my life who have contributed in some way to this book's creation. I know I'll never be able to mention them all by name, but know that my heart is full of gratitude for all of you.

Thank you to my amazing readers, who provided me with feedback, wisdom, tough questions, and encouragement. Kia Corthron (my sister, a trailblazing writer as well as a beautiful human being), Tom Matthew Wolfe (more about him in a moment), and these rock stars: Neal Adelman, Emily Bradley, Aleah Chapin, Tasha Gordon-Solmon, Kelly Ramsey, Nova Ren Suma, Cory Silverberg, Cori Thomas, and Chris Van Strander. Thank you to Beth Blickers, my intrepid playwriting agent, for giving me fantastic notes on an early draft and for introducing me to the force of nature that is Laurie Liss. Thank you, Laurie and Sterling Lord Literistic, Inc., for your unwavering support of me and this book and for being awesome in general.

I can't thank the lovely people at Simon & Schuster/Simon Pulse enough for taking a chance on this story. And to my incomparable editors, Fiona Simpson and Michael Strother: Thank for your tireless work, brilliant editing, and all you've given to this process. I am indebted to you both.

I am so fortunate to have been supported by the following institutions at different stages of the writing process: the MacDowell Colony (where I worked on an early draft and then returned two years later to work on the final draft), Djerassi Resident Artists Program, Hawthornden International Writers Retreat in Scotland, and the angels at New Dramatists in New York City, who let me stay in "Seventh Heaven" for several uninterrupted days to pump out a fresh draft, even though I lived a forty-minute subway ride away.

I want to again thank Tom for being the most supportive, funny, kind, soulful, intelligent husband I could've ever wanted. I'm a lucky lady.

Lastly, to the families of Trayvon Martin, Tamir Rice, Michael Brown, Eric Garner, Sandra Bland, Symone Marshall, Akai Gurley, Alton Sterling, Philando Castile, Lonnie Hamilton, Keith Childress, Bettie Jones, Kevin Matthews, Leroy Browning, Roy Nelson, Miguel Espinal, Nathaniel Pickett, Tiara Thomas, Cornelius Brown, Chandra Weaver, Jamar Clark, Richard Perkins, Stephen Tooson, Michael Lee Marshall, Alonzo Smith, Yvens Seide, Anthony Ashford, Lamontez Jones, Rayshaun Cole, Paterson Brown, Christopher Kimble, Junior Prosper, Keith McLeod, Wayne Wheeler, India Kager, Tyree Crawford, James Carney III, Felix Kumi, Wendell Hall, Asshams Manley, Christian Taylor, Troy Robinson, Brian Day, Michael Sabbie, Billy Ray Davis, Samuel Dubose, Darrius Stewart, Albert Davis, George Mann, Jonathon Sanders, Victor Larosa III, Kevin Judson, Spencer McCain, Kevin Bajoie, Zamiel Crawford, Jermaine Benjamin, Kris Jackson, Alan Craig Williams, Ross Anthony, Richard Gregory Davis, Markus Clark, Lorenzo Hayes, D'Angelo Stallworth, Dajuan Graham, Brendon Glenn, Reginald Moore, Nuwnah Laroche, Jason Champion, Bryan Overstreet, Terrance Kellom, David Felix, Lashonda Ruth Belk, Gregory Daquan, Samuel Harrell, Freddie Gray, Norman Cooper, Brian Acton, Darrell Brown, Frank Shephard III, Walter Scott, Donald "Dontay" Ivy, Eric Harris,

Phillip White, Dominick Wise, Jason Moland, Nicholas Thomas, Denzel Brown, Brandon Jones, Askari Roberts, Terrance Moxley, Anthony Hill, Bernard Moore, Naeschylus Vinzant, Tony Robinson, Charly Leundeu "Africa" Keunang, Darrell Gatewood, Deontre Dorsey, Thomas Allen Jr., Calvon Reid, Terry Price, Natasha McKenna, Jeremy Lett, Alvin Haynes, Tiano Meton, Andre Larone Murphy Sr., Brian Pickett, Leslie Sapp, Matthew Ajibade, and many, *many* others: May you find peace. May this nation be cured.

ABOUT THE AUTHOR

Kara Lee Corthron lives and writes in New York City. She's written many plays that have been performed around the US, including *AliceGraceAnon*, *Welcome to Fear City*, *Listen for the Light*, and *Holly Down in Heaven*, which won her the Princess Grace Award (and a dance with Prince Albert II of Monaco). *The Truth of Right Now* is her first novel.

THE FORTY RIDERS

To everyone in the remote town of Powder
Springs he was Joe Smith, husband, father
and baker. Not even his wife and sons knew
his true identity. His secret would have
remained, but one sunny morning Trent
Hardin led forty riders into town to execute
the most daring robbery of his career. He
planned to take control of the town and was
determined that nothing would stand in his
way. None of the outlaws suspected that one
man was preparing to finish a job he had
started many years earlier. Only then would
they all know who Joe Smith really was...

Other DALES Titles
In Large Print

JANIE BOLITHO
Wound For Wound

BEN BRIDGES
Gunsmoke Is Grey

PETER CHAMBERS
A Miniature Murder Mystery

CHRISTOPHER CORAM
Murder Beneath The Trees

SONIA DEANE
The Affair Of Doctor Rutland

GILLIAN LINSCOTT
Crown Witness

PHILIP McCUTCHAN
The Bright Red Business

THE FORTY RIDERS